Chapter One

My stomach knotted when I saw the strange car in my driveway and discovered my key wouldn't open the front door. Deadbolt was locked.

A stereo blared from inside. The door vibrated as if my house had been possessed. I couldn't imagine my husband blasting music. He'd always complained about loud noise in the morning. When I left an hour ago, he was asleep. Or appeared to be.

As the Eagles belted out *Heartache Tonight*, I punched the doorbell until snow clouds buried the sun. No response.

Dad used to say, "Always trust your gut."

My gut screamed disaster, reminding me of the day I got the tragic news about Mom and Dad. They'd died in a plane crash on their way from Atlanta to Ethiopia.

Justice's Journal

(Previous edition A Message in the Roses)

Sandy Semerad

Print ISBNs

Amazon print 9780228626756
Ingram Spark 9780228626763
Barnes & Noble 9780228626770

BWL Publishing Inc.

Books we love to write ...
Authors around the world.

http://bwlpublishing.ca

Table of Contents

I shook off that sad memory and focused on trying to get inside the house. Kyle didn't expect me home. He thought I was interviewing Police Chief Barnum about the recent shooting death in our community.

My job, as a crime reporter, was to find out what happened. Why did the police arrest four black teens for the murder of a white teen? Were their arrests racially motivated? Barnum had promised to give me the full scoop.

Unfortunately, my car broke down.

Tyrone, of Ty's Wrecker and Repair, kindly offered to take me to my appointment in his tow truck. But I had him drop me off at my house so I could drive Mom's old Cadillac to my meeting. I can't stand to be without wheels.

I couldn't get the Caddy out of the garage because Kyle had blocked it with his Alfa Romeo. The other car, a red Thunderbird, was parked beside Kyle's.

How inconsiderate. I wanted to protest his rudeness, but I couldn't get in the house.

I zipped up my leather jacket against the icy wind and inspected the unfamiliar Thunderbird. It had a Georgia tag with the letters "Hot stuff," and a graduation tassel hanging from the rear-view mirror.

When I peered through the T-Bird's windows, I saw spiral notebooks, crumpled up paper bags and a pizza box. I pulled at the door handles. Locked.

Who was visiting my husband? And why was he up this early, blasting the roof off? He'd worked late last night, which suited his nocturnal clock.

I'm usually up and out with the chickens. This morning I'd left the house before seven, in plenty of time to stop by the newspaper office before driving to my interview with Barnum. If my car hadn't died, I would have arrived early.

I stomped my feet like an angry toddler. My tantrum and the fierce wind dislodged my hair from its bun. Unruly strands whipped my face as I pounded on the front door and rang the bell.

Kyle had some nerve, locking me out. This house has been in my family forever.

I've lived here most of my twenty-five years. My closest neighbor and buddy, Freemont, said my home, with its white pillars and large veranda, reminded him of Tara in *Gone with the Wind*.

After I lost Mom and Dad, the so-called "classic antebellum" house I inherited became more of a burden than a home. I'd gladly trade this old relic and all my possessions, if only I could turn back the clock and stop my parents from boarding their fatal flight.

I probably wouldn't have married Kyle if they'd been alive to advise me against it. Sadly, they weren't, and I fell in lust too quickly.

Knowing Dad, he would have broken down the door. Mom would have said, "Be patient. Patience is a virtue."

"Give me patience," I whispered as I followed the veranda to the back porch. I thought I could get in through the porch entry, but the screen door wouldn't budge. The slide lock was engaged.

Burning with rage, I ran back to the front of the house and rang the doorbell again. I could barely hear the chimes above the blaring stereo of Bruce Springsteen's *I'm on Fire*.

I screamed like a mad banshee, or what I thought a mad banshee might sound like. I yelled loud enough to be heard from miles away. My hollering would have woken the dead.

After a while, I gave my burning lungs a rest, and glanced at my wristwatch. He'd given me this watch to celebrate our one-year wedding anniversary. I found out he'd charged it on his American Express card and couldn't afford to pay the bill. He even had the audacity to ask me to pay for it. For crying out loud, what kind of man surprises his wife with a gift she didn't ask for, then asks her to fork out the cash for it? I'm glad I had sense enough to keep our bank accounts separate, or else he would have bled me dry.

My expensive timepiece showed 8:30 a.m. I needed to call Barnum to reschedule, pronto. At least the earsplitting music had finally stopped.

I pushed on the doorbell again. The chimes echoed loudly. I waited and waited. No Kyle.

I knelt to pick up the stone planter from the veranda. A pang of guilt warned me against what I felt compelled to do. Mom loved these windows. She called them "sentinels." They're nearly as old as the house.

I gripped the giant vase in both hands, bent my knees for leverage and drew back the urn. As I started to throw it, the front door creaked open.

My husband's handsome face appeared, looking like Hamlet seeing his father's ghost. Kyle had played Hamlet several times for the Shakespeare Festival. His wavy hair, the color of a copper penny, was all mussed. His two-day stubble gave him a rugged bad-boy look. He had on a beige long-sleeved tee-shirt, open in the front to show wisps of chest hair. His snug corduroy jeans displayed his abundant manhood. His brown eyes glared at me like I was crazy Ophelia.

He stepped outside and grabbed the planter out of my arms. "What's wrong, love?" His mouth looked puffy, and he seemed to be exaggerating his Irish brogue, the one he used to charm my pants off. He wrapped his arms around me as if he thought I needed a strait jacket.

I shoved him away and walked inside to see what he was hiding. Lo and behold, I ran smack dab into a young woman about six feet tall and voluptuous.

I'm her opposite; blonde, five-seven, and skinny. Mom used to say I looked like a popular model, the one with the gap like mine between her front teeth, but of course, my mom would say that.

Kyle's lady friend tossed back her silky long hair, the color of last night's sunset—reddish orange. She looked me up and down.

My messy hair was frightful, but the rest of me appeared decent, I thought. I'd worn my favorite black dress, leather jacket and heels. Kyle's paramour had on tight blue jeans and a velour sweater that matched her hair. Her sweater was wrong side out, as if she'd dressed in a hurry, in the dark.

She glanced at the tiny watch on her wrist. "Oh, no, I'm late for work."

"Who are you?" I spat out.

Rather than answer and explain why she was in my house with my husband, she turned toward Kyle.

He introduced her. "Carrie Sue, this is Maryann Nielson. She's Blanche in Streetcar. We've been going over her lines."

I bit my tongue and considered his pitiful excuse. He directs plays for Stage Atlanta at night. In the afternoons he teaches two college classes, with ample time to coach actors at the college or at the theatre. I saw no legitimate reason for him to invite this woman to our home.

Maryann's lips twitched. "Hi," she said. Her green eyes ping-ponged from me to Kyle. "Thanks, Kyle. See you later." With that, she dashed away, jumped into her red Thunderbird, and sped down the long circular driveway like a racecar driver.

I glared at him. "You and Maryann have been screwing around, haven't you?"

Kyle gave me a stern stare. "No, Carrie Sue. Maryann called this morning and asked me to help her get into character. You know how it is. Opening Night jitters. She's nervous, unsure of herself."

I gasped in disgust. "You think I'm stupid enough to believe you were rehearsing with the stereo blaring the way it was?" I slammed my hands on my hips to keep from slapping him.

He rolled his eyes. "I turned on the stereo to try to wake up. And when Maryann arrived, I thought it'd be more appropriate to rehearse on the back porch." He stepped closer, thinking he could charm me. "And I forgot to turn the music off, love. I'm sorry."

I slapped his chest, pushing him away. "Don't give me that crap. You weren't on the porch. I walked back there trying to get in the house after I discovered my key wouldn't open the front door, because you'd engaged the deadbolt to lock me out."

Rather than argue, he strolled outside like a tomcat on the prowl, and looked around. After a moment, he wandered back in. "Where's your little car?"

"That's none of your concern."

He frowned. "Did it break down again?"

Seething with anger, I refused to answer.

"If your car broke down, why didn't you call me?"

"Get real. You wouldn't have heard the phone above the blaring music. Plus, you were preoccupied with Maryann."

He grabbed my arms. "Stop it, Carrie Sue. I love you. Don't you know that?"

"Get your filthy hands off me." I pushed him backwards.

"You're overreacting." Tears welled in his deceitful eyes.

I turned away, determined not to let this Shakespearian Iago deceive me again. He might be a great actor, but he didn't have a sincere fiber in his body.

He grabbed my waist and pulled my butt against his sex. "I think I know what you need, baby."

I poked him as hard as I could with my elbows. "Get out of my house," I shouted.

His arms tightened around my waist. "You don't mean that."

I elbowed him again and stepped toward the antique hunt board. Dad used to keep his snub nose pistol in the top drawer. It was the same type of gun Jack Ruby used to kill Lee Harvey Oswald.

I didn't find the gun but spotted Mom's stainless steel letter opener. She called this her "paper knife."

I wrapped my fingers around the handle, not intending to kill him. My main purpose was to get him out of the house and away from me, but I must admit, the thought of destroying his manhood crossed my mind.

I pivoted toward Kyle, holding the letter opener like the murderer in the movie Psycho. Kyle's eyes widened. He jumped back.

My rage had startled him. Good, he deserved to be afraid.

"Philandering snake," I shouted.

His expression changed from fearful to ferocious, as if I were a burglar who'd broken into the house. He growled and lunged toward me like Bruce Lee, his hands and feet chopping all over the place.

I jumped away, but not quickly enough. He whacked at my hand, and I lost my grip on my weapon. It flipped wildly through the air.

I imagined the knife coming down and piercing his heart, but it clanged to the floor, missing him by inches. I drew my hand back, intending to slap him from now until Sunday. Before I could, he turned and strutted out.

As I listened to his car scratch off in the driveway, I started trembling. I pressed my back against the door and slid down to the floor, sobbing. His betrayal hurt like a stab in the heart.

I told myself he wasn't worth this pain. I never should have married him. I'd dated

Kyle for only six months before I agreed to become his wife. He'd been married twice before. Those marriages failed, because his previous wives didn't want an open relationship, he'd said.

Before I married him, I insisted on an exclusive union, and he had agreed to forsake all others. I was naive enough to believe him. I should have known he wouldn't change.

I inhaled slow, deep breaths to steady myself enough to call Chief Barnum and apologize for missing our appointment.

"Everyone has car problems now and then," he said and agreed to meet me in the afternoon. I hoped he couldn't hear the self-doubt in my voice. I'd lost all confidence in myself as a woman and questioned my ability to write a decent article before my deadline.

I gritted my teeth, got into the Caddy, and drove out. Someone once said, "Most of life is showing up," and I wanted to believe that.

As I pulled onto Freedom Lane, my hands were still shaking. I weaved from side to side on the narrow, winding street, named in honor of the slaves who'd escaped my ancestors' cotton plantation a century ago.

My grandmother and my parents eventually broke that cycle of prejudice. They were progressives for peace. Mom and Dad frequently talked about the importance of President Abraham Lincoln's

Emancipation Proclamation, and when I learned his Gettysburg Address, as required in school, Mom said I should insert the word women, and say "all men and women were created equal."

They also admired Dr. Martin Luther King, and prominently displayed a photo of them both taken with Dr. King at his *I Have a Dream* speech in front of the Lincoln Memorial in Washington, DC.

I now know my parents were a hard act to follow, but in my rebellious teen years, I thought every word they uttered was pure crap. I wanted to be their complete opposite and find my own identity. Cheesy, I know. They should have disowned me, but they kept saying they loved me, and understood. They were young once, they said. Back then I couldn't imagine my parents as young, and unfortunately, I gave them hell and no reason to be proud of me.

Would they be proud of me now? I pondered the question as I turned on the radio and listened to Bob Seger singing *Against the Wind*.

My whole body throbbed like it'd been stung by wasps. Dad almost died from wasp-stings once, and would have, according to the doctor, if not for Mom's quick response.

If Mom had been riding in this car with me, she would have said "slow down and smell the roses," but I wouldn't stop speeding, not even around the hair-pin curves.

An old truck honked like crazy and barreled toward me. I swerved to miss it; then froze like a helpless ninny. His tires squealed and plowed into a patch of pine trees.

I opened the door to apologize and offer aid. The irate driver rolled down his window and cursed in Spanish. He reminded me of Fidel Castro, and I recalled when Castro allowed Cubans to flee to America several years ago. We later discovered some of the exiles had been released from jails and mental institutions.

As I waited for the man to stop yelling, I tried to think of something to diffuse his anger. I'd taken two Spanish courses in college.

"Lo siento. Fue sin quere," I said, trying to apologize for the accident.

He gunned the accelerator and glared at me like a charging bull. His tires stirred up a murky cloud of Georgia red clay.

"Drive away," I told myself. "Don't be a target."

I cranked up the Caddy as his truck plunged forward out of the mud. I expected him to aim his vehicle at me, but he sped off down the road in a haze of dust, dragging a baby pine tree caught under his back bumper.

As he disappeared, I took deep breaths to relieve the tension, and drove to a grassy area where I could rest until my hands stopped trembling. I sat in the car with the motor running, radio on, and heat blowing full blast.

Two buzzards circled overhead, probably waiting for me to die. I stared at them until the news came on.

"Cuban detainees freed eighty-nine hostages, after signing an agreement that ended a siege at the Atlanta Penitentiary, the longest prison uprising in U.S. history," the newsman reported.

I thought of that angry trucker and his fierce eyes. A shiver ran up my spine. Had he escaped the Atlanta Pen?

Chapter Two

The Southern Journal resides in a three-story Victorian house, all decked out for the holidays. Lisa Anderson and her husband Thomas endangered life and limb, stringing a gazillion lights around the roof and windows. Lisa was the office secretary and circulation manager. Thomas was a retired journalism professor. He often helped Marcus Handley, the publisher and managing editor, in whatever capacity was needed.

I'd sold the newspaper and building to Marcus a few months after I'd lost my parents. He'd been my mentor since Dad hired him seven years ago. Under his leadership, the Southern Journal had won several awards and honored the tradition Dad started: *Fight injustice. Write the truth.*

Our weekly covered all of Atlanta's Southside. Marcus had assigned me the crime beat. I also wrote a personal column and feature articles.

I grimaced at the thought of going inside, but I couldn't avoid it. I needed my Tandy. It was an advanced word processor. I'd become entirely too dependent on mine since Marcus bought them for the staff. We could now send our stories via telephone lines from wherever we were, which was convenient and a time-saver. I could type my interviews, rather than try to decipher my speed writing.

A sick dread washed over me, and I couldn't shake it. My eyes looked red in the mirror of my powder compact. My hair was a mess. I hated to face the crew like this. Journalists are buzzards. They can smell weakness and pain. I expected a barrage of nosy questions.

I redid my hair bun, rested my forehead on the steering wheel and remembered what Mom used to say, "In ten years you'll forget all about this." Perhaps she was right, but ten years seemed like an eternity.

At the tap on my window, I jumped up like a Jack-in-the-box. Marcus was frowning and holding my little computer like a weapon. Without the scowl, he resembled those pictures of Jesus featured in Sunday school books. His mustache, beard and long hair made him appear older than thirty-five. I often found it difficult to believe he was only ten years my senior.

Dad used to say Marcus was wiser and had endured more than people twice his age. This afternoon he wore jeans and a V-neck blue sweater, giving me a peek at his powerful chest.

A compulsive runner, he often ran to and from work. He lived three miles away in an old Georgian Colonial he was restoring.

When Dad hired him, he came to our house for dinner and stayed the night. My body tingled when I first saw him. He looked like Superman with facial hair.

I exhaled a sigh and forced a smile as I rolled down the window. "Hi Marcus. What's up?"

He tapped the Tandy. "I couldn't find the story on the shooting in here, Carrie."

I inhaled his sexy, musky scent and chewed on my lower lip to keep from crying. I'd rather stand nude in freezing rain than cry in front of Marcus. "I haven't written it yet. I had to reschedule with Barnum." I glanced at my watch. "I need to get over there now."

His dark blue eyes bored into mine as if he could read my soul. "Why'd you have to reschedule?" He touched his beard as gently as he might stroke a lover. Dad once told me he heard Marcus play Beethoven's Moonlight Sonata on the piano. I tried to imagine these masterful hands dancing across piano keys - though I couldn't reconcile that image with what Dad said about Marcus flying B-52s and dropping bombs.

"It's a long story. No time to tell it."

He leaned through my open window and whispered, "Are you all right, Carrie? You don't look well."

I closed my eyes to hide. "Gee, thanks."

"If you need me to interview Barnum and write the story, I will." He touched my shoulder.

His fingers sent an electric charge. "I'm fine, just pissed off. My car broke down, and I had to postpone the interview. Don't worry. I'll get the article together in time."

He exhaled a grunt. "I need that story before deadline."

"Of course," I barked. "I'm in no mood for your condescending attitude." I snatched the computer and cranked up the Cadillac.

As I drove away, I regretted my words. I ought to have known better than to misdirect my anger at Marcus. He was an unpredictable, grouchy man. He expected perfection and didn't tolerate disrespect. What if he fired me for spouting off at him?

Chapter Three

Chief Barnum's office resided inside the belly of the College Station police building, an ugly concrete box, hogging the street corner. I parked, took deep breaths, and slid my little word processor inside my heavy tote, which was already crammed full of reporters' notebooks, cosmetic items, and a change of clothes, tampons, clean underwear and my trusty Olympus camera.

I needed to take another picture of Chief Barnum. We had several photos of him in the can, but Barnum claimed they made him look like a fat convict. He'd lost quite a bit of weight recently and was justifiably proud of that accomplishment.

I sucked in my gut, pulled my shoulders back and walked through the double doors like I owned the place. My boots clopped like horse-hooves on the linoleum, as I headed down the hall.

The door to Dora Lee Thompson's office was closed. She was Barnum's secretary, and no one entered his office without going through her first. I stopped for a moment and took a few more deep breaths to compose myself before I eased the door open.

Dora Lee faced the back wall. She appeared to be copying something on the Xerox machine. Her lavender knit dress clung to her rear end. She looked like a model in a fashion magazine. Her long dark hair draped her shoulders.

She arranged the copied pages into three separate stacks and stapled each pile. When she turned around, she gasped and slapped the papers to her chest. "You scared me to death, Carrie Sue. When did you get here?"

"I just walked in."

"The Chief will be back soon. Time got away from us." She plopped down in the chair behind her desk and slammed the copied papers on top. "I thought I'd never finish transcribing these."

I nodded at the stack of papers. "What are those?"

"Police interviews, you know, of the boys arrested for killing Preston Campbell. Took me forever to transcribe." Dora Lee glanced at the Coca-Cola clock on the wall. "Nev Powers will be here any minute. He's taking these over to Wally's office."

"You mean, Wallace Sheppard, Fulton County D.A.?"

She nodded. "Yeah. Thank God I finished in time. I don't need Nev breathing down my neck." She twisted her mouth into a quirky grin. "You know how he can be." She threw up her hands in a gesture of surrender.

"Of course, you do. Y'all dated in high school, or at least, that's what he tells everybody." She lowers her voice to a whisper, "I was surprised you'd date him. He talks down to people and he's narrow-minded. Don't you think?"

My face burned with embarrassment. "Nev is exaggerating, as he tends to do. I thought we'd talked about this before, Dora Lee?"

"Yes, but you changed the subject and evaded my question."

"We had only one date."

Dora Lee's brown eyes widened as if she wanted me to elaborate. I had sense enough to keep my mouth shut. Knowledge is power, I'd learned, and gossip in the workplace was anathema.

I sat in the chair opposite her. "That was years ago, Dora Lee." I gritted my teeth. I needed to stay professional, not puke up all my personal stuff.

She smiled and blinked, as if processing information. "Nev said y'all went to different schools."

"He played quarterback for Fulton County High. I went to Justice Academy."

She nodded. "I heard your grandma started that school."

"That's right. She did." I shuffled through my tote, pretending to look for something. Stay calm, I told myself.

She propped her elbows on her desk. "I'm always giving you scoops. 'Bout time

25

you gave me one." She giggled, and I wondered how she could find humor in anything so silly. I couldn't remember the last time I'd enjoyed a silly laugh.

"How'd you and Nev get together?"

"I met him at the Varsity. One thing led to another. We went to a movie. Nothing much to talk about."

I didn't dare tell Dora Lee that Nev Powers lost his temper at the movie and called Jimmy Johnson a "coon," then punched him in the face. Nev said he attacked Jimmy because I flirted with him. Nev went on to say, Jimmy looked like the drunk driver who caused the automobile accident that paralyzed his Mom and killed his twin brother Nathan. If I regurgitated all that crap, Dora Lee might use it against Nev, and he'd end up resenting us both.

"Speaking of Nev, before he gets here, I'd like a copy of those police interviews, please." I held out my hand, expecting her to grant my request.

She stared wide-eyed, as if I'd asked her to swallow poison. "This is an on-going investigation, Carrie Sue."

"I know, but the Chief will have to share them with the legal eagles. And I'll get a copy eventually, anyway." I tried to look sincere as I waggled my outstretched fingers. "I won't tell anyone. You know you can trust me." She'd given me information before, and I'd never revealed her as a source.

She and I eyeballed each other for a moment. Then she stood abruptly, walked over to me, opened my tote and crammed in one of the little stacks she'd stapled together. "Don't you dare tell a soul, Carrie Sue." She shook her finger like a teacher scolding a child. "I'll get fired, and I need this job. I'm a single mother of a four-year-old daughter with a sorry ex, who's negligent on his child support."

"I won't tell a soul. I promise." I gave her what I hoped was a reassuring smile. "Thanks for scoring one for the First Amendment."

As Dora Lee rushed to make another copy, Nev walked in, dapper in a Reaganesque brown suit and wide-striped tie. His chest seemed a little bulky from the shoulder holster, gun and ammo pouch that detectives wore. His boyish face hadn't changed much since high school. His short brown hair stuck up like a well-used brush. His forehead was almost as long as the rest of his face, which made him appear intellectual, although he claimed to be "a good ole boy."

"Hello, Nev," I said, loudly, to alert Dora Lee, so she wouldn't pass any comments and incriminate herself.

Nev flashed his tiger eyes. "Well, well, well."

Dora Lee turned from the Xerox. She gave him a tight-lipped smile. "That's a deep subject, Nev."

"I'm a deep guy." He shifted his eyes toward me. "Carrie Sue, you doing any good?"

"Depends on your point of view, Nev. Right now, I'm waiting to interview the Chief."

"He'll be along shortly," Dora Lee said, as if she hadn't already told me this.

Dora Lee stapled and handed a stack of papers to Nev. He flipped through the pages. His eyes zipped from left to right as if he were speed reading.

Silence enveloped the room. I embraced it like an old friend. A quote from Abraham Lincoln kept running through my head: *It's better to remain silent and be thought a fool than to speak out and remove all doubt.*

When Chief Barnum strolled in, wearing a dark grey suit a size too big, Dora Lee sighed in relief. Barnum was a tall, bulky Tennessee Ernie Ford look-alike, with the same high cheekbones, long nose, mustache, and coarse, slicked-back hair. Dora Lee once told me he did a fair imitation of Ford singing Sixteen Tons.

He placed his large hands on Nev's shoulders. "Thanks for taking those over."

Nev backed away. "Sure thing, Chief." He bowed toward me and Dora Lee. "Try to stay out of trouble, ladies."

Dora Lee and I raised our eyebrows at his condescending remark. She seemed to be holding her breath. I crossed my legs and nervously swung my top foot to offset the sadness seeping into my bones.

Nev turned to face Chief Barnum. "I'm gonna read these statements over carefully before I give them to the D.A. I wanna make sure they're accurate."

Chief Barnum frowned. "Dora Lee's a stickler for accuracy, you know that."

Nev grunted a response, pushed the door open and walked out. "See you later."

After Nev left, Barnum smiled at me. "Hi, Carrie Sue. Hope you haven't been waiting long."

I pushed my stiff, achy body out of the chair. "No, I just got here, Chief. Sorry for missing our appointment this morning. I know how busy you are."

"No busier than anyone else. You get your car fixed?"

"Not yet. I'm driving Mom's old Cadillac. At least it runs."

He motioned for me to follow him. "That's good. Come on in."

He plopped down behind his mahogany desk with its mountain of papers. He had forbidden Dora Lee to straighten it. "He can usually find what he's looking for on top of his messy desk, but it drives me nuts," Dora Lee once told me in private.

I sat in the worn leather chair directly across from him, trying not to look at the sad-eyed buck with antlers mounted on the wall. Beside the buck's head was a sign that said, *A clean desk is a sign of a sick mind.*

Next to the slogan was a photo of Barnum with President Reagan. Another photo showed a younger Barnum as deputy with the Forsyth County Sheriff's Department. He grew up in Cumming, where he lived until moving to College Station to become the chief of police.

As I pulled out my camera and focused on Barnum's face, he picked up a paper from his messy desk and pretended to study it as I snapped his photo.

After taking several shots, I stuffed the camera inside my tote and withdrew my little computer, maneuvering the stapled pages from Dora Lee to the bottom of the bag. Right on cue, she walked in with a beige file folder and handed it to him.

When my Tandy booted up, I said, "Tell me about the victim of last night's shooting."

Barnum opened the file from Dora Lee, withdrew his reading glasses from a breast pocket and positioned them on the bridge of his long nose. "Preston Campbell, sixteen, Caucasian; performed odd jobs at the Methodist Church. He was walking home from church when he was shot in the back. He died at the scene. Robbery seems to be the motive. His father Hampton Campbell identified the body lying in a pool of blood at the scene. Preston had decided to walk home from church that night, Mr. Campbell said. When his son didn't come home, Mr. Campbell came looking for him."

I asked him to verify the spelling of Preston's name. Then I asked, "Which school did he attend?"

"Justice Academy. Didn't your grandmother start that?"

"Yes, my paternal Grandmother, Elizabeth Ann Justice."

"I've seen the plaque. What inspired her to start a school?" He pulled off his glasses and stared at me, as if waiting for my answer. Was he trying to get me off track and avoid a lengthy interrogation?

Rather than disclose my suspicions, I answered him. "She died before I was born, unfortunately. But according to her journal, she started Justice Academy because she didn't think the public school system would integrate, as required by law. Only a few students attended back then. She drove them to and from school and taught the classes. She even provided breakfast and lunch free for the students who couldn't pay."

He nodded. "Several hundred attend now, don't they?"

I glanced down, embarrassed I couldn't recall the exact number. "I'm not sure how many, but I know the administration tries to keep a good ratio of blacks and whites. Some Asian students attend, too." I studied my computer screen. "Getting back to Preston Campbell, you said robbery was the motive. Is that correct?"

"That's what we've determined. We've interviewed the suspects. A witness heard one of the boys brag about shooting Preston. But Preston didn't have money on him when he was gunned down."

As I typed in what Barnum said, he stood and sauntered into Dora Lee's office. "Make Carrie Sue a copy of the addresses of the victim and the suspects, Dora Lee." He waited at the doorway until she handed him a sheet of paper with the requested information.

After he offered the info to me, he asked, "What else do you need to know?" He sat and drummed his fingers on his desk.

"Where exactly did the shooting occur?"

"On Hemphill, near Virginia Ave, a few blocks from where Preston lived."

"Whom did you arrest for Preston's murder?"

"Four black youths, all members of the same gang. Jeremy Andrews, age sixteen, Calvin Newson, age fourteen, Leroy Cortez, age sixteen and Tatum Brookins, age fifteen."

I glanced at the sheet Barnum had given me to make sure their names and ages were included. "How did you discover these boys were members of a gang? What's the name of the gang?"

"Bad and Black."

"Were they wearing clothing identifying them as belonging to this gang?"

"No. We gathered that information from other sources."

"What sources?"

"I can't divulge that right now, Carrie Sue. This is all under investigation."

"Did any of the youths admit to being part of a gang?"

"No."

"Chief, if you claim these youths are members of a black gang, eventually you'll have to prove it."

"I do have proof. I'm just not ready to share it with you yet, Carrie Sue."

"Why did you arrest these four?"

"Like I said, we have witnesses, and we have the boys' statements."

Even though Dora Lee had given me copies of the statements, I tried to get copies from Barnum in order to protect her. "I'd like to read their statements please."

"You know I can't give you that now, Carrie Sue. They're not for publication."

"Then tell me what you know for sure."

"The suspects ganged up on Preston. They all worked together to commit the crime."

"Are you saying all the suspects have admitted to this?"

"More or less."

"What do you mean, more or less?"

"It's like I said. We gathered from their statements that they worked together to rob and kill Preston Campbell."

"Other than the suspects, who are your witnesses?"

"We're not revealing that information yet, Carrie Sue, but we think we have the murder weapon, a twenty-two pistol, found in Jeremy Andrews' car."

"Did any of the youths admit to shooting and killing Preston?"

"The suspects identified two possible shooters, but they're blaming one another, which is typical."

"Who are the two possible shooters?"

"Jeremy Andrews and Calvin Newson."

"Are you still holding all four suspects?"

"We are."

"Where?"

"Juvenile Detention Center."

I glanced at the sheet Barnum had given me with the addresses of the suspects. "Do all of the suspects live in the same area?"

"Yes, they live in the projects, you know, public housing."

"Have these boys been in trouble with the law before?"

"I would almost swear to it, but we're in the process of gathering all of that information now."

"What time did the shooting occur?"

"Around eight...eight-thirty, two nights ago."

"Where did the suspects attend school?"

"All except Tatum Brookins were bused to Tanksley High in DeKalb County under the Majority-to-Minority program. You know how that works. If you're in a public school where you're in the majority, you can get permission to go to another public school where you're in the minority."

Barnum frowned, shook his head and closed his eyes as if it pained him to continue this interview. "Tanksley High is mostly black now, due to all the bussing going on. Also, all the white folks have moved farther north or they're putting their kids in private schools that are white. That means the efforts to desegregate aren't working. Bussing isn't doing a damn thing to integrate the school system. Tanksley used to be majority white. The bussed kids spend too much time on the bus, going to and from. By the time they get home, it's dark, they're hungry and frustrated, and want to hang out and get in trouble."

I interrupted Barnum. "Where did Tatum Brookins go to school? Didn't you say all the youths except Tatum went to Tanksley?"

"Brookins attended College Station High."

"If Tatum Brookins attended a different school from the others, how is it likely they all belonged to the same gang?"

"It happens. They live in the projects."

I took a moment to read through my notes. "Thanks for your time, Chief. If I have other questions, I'll call you." Little did he know I had a bounty of information, thanks to Dora Lee.

Chapter Four

I walked back to the corner toward the giant magnolia tree where I'd parked the Cadillac. One of my favorite places to write was in my car, parked in a safe, private location. If any place was safe, it should be the police station. Or so I thought.

I scooted my seat back, pulled out my computer and read through my notes again. I tried to think of a clever lead, but my mind wouldn't cooperate. It kept going back to the horrible moment when I caught Kyle cheating.

A reddish gold sunset had filled the sky by the time I'd written a semblance of an article. I read it and grimaced. Not good.

I tried to meditate, reciting the mantra "om" to spark my creativity. I imagined Marcus pacing the floor like a caged lion, while waiting for this article. He couldn't put the paper to bed without it, a front-page story. I could almost feel his petulance, like the chilly air seeping through the car windows.

Regardless, my conscience, and my professional pride, wouldn't allow me to give him a half-ass, one-sided article when I suspected a more complete story could be found in the police interviews.

I flipped through the stack of interviews Dora Lee had given me. The first statement was from Tim Dillon. Officer Lewis Stanley had recorded his statement. Nev Powers asked the questions.

Chief Barnum hadn't mentioned Dillon's name in connection with Preston Campbell's alleged murder, but as I read, I discovered Dillon was a witness. He told Nev he was riding the bus with Calvin Newson when Calvin admitted he shot Preston Campbell with Jeremy Andrews' gun.

Dillon said he knew Jeremy and the name of the third boy involved, Leroy Cortez, but he didn't mention Tatum Brookins.

That didn't make sense. From what Chief Barnum said, four boys had been arrested, and they were all members of the gang Bad and Black. Yet, Dillon said nothing about a gang and only mentioned three teens, leaving out Tatum, who was arrested anyway. Why?

I riffled through the stack of interviews, searching for another witness. When I couldn't find one, I read the statement from Tatum Brookins. His mother had signed a paper waiving his Miranda rights. Why? It would have been better to remain silent and request an attorney.

Nev asked Tatum what he was doing the night Preston was shot and killed.

Tatum said he went to the grocery store to buy donuts, but Jeremy, Calvin and Leroy went to shoplift. When Calvin saw Preston Campbell, he wanted to rob him, Tatum said Calvin got the gun from Leroy, because Leroy was holding it for Jeremy. Tatum said Calvin didn't think a twenty-two pistol could kill anyone. Tatum stated he warned Calvin and the others not to bother Preston, and then walked away. He was two houses up, he said, when he heard a gunshot. He saw a lady named Ms. Sikes. "She in a wheelchair and there was a guy-I forget his name-he do her laundry. He brings it to her," Tatum said. "That guy, he say, 'Hello,' to me," Tatum stated.

I paused from reading. Was Tatum referring to my neighbor and friend Freemont Jackson? Freemont owned and operated Jackson Laundry. He ran his mother's business, after she passed, out of his home, as she had. Just about everyone had called her Mama Jackson. She died of a heart attack a year after Mom and Dad were killed.

I stared out in the darkness. Were the police planning to interview Freemont?

The night had killed the sunset, Marcus probably wanted to kill me, but he also wanted a balanced story, not a regurgitation of what Chief Barnum said. So, I continued reading.

Next in the stack of interviews, I found Jeremy Andrews' statement. Barnum said, police discovered the twenty-two pistol in his parents' car. Jeremy's father Joseph had also signed a paper agreeing to waive his son's rights.

Sixteen-year-old Jeremy claimed Calvin robbed and shot Preston with Leroy's gun. The gun in his car belonged to his sister's boyfriend, and was not the gun used in the shooting, Jeremy stated. He mentioned nothing about Tatum being involved.

One of the last interviews was with fourteen-year-old Calvin Newson. His mother Clarissa had also waived his rights.

Calvin stated that Jeremy ran up to Preston with the gun and shot him. Calvin said Tatum told all of them to leave Preston alone. Then Tatum left the scene.

Next, I glanced at the statement from sixteen-year-old Leroy Cortez. Like the others, he waived his rights. Nev questioned him in the presence of his mother Lisa Cortez.

Leroy claimed all four boys walked out of the grocery store when Calvin spotted Preston. Calvin wanted to jump him, Leroy said, but Tatum said, "Naw, I ain't touching the dude," according to Leroy.

Leroy said he and Tatum walked a different way, but Calvin and Jeremy went up the street toward Preston. Leroy said he gave Calvin the gun because Jeremy told him to, but later when he talked to Calvin, Leroy said he found out Jeremy took the gun, jumped on Preston and started hitting him.

"When Jeremy said he shot the dude right in the back. I tell him, 'They catch you, they gonna lock you up,'" Leroy stated.

After I read Leroy's statement and polished my article, I wrote down two questions to consider later: 1. Why was Tatum arrested? 2. Why did Barnum say the arrested youths were gang members?

I heard a knock on my widow and looked up at a tall, dark man. He wore a wool cap, pulled down low over his forehead. Blood raced to my head. The man looked like a burglar.

"Oh no," I whispered and groped for my car keys, but they weren't in the ignition, though I'd started the car not long ago to turn on the heat. I couldn't remember pulling the keys out. My heart hammered as I searched. They weren't on the floorboard or between the seats.

The stranger sprayed my windshield with what appeared to be water and wiped it off with a rag. When he'd finished, he smiled and folded his hands in prayer, bowing slightly.

As I studied him, I began to relax. He looked like a humble man. Did he need money for food, alcohol or drugs? Who was I to judge? He'd performed a service. He'd clean my windshield.

I reached inside my tote for my billfold, and miraculously found my bunch of keys. From the money folder, I took out a five and rolled down the window. The cold air swooshed in.

I shivered as he grabbed the wrinkled Lincoln and squeezed my hand. "Thank you, Ma'am." He smiled. No front teeth. "I'm warm from your gift. God bless you. You have given to the least of men and so you have given to my Father who is in heaven."

I inhaled the cold air along with his gratitude. All at once, my body felt lighter, less encumbered. This poor man had so little. Yet he could articulate his appreciation better than most. Why shouldn't I be thankful as well?

Chapter Five

As I pulled up to the Southern Journal building, I saw Marcus sitting on the front steps, bathed in a flood of Christmas lights. He wasn't pacing the floor as I had imagined, but he looked downright angry. I zipped up my leather jacket against the wind and jumped out to face his rage.

I noticed he was puffing on a cigarette. I'd never seen him smoke before, but I knew little about his personal life and habits.

Marcus grew up in Irvine, California. He earned a master's degree in journalism from Whittier College, joined the Air Force, and flew B-52s during the Vietnam era. As a flight commander, he'd won several medals. He married a journalist, Susan Silverman, who died in a helicopter crash, while covering the war in Vietnam.

I walked up to him with my brave face on. "I didn't know you smoked, Marcus. I thought you valued your health."

He stomped out the cigarette. "I've quit."

"Obviously not." I sat beside him on the step. The heat from his body warmed me as I opened my computer to the shooting story.

Marcus read through the article. "I left a space above the fold. This should fit."

"I want to apologize for what I said to you earlier. I was out of line."

He nodded but said nothing.

"I'm sorry it took me this long to get the story together. There are extenuating circumstances, and there's much more to it than what you see here. So, we need to talk."

He stroked his beard. "Your husband has left several urgent messages. Lisa put them on your desk." He studied my face, as if it held a tragic novel.

"Kyle and I are not going to make it, and I'd rather not go into the reason why. I'll need to stay here in one of the bedrooms upstairs for a night or two."

He frowned. "Ordinarily that would be fine. But I'm staying here until the workers at my house finish tearing down one of the walls and redoing the electrical system." His warm breath steamed out in the cold air. "My better judgment tells me it wouldn't be a good idea."

My face burned with anger. I'd sold him this building and this newspaper. Why shouldn't he help me out in my time of need? "There are two bedrooms on the third floor." I gulped a breath. "I'm desperate. I need to stay here."

He scowled. "Wouldn't you feel uncomfortable?"

I avoided his shrewd stare. "No, not at all. I'll feel safer here than at my house." I didn't dare ask him if he'd feel uncomfortable. He may have said yes.

"All right, Carrie. If you're fine with it, I'm fine with it."

I flushed with relief. "Thank you." On impulse, I hugged him, squeezing tighter and longer than I should have. I loved the feel of his strong, warm body.

He pulled away, stood and walked inside without saying a word. I followed him into his office and closed the door. I started to tell him about the transcripts I'd gotten from Dora Lee, but I was struck dumb when I noticed how his jeans winged out in front. Holy Mother of God, he may look like a combination of Jesus and Superman, but he was endowed like Goliath. Did my impulsive hug cause this reaction?

As I pondered this, I noticed an eight-by-ten of a beautiful blonde woman by his desktop computer. The photo was signed, *To the love of my life, forever yours, Susan.*

I picked up the photo. This was a picture of his late wife. I wanted to ask him about her, but I didn't dare.

He snatched her picture from me and threw it in a desk drawer. I gulped the sexually charged air. If we'd been in a car with the windows rolled up, the glass would have fogged over for sure. We both needed our bones jumped, but his cold eyes of steel were in denial, and I was too stunned to respond.

44

I forced my eyes away from his erection and stared at the large black binders against the back wall. These binders contained recent issues of the Southern Journal. The older newspapers were stored on the second and third floors in the Archives.

I noticed a bottle of Jack Daniels on one of his shelves. I'd never seen Marcus drink whiskey, but I'd never seen him smoke a cigarette until a few minutes ago. Was he planning to get hammered later? My gut told me, yes.

I watched him out of the corner of my eye. He attached my Tandy to the desktop computer and typed in the code on the top of my article to send it to the main frame for printing.

"You need to call your husband," he said, staring at the computer screen.

I saw red. "Excuse me? You're telling me what to do in my personal life when you guard your privacy like an alligator protecting her young?"

He still stared at the computer screen, as if he found it more interesting than my face. "I don't know your situation, Carrie, but if you don't call him, he'll become even more obsessive than he already is. He's called here half a dozen times. If he doesn't hear from you tonight, he might come by. I don't want him here. I don't think you do either. Isn't that why you're staying upstairs? You want to avoid him."

"I don't give a damn what Kyle does." I yelled, stomped out of his office, ran to the bathroom and slammed the door.

When I cooled down, I came to my senses. Marcus was probably right, but the thought of calling Kyle made my stomach tighten into a sick knot.

I washed my hands, splashed cold water on my face, walked to my cubbyhole desk and dialed the number for Stage Atlanta. The machine answered with a breathy woman's voice, probably Maryann's, reciting the times and dates for performances, and directions to the theatre.

After the beep, I said, "This is Carrie Sue Justice. Tell Kyle Holland not to call me again. I'm alive and well and staying with a friend. I'll be in touch later with regard to my plans."

I slammed the phone down and took a moment to relax before I called Freemont Jackson. If I had a brother, I'd want him to be exactly like Freemont.

"I'm your black brother," he often said.

We share an amazing history. In the 1800s, my double great-grandmother Charlotte willed his double great-grandmother Georgia her freedom, along with an acre of property and a small house. But the laws governing the Southern states prohibited slaves from being free and owning property. I learned this from Granny Justice's journal. Thanks to her tireless research, Freemont's ancestors were able to claim their property.

After Freemont's Mom died of a heart attack, he inherited the house, the land, and Mama Jackson's laundry business, but his ultimate plan was to teach Black History.

He answered on the first ring. "Jackson's Laundry."

"Hi, it's me, Carrie Sue."

"Hey there, long time, no see."

"I know. We've both been too busy. How are you?"

"Not enough hours in the day. You don't sound good. Are you okay?"

"No," I whispered. "My car broke down this morning, and I came home early to find Kyle with another woman."

"Oh, no, honey. I'm so sorry. Where're you now?"

"I'm at work, that's why I'm whispering."

"You want me to kick his ass?"

Freemont was a giant of a man, about six-six, built like a battering-ram, but he had a gentle soul. He turned down a football scholarship from the University of Georgia, because of his Mama's weak heart. Every time he got hurt playing ball, she'd have to swallow a nitroglycerine tablet. But no matter how much he sacrificed to protect his Mama, her soft, tired heart eventually gave out. "Kyle's not worth your time, Free."

"What are you planning to do?"

"Divorce his ass."

"Are you driving home tonight?"

47

"No, I don't want to run into him. I'm at the newspaper. I'm planning to stay in one of the bedrooms upstairs. I'll write Kyle a letter, telling him he has two days to get his stuff from the house. After that, I'll have the locks changed."

"You want me to deliver the letter?"

"Thanks, Free, but I hate to put you in the middle of this."

"Don't worry about it. I'll be happy to help."

"I need to contact a lawyer first and think about what I'm going to say. But I didn't call you to talk about Kyle...although I must admit I feel better after venting."

"Vent as much as you need to, I'm here."

"I know, Free, thank you. The real reason I called was to ask if you know anything about the College Station teenager who got shot and killed two nights ago."

"Word on the street is local boys were arrested."

"Yes, but one of those boys, Tatum Brookins, wasn't even at the scene when the shooting occurred. Police arrested him anyway."

"You know this for certain?"

"Don't tell anyone, but I read the police transcripts. Tatum told police he warned the others not to hurt Preston, which was verified by the other suspects in their statements. Tatum also stated he saw someone delivering laundry to Ms. Sikes.

Was that you? If it was, maybe you can identify Tatum, and he'll walk."

"Was that Wednesday night?"

"That's right."

"I did see a kid. He was alone. If I saw him again, I might recognize him. Kids usually hang out together. Why was he arrested?"

"Wrong place, wrong time, I'm not sure. Police are saying the boys were members of a black gang. Maybe they're thinking the more the merrier. But we need to talk about this privately, sometime tomorrow if you can spare the time."

"Come on over for supper around six. I'll cook the vegetables I put up in the freezer and fry some cornbread."

My stomach growled at the mention of food. "Sounds wonderful. Wish I had some now. Are the vegetables from your garden?"

"Yep, they are."

"I don't know how you find the time to run your business, go to college and take care of your Mama's Garden."

He laughed. "And don't forget I take great care of our roses, too."

He was talking about the blanket of roses, separating my property from his. The Jacque Cartier's have been blooming since the 1800s, according to Granny Justice's journal. "Yes, and you're also known for your humility."

"What are you talking about, girl? I'm not humble. I'm mean as a snake."

Chapter Six

After I said goodbye to Freemont, I ordered a large pizza, and searched for Marcus. He wasn't in his office, but I found him in the production room, armed with a paste-up knife, hovering over the light table.

I loved watching him. His artist's touch reminded me of Dad's. "I took a new picture of a slimmer Chief Barnum."

He grimaced. "No room, no time."

"Another thing, I have copies of the police interviews of the four suspects."

He looked up from bordering my article with tape and listened as I explained. When I stopped talking, he smiled, and I got a glimpse of his beautiful teeth.

"Now I understand why it took you so long to get back here. You were reading those statements." He turned away to stare at the front page. "I'd like to run them verbatim in the next issue."

"You know I want to, Marcus, but if we publish too soon, Dora Lee may lose her job."

"No one can prove Dora Lee gave them to you."

"I'm not so sure about that. Nev came in soon after I'd stuffed them in my tote.

Knowing Nev as I do, and I've known him since high school, he might put two and two together and blame Dora Lee."

With a heavy sigh, Marcus ran the roller over the front page. I waited for his response and smiled at my above-the-fold article with the headline I wrote: Four youths arrested for slaying teen. I felt relieved Marcus didn't substitute "youth gang" for "four youths."

As if he'd heard my thoughts, he said "In my opinion that gang stuff is nonsense. See if you can get a duplicate copy of those interviews from one of the lawyers. That way we'll have a different source, and we won't incriminate Dora Lee."

Before I could respond, Lisa waltzed in. Fortyish and attractive, with thick, shoulder-length flaxen hair and blue eyes, her face reminded me of a Kewpie Doll. She wore red lipstick painted outside the lines of her mouth. On Fridays, during deadline, she often said she removed her receptionist/secretary's hat, put on her circulation manager's hat and dressed down. She had on jeans, a yellow turtle-neck sweater, and tennis shoes.

Lisa hugged me, and I got a whiff of her gardenia perfume. "Your husband has been calling like crazy."

"I know. I called him. He knows I'm alive and well."

"I'm glad," she smiled and pursed her lips as she studied my face. To avoid an inquisition, I rushed out to get the pizza I'd ordered.

I left half of the pizza in the break room for the guys who ran the presses and carried the rest along with my heavy tote up three flights of stairs.

Mom had decorated the third floor with antiques, and as I inhaled the old furniture smell, I remembered how she'd forced me to traipse along while she bargained for relics.

I walked to the kitchen area and placed the pizza on the table. I poured myself a glass of water from the refrigerator's spout, though I had a hankering for beer.

I looked inside the fridge and found a six-pack of Heineken and plenty of food: sliced turkey, lettuce, tomatoes, mayonnaise, mustard, yogurt, oranges, grapefruit, peaches and other stuff.

I opened a beer and guzzled it down with the pizza. Cleanup took about a minute.

I walked down the hall and peered into the bedroom on the left. It had a blue duffle bag on the burgundy and black rug. Marcus had claimed this room. The bed, a black mid-century four poster, was haphazardly made, the maroon spread askew. A book entitled Greek Tragedies had been placed on the round marble table next to the bed. I once took a course on Greek literature, in which Professor Jacobs said, "Reading tragedy makes us feel better about our own life."

I leafed through the book and lingered for a while in that room. I loved inhaling the spicy, musky smell.

My loitering came to an end when I heard footfalls on the stairs. I scurried to the bedroom across the hall, closed the door and plopped on the bed.

I gulped deep breaths to calm my hammering heart and gazed up at the filmy white canopy draping the four mahogany posts. The little girl in me wanted to believe in "happily ever after" even though the grown up me knew it was a fairytale.

I jumped up when I heard a knock. "Carrie, are you in there?"

I answered a weak, "Yes."

"Are you okay?"

I wiped my eyes and smoothed my hair before I opened the door to face him. "I'm alive. What about you?"

His mouth smiled, though his eyes appeared sad. He gripped a bottle of Jack Daniels—probably the same one I'd spotted in his office earlier.

I pointed to the bottle. "Are you sharing?"

He nodded and walked down the hall toward the kitchen. I followed him.

He grabbed two small glasses from the cupboard, positioned two fingers near the bottom of each glass and poured booze up to his top finger. Dad used to pour shots this way.

After he handed me my portion of the whiskey, he gulped his down like a cowboy in an old western movie.

I sipped mine slowly. It burned going down. I disliked hard liquor. I preferred a glass of wine or a beer, but I couldn't miss this opportunity to share a personal moment with Marcus. He looked like the sexiest man alive as he sat across from me and poured himself a second shot.

"Would you like another?" he asked, picking up my glass.

"I'd better not. I might go crazy on you. I've never been able to hold my liquor with dignity."

He sat in the chair next to mine and cocked his head to one side. He seemed to be studying my face, as if he thought I was the most intriguing person he'd ever seen. His eyes lingered on mine as he capped the bottle. I thought I sensed his desire, but maybe it was the whiskey blurring my judgment.

He wrapped his left arm around the back of his chair and spread his long legs out. With his other hand, he stroked his beard. "Do you need to talk about what's bothering you, Carrie?"

My mouth fell open. I couldn't believe this ultra-private man had asked me to spill my guts when he'd never shared a damn thing about himself. "Maybe I will have another drink."

He uncapped the Jack, poured two fingers and handed me my glass. "You said you and Kyle were having problems."

I took a sip. Marcus gazed at me in a way he'd never done before. I felt naked.

His index finger encircled the rim of his glass. "Perhaps I can give you a male's perspective."

"I've already made up my mind. I'm divorcing Kyle."

"Why?"

I drank the whisky in my glass before I answered. "He cheated on me. I caught him with another woman this morning; one of the actresses in the play he's directing. He had the nerve to invite her to our house after I'd left for work. He didn't expect me home." My lips trembled and I felt tears spilling down my cheeks.

Marcus stood but said nothing as he walked down the hall to the bathroom. Damn him, he invited me to open up and I shared my private hurt, but he left without saying a word, I thought. I wanted to leave and get the hell out, but my legs wobbled and refused to function.

I was holding on to the table to steady myself when Marcus came back. He offered me a wad of toilet paper. I wiped my face and blew my nose with it.

My legs buckled, and I plopped in the chair again. He sat and scooted closer to me. "I'm sorry you're hurting, Carrie. Everyone who knows you knows you're a good person.

You have a good heart. You're talented and intelligent. You work hard. You're always pushing yourself above and beyond the call of duty. And as you reminded me a moment ago, you're alive. Kyle's cheating is his failure, not yours; his loss, not yours. I think you deserve better, but I don't know Kyle. You need to decide what's best for you. If you love him, you may want to give him another chance, and try marriage counseling."

I screwed up my face in disgust. "I don't love Kyle. I don't think I ever loved him. I never really knew him. I saw what I wanted to see, but I was mistaken. Many times. I've suspected he cheated on me, but I didn't want to believe it, so I denied it to myself. Does that make sense?"

Marcus nodded. "Why'd you marry him?"

"I don't know. At first, I had no intention of even dating him. He was one of my professors. I needed an elective and took his dramatic literature class. The first day of class he undressed me with his eyes, a definite red flag. The second day of class, he performed Playboy of the Western World. That's a play written by an Irish playwright, and as I think about it now, his performance that day should have been another red flag. Two weeks later, he asked me out. I told him I wouldn't feel right about dating one of my professors. After the quarter ended, he asked me out again, and I agreed."

The whiskey had loosened my tongue, and I couldn't seem to stop it from wagging. "I guess you might say I let him seduce me with candlelight dinners and romantic drives. I should have ended it when I found out Kyle was going through his second divorce, but like a fool, I ignored all the red flags and became wife number three. The sad truth is, after I lost Mom and Dad, I needed to feel part of a family again, and Kyle made me feel beautiful and desirable. After we married, everything changed. No more romance. It's been weeks and weeks since we've had sex. I blamed it on our crazy schedules. Now I know he's been getting sex elsewhere."

Marcus exhaled loudly and rubbed his eyes. "Kyle doesn't deserve you."

I reached out and touched his beard. It felt softer than I'd imagined. "I know you've been grieving, Marcus. Your grief has created a barrier that says, 'Stay away.' This is the first time you've asked me anything about my private life. We've always talked about work, never about anything personal, and I often feel like I'm always struggling, trying to measure up to you and your perfectionism."

His dark eyes stared at me. "I want the best for you, Carrie, and if I've pushed you, it's only because I want you to reach your full potential. As to grief, everyone grieves differently, and when tragedy strikes, it's not easy coming back to life. That I know." He sucked in a breath. "Is there anything I can do to help you?"

"Yes, there is." I took his face in my hands. "You can make love to me." I kissed him full on his mouth. Before catching Kyle cheating this morning, I would have never considered betraying him or sinking to his level. Maybe I was seeking revenge. I don't know. I'd lost control, obviously. I desperately needed to be held and kissed and made love to. Did I feel guilty? No.

He growled like a captured lion, sucked my lips into his and lifted me from my chair. His urgent desire seemed to match mine. I trembled all over in anticipation as I unzipped his jeans to free his erection.

When I touched him, he placed his hands on my shoulders and pushed me away. "Carrie, you're very beautiful, but you're vulnerable right now." His sad eyes stared into mine. "And we both have a buzz. We're not thinking clearly. I can't take advantage of you in this situation."

I wanted to slap him. Had I imagined his hunger? I'd never been kissed like that before. Never felt that kind of spark. "I want you to take advantage of me, Marcus. Um, I mean, you're not taking advantage of me. I'm an adult. You're an adult. We need this."

His mournful eyes studied mine. "Carrie, you're still married, and going through heartbreak. If I don't control myself, I'm being unfair to you. Also, I don't want us to have problems in our working relationship."

Lost in his penetrating stare, my brain couldn't process what he was saying. His words didn't match the passion I saw on his face. His lips trembled, and I wanted desperately to kiss them again.

I heard what sounded like rain on the roof and a loud screaming noise, human, not animal. It seemed to be coming from outside. Marcus turned his head toward the commotion. "Something's wrong. You stay here. I'll go see what's going on."

"I'll come with you," I said.

"No, no, you stay. I'll be right back." With that, he bounded down the stairs.

The screaming penetrated the thick walls of the house. Most of the structure had been remodeled to make way for offices, libraries, a printing press and living quarters, but the strong outer walls remained.

My heart raced in fear for Marcus. I told myself he was tall and muscular, a trained soldier. He'd survived Vietnam. Why wouldn't he survive this?

As I pondered that question, my gut tightened, warning me. I imagined a gun-toting, angry person wanting to kill someone, anyone.

I staggered to the archives room and glanced out the pointed window. I saw pouring rain. Lightning snaked through the sky. Thunder crashed in the distance. I no longer heard the screaming.

From my viewpoint, I saw only the bottom steps of the building and the street.

Streetlamps emitted a foggy glow and in the faint light I searched for anything that appeared suspicious. I spotted Kyle's Alfa Romeo, parked between Mom's Caddy and Marcus' jeep.

Damn son of a bitch. He was the one who'd been yelling, as if imitating how I'd screamed that morning when I couldn't get in the house. He should have been arrested for disturbing the peace. Lord knows, he'd disturbed the piece I was trying to get from Marcus.

I locked the door and sat against it in a fetal position. Fatigue washed over me as I waited for what seemed like an eternity. My brain recalled every painful experience of my past. I was sobbing like a child when I heard the knock on the door.

"Open up," Marcus demanded.

I peered through the keyhole to see if Kyle might be with him, but I couldn't see a damn thing. No way would I open the door. "What's going on?" I shouted.

"Kyle's drunk," Marcus said. "I called a cab to take him to your house. Is that okay?"

"Fine," I yelled at the closed door.

"He wanted to sleep it off in his car, but I told him that wouldn't be a good idea. I took his car keys so he couldn't drive. I also told him you were staying with a friend."

Chapter Seven

After Marcus left the archive room, I staggered to the bathroom to wash off the grime and frustration. My feet slipped from under me as I stepped in the tub to shower. I fell hard on my butt and sat there for a while, waiting for the spray to sober me up enough to stand and wash myself.

When I finished my shower, I tucked a towel around my body and walked out to the hallway. Marcus had his door closed.

I knocked. "Marcus?" My heart raced, as I waited for him to answer.

"We'll talk tomorrow, Carrie," he said, without bothering to open the door. "You've had a rough day. Sleep well."

My heart sank as I crossed the hall, slammed my bedroom door, and grabbed my Atlanta Braves tee-shirt from my tote.

Dad bought it April 15, 1974, the night Hank Aaron surpassed Babe Ruth's home run record in the fourth inning against the Los Angeles Dodgers. I was twelve at the time. We cheered ourselves hoarse. Dad later showed me a newspaper article in which Aaron was quoted as saying, "On the field blacks have been able to be super giants. But once the playing days are over, this is the end of it, and we go to the back of the bus again." I started carrying this tee everywhere after Mom and Dad died.

Our laws were created to protect all citizens equally, but they didn't. They protected the rich and influential, sure, but not the poor and unconnected. Our laws didn't protect Tatum Brookins. He was arrested. But why? He appeared to be innocent, and if I sat around, feeling sorry for myself, an innocent teenager might be convicted of a crime he didn't commit. My parents raised me better than that.

"I promise I'll do my best to help," I whispered a silent vow to them. "Come hell or high water."

Chapter Eight

December 9

I awoke with a throbbing headache, a hangover from the whiskey. My watch showed nine-twenty-five. I'd slept late for the first time in years. It was Saturday and I didn't give a shit, though I suffered pangs of embarrassment for the way I'd behaved. Why had I spilled my guts to Marcus and asked him to make love to me?

I swallowed two aspirins then crept out of bed, shivering. Marcus had turned the thermostat down to sixty-five. I turned it up to seventy-four.

His bedroom door was open. I peeked in. The maroon spread had been thrown over rumpled covers, but he wasn't in there. I smelled coffee brewing, but he wasn't in the kitchen.

I walked to the bathroom to check my sad face in the mirror. My hair stuck out in all directions. I picked up the black comb on the edge of the sink and captured the mess into a ponytail. I could do this without looking at myself in the mirror.

After I splashed water on my face, brushed my teeth with Marcus' toothbrush, I put on jeans, a beige turtle-neck sweater, and boots.

I rarely wore makeup, except for special occasions like parties or the premier of a play. When I got all dolled up, I'd been told I looked like Barbie, though it was never my intention to look like a doll. I considered myself a serious journalist, and to do my job properly, I thought I should appear professional.

That morning I could have used a compliment. I felt insecure and unattractive, probably due to Kyle's cheating. A little insecure voice in my head kept telling me I needed to make more of an effort to be more attractive.

I patted my cheeks with peach blusher, applied Cherries in the Snow lipstick and brushed my lashes with mascara. Mom used to say I was lucky to have dark lashes and brows. Hers were fair but beautiful. She looked like the French actress Catherine Deneuve. When Dad first met her, he said her beauty intoxicated him. Mom said it was her Chanel perfume. After she died, I started wearing that same fragrance.

Strange as this may sound, it made me feel close to her. I took out the little dispenser and spritzed some behind my ears.

I spotted the latest edition of the newspaper on the kitchen table. On top of the paper, Marcus had left a note, written in his big, right-slanting scrawl: "Great job. I want to read the transcripts of the police interviews. I'm at home dealing with contractors." He'd written his home number, as if I didn't know it already. "I'll be back soon. Drink plenty of water. It'll flush away the booze, and you'll feel better."

He sounded like Dad, telling me to drink water; it suddenly occurred to me Marcus had assumed a fatherly role at work, but he'd never interfered or asked me squat about my personal life. When I announced my engagement to Kyle, everyone at the office congratulated me, except Marcus. He said nothing, nada.

He didn't even offer to give me away at my wedding. It would have been nice not to walk down the aisle solo. At the wedding party afterwards, he'd left early. He didn't wish me well or say goodbye, but last night I got a glimpse of a man I never knew existed, and we'd turned a corner in our relationship, I thought.

I poured a glass of water from the fridge spout and grabbed a coffee mug that said, *"An investment in knowledge always pays the best interest,"* Benjamin Franklin. I filled the cup with the brew from the coffee machine. Marcus had given me a coffee maker like this as a wedding present.

I drank the coffee and reflected on my screwed-up life. I needed a divorce lawyer pronto. Sam Abrams should be able to help. He was a partner with one of the largest law firms in Atlanta--Abrams, Silkman, McBride and Johnson. He'd handled my parents' estate, as well as the sale of this building and newspaper to Marcus.

I dialed his office number from the kitchen wall phone but got voicemail.

I left a message there and then dialed his home. He'd often said, "If you need anything, don't hesitate to call."

"Hello, this is Janet."

"Hi, Janet, it's Carrie Sue Justice. Sorry to bother you, but I have an urgent matter to discuss with Sam. Is he available?"

"He's out back, Carrie Sue, trying to finish his 'Honey Do' list. Hold on a minute. I'll get him."

Janet yelled, "Samuel!"

After a few minutes, I heard what sounded like a forceful exhale. "Whew, you might have saved me from a heart attack, Carrie Sue. Janet's got me sawing down two dead trees. That woman has no mercy." As he spoke, I visualized him, tall and stout, with a shock of silver hair and a cherubic face. He looked more like a priest than an influential business lawyer. "How've you been, Carrie Sue?"

"I'm hanging on."

"Janet said you have an emergency."

"I need a good divorce lawyer."

After a long pause, he asked, "For you?"

"Kyle is cheating, and I don't want to be married to him anymore."

"Do you have proof of his cheating?"

"I caught him cheating on me yesterday morning. He wasn't expecting me home. It's the first time I've caught him, but I'm sure it's not the first time he's cheated."

"Oh Lordy, I'm sorry. I don't handle divorces, but Debbie Jasper and Henry Salvo at our firm are two of the best. Do you want a bad ass who'll hang his balls up in the middle of Atlanta if necessary, or do you want a nice lawyer?"

I laughed, despite the graveness of my situation. "I want someone who'll get me out of this damn marriage as soon as possible. I don't want anything from Kyle, but I don't want him taking anything that's mine. I just want him out of my house and out of my life. Do you see a problem with that?"

"It's your home, Carrie Sue. It's the home you grew up in and the home you inherited from your parents, and you're within your rights to change the locks and do whatever you feel is necessary to protect yourself from someone you don't trust. But that doesn't include maiming or murdering him, even if you want to."

I laughed. "I threatened his manhood with a letter opener. Unfortunately, I didn't succeed."

"Oh Lordy. I'd advise you to stay away from Kyle. As to the best attorney for you, I recommend Debbie Jasper. She's one tough cookie. I'll have her call you."

"Thank you, Sam. Tell her to call me at work, not at home." I recited the phone number. "I'd like to talk to her this morning if possible. I'll be in the office for a while. If I don't answer, she can leave a message on the machine."

"Will do. Sorry this happened to you, Carrie Sue. At least there are no children involved."

"Except for the one I married."

Sam laughed. "Before I forget, Janet said to tell you she loves your articles and columns. This morning I saw what you wrote about the shooting death in College Station. Karl Silkman at our firm is representing one of the boys charged."

"Which one?"

"It's Tate. . ."

"Tatum Brookins?"

"That's right."

"Sam, I need to talk to Karl Silkman right away. I have some important information that might help him defend Tatum."

"All right, I'll have both Karl and Debbie give you a call."

After I said goodbye to Sam, I punched in Freemont's number. His answering machine came on.

I left a message. "It's a quarter to eleven, Free. I'll wait at my office for you to pick up the note to Kyle, but if you're too busy or forget, it's okay. See you tonight for supper."

I walked down to my cubby office and scribbled out a letter to Kyle. I rehashed all the ugliness of yesterday and noted the many times I'd suspected him of cheating. No words seemed adequate to express the violation I felt.

In conclusion I wrote, "I want a divorce. I'm not asking for anything from you. I'll have a lawyer draw up the necessary documents for us to sign. Collect your belongings from the house within the next twenty-four hours."

The phone rang soon after I'd read through what I'd written. "Carrie Sue speaking."

"Hi Carrie Sue, I'm Debbie Jasper. Sam Abrams asked me to call you." Her voice was precise and deep; she would have made a good news anchor.

"Yes, when can we get together?"

"I can meet with you Monday morning at nine." She recited the address, though I already knew where she was located.

"Sounds good."

"Sam said you want to hurry this process along. I don't see a problem. If uncontested, we can usually finalize within thirty to forty days. There are no children involved, right?"

"That's right." I took an envelope out of my desk, folded the letter to Kyle, placed it inside and wrote his name on the outside.

"Carrie Sue, before we meet on Monday, I want you to write a marriage story and a divorce story, pertaining to you and your spouse."

"What do you mean by marriage story and divorce story?"

"Describe the kind of marriage you have and why you want a divorce."

"I'd rather tell you when we get together."

"Take my word for it, Carrie Sue. You'll leave out important details unless you write them down."

"This feels like a homework assignment."

Debbie laughed. "I'm not asking for a literary masterpiece. Think in terms of a chronology of your life with your spouse that will allow me to comprehend the situation. You can be as brief as you like. In fact, I prefer brevity."

I sighed, "Okay."

As I hung up the phone, I heard knocking on the front door. Probably Freemont coming by to pick up Kyle's letter.

I peeked out a window at the front of the building and cringed at the sight of Kyle in frayed jeans. His turtle-neck sweater matched his copper hair. He massaged his arms, hugged himself and looked like he was shivering in his black-leather biker's jacket.

Hoping he'd leave, I backed away from the door. After a moment, the knocking stopped and I peeked out again to see Kyle talking to Lindsey Jernigan, the features editor, a stunning woman, about thirty, with shoulder-length, black hair, and porcelain skin. She often said she was as white as Dracula's bride. Her brown eyes were wide as if enthralled in conversation with my cheating husband. She batted her long lashes, finger-combed her hair with one hand and held her keys and briefcase in the other.

I rushed toward my desk, grabbed my tote to hide upstairs. But before I could escape, my desk phone rang.

I answered, "This is Carrie Sue."

"Hello, Carrie Sue." His voice sounded deep, assertive. "I'm Karl Silkman. Sam Abrams asked me to give you a call. He said you had information regarding Tatum Brookins."

"Yes."

"There she is," Lindsey said, strutting in with Kyle. "Hi, Carrie Sue, look who's here."

I pointed to the phone, a signal not to bother me. Kyle flashed goo-goo eyes like a teenager in love. Had he already forgotten I'd caught him with Maryann yesterday, and tried to stab him with a letter opener?

I turned my back to him, but the asshole started kissing my neck. I stepped away, handed him the letter I'd written and continued my conversation with Silkman.

"I need to meet with you in person, Mr. Silkman and share some vital information."

"I'm at the office now if you want to come over." He gave me the address and office number.

I stuffed my Tandy inside my tote and positioned the strap over my arm. "Yes, I know where you are, and I'm on my way.

I hung up the phone and brushed past Kyle as Marcus walked in, wearing a hooded sweat jacket, running shorts and shoes. His handsome face glistened with perspiration, despite the cold outside.

Lindsey said, "Wow, hi Marcus, you're looking good."

Without a word, Marcus walked into his office. When he came out, I recognized the star shaped holder in his right hand. He'd taken Kyle's keys last night to prevent him from driving drunk. He handed the keys to Kyle.

I rushed toward the front door, "Got to go. I have an appointment with the lawyer defending Tatum Brookins. Remember, Marcus, we talked about him? He's one of the boys arrested for allegedly shooting and killing Preston Campbell."

"I'll drive you," Kyle said.

"No. I need my wheels and you need yours."

"We need to talk," Kyle said, following me.

I hated airing my dirty laundry in public. Marcus knew about Kyle's cheating, but Lindsey didn't, and she thrived on gossip. "Not now, Kyle. I don't have time. I need to go."

I heard Marcus behind me. "What's the attorney's name, Carrie?"

I turned to face him. "Karl Silkman."

Marcus stroked his beard. "I read or heard something about him recently. He's a son of holocaust survivors, does quite a bit of pro bono work. I'd like to be present at that meeting if you don't mind. Are you meeting him at his office?"

"Yes. He's in the same building with Sam Abrams."

"I'll shower and change and see you over there."

"Okay." I opened the front door and ran down the stairs toward the Cadillac.

Kyle raced after me, grabbing my arm and the handle of my tote. "Let me help you with that."

"No, Kyle, let go. I don't need your help. Read the letter I gave you. Everything I have to say to you is in there."

"Be reasonable, Carrie Sue." He tugged hard and snatched my tote from me.

"Damn you, Kyle, give that back."

"Not until after we talk. I'll ride with you to your appointment and catch the train to the theatre."

"No." I stomped my feet. "If you don't give me back my bag, I'm calling police."

Kyle smirked as if I'd told him a joke. "Oh, come on. Don't be stupid."

I ran back up the stairs to make good on my threat as Marcus jogged past me and grabbed my bag from Kyle. "You'd better leave, Kyle."

"This is none of your business, Marcus. Carrie Sue is my wife."

"Carrie is her own person, and I won't allow you to bully her and take her things."

My trembling hands accepted my tote from Marcus. I thanked him and thought about the last time Kyle lost his temper. I'd asked him why he and a young woman, he called his "star student," disappeared from a party at our house. In response, he'd smashed a bottle of red wine on the kitchen floor.

I couldn't seem to shake the awful memory as I drove to Silkman's office. Kyle tailed me over there. I took several twists and turns but couldn't lose him.

When I pulled into the parking garage beneath the tall grey building housing Abrams, Silkman, McBride and Johnson, a guard in a tan uniform greeted me. He wore a holstered pistol on his belt.

I introduced myself and said I had an appointment with Silkman.

"Yes, he's expecting you. Pull up over there." He directed me to a parking spot near the elevator.

"A man followed me over here, and I'm a little threatened." I gave the guard a description of Kyle and his car, "I'm concerned he's close by."

He nodded. "I'll be on the lookout. Do you want Mr. Silkman to come down and meet you?"

"No, that's okay."

From the parking garage, I rode the elevator to the tenth floor. As the doors slid open, I heard echoing footfalls. Rather than step out onto the empty hallway, I froze and held the elevator door open in case I needed to make a quick getaway.

A man about five-ten, with salt-and-pepper hair, black beard and mustache appeared from around the corner. "Carrie Sue? I'm Karl Silkman." He walked up to me and extended his hand. His smiling brown eyes and regal nose dominated his narrow face. He wore a crisp blue shirt with grey, pinstriped trousers.

I returned his firm grip. Dad always said, "Shake hands like you mean it; show your strength."

"I heard you have a stalker, Carrie Sue."

"I don't know if you'd call my soon-to-be ex-husband a stalker, but he did follow me over here. It's a long story."

Silkman's brown eyes narrowed. "Well, you need to be careful. Does he have a history of violent behavior?"

I shrugged, not knowing how to answer. Was hurling a wine bottle and snatching my tote from me considered violent? Kyle would probably say I was violent for threatening him with a letter opener. "No, not really."

He nodded and motioned for me to follow him. "Let's see what you've got."

We walked inside a glass-enclosed reception area. "Marcus Handley should be joining us soon. Maybe we should wait for him."

Silkman picked up the phone at the front desk. "Henry, let me know when Marcus Handley arrives."

Silkman directed me into his large office, furnished with a striped sofa and matching chairs. It smelled of ink and old newspapers, like the archives at the Southern Journal. Legal reference books lined three of the walls. I noticed a few literary novels among them: The Confessions of Nat Turner and Sophie's Choice, by William Styron. On the wall behind Silkman's desk were stark black and white photos. I studied them before I sat. "Where were these photos taken?"

"Auschwitz. The Nazi Concentration Camp in Poland."

I remembered what Marcus had said about Silkman being a son of Holocaust survivors. "Horrifying," I said.

Silkman swiveled his chair around to face the pictures. "My wife Eva thinks these are too depressing to be in here, but I don't think we should never forget. In Auschwitz alone, the Nazis killed millions.

I stared at the sad photos of sweet-faced children trapped behind a barbed-wire fence. Guards inspected crowds of adults and youngsters. Gas chambers and piles of bodies. I'd read somewhere the Nazis may have killed up to eight million people during Hitler's reign. How did Silkman's parents survive the holocaust? I was just about to ask him when his phone rang.

He grabbed it on the first ring. "Thanks, Henry. I'll meet him by the elevator." He put the phone back in its cradle. "Be right back."

As he walked out, I reached inside my tote and withdrew the transcribed statements of Tatum Brookins, Jeremy Andrews, Calvin Newson, Leroy Cortez. They also included Tim Dillon's statement. Dillon was the witness who Calvin allegedly talked to after the shooting.

My heart flip-flopped when Marcus walked in. He gave me one of his rare smiles and sat in the chair next to mine. He smelled soap clean, and looked handsome in a brown corduroy sports coat, white shirt, tan trousers and polished brown loafers.

I held up the stack of papers Dora Lee had given me. "Sorry I didn't have time to make copies of these."

Silkman grabbed them. "I'll make three."

After Silkman left the room, Marcus gave me a penetrating stare. "How're you doing?"

I had to bite my lip to hold back the tears. "I'm better, thanks, but I'm sorry you had to intervene today."

Marcus sighed. "Don't apologize."

I touched his arm. "Kyle got angry and acted badly, because I gave him a letter explaining why I'm divorcing him. He wanted to talk, and I didn't want to listen to his crap."

Marcus leaned in and whispered, "Carrie, there's never a justifiable reason for a man to bully a woman. You aren't responsible for Kyle's bad behavior. It's his problem, not yours, and from what I saw today, and last night when he was drunk, you need to protect yourself."

"I have an appointment on Monday morning with a divorce lawyer." I sighed, thinking about the assignment Debbie had given me. "She wants me to write her a marriage story and a divorce story."

Marcus stretched out his long legs, crossing them at the ankles. "Be sure to include how he bullied you today. I'm sure it wasn't the first time." He cocked his head sideways and gave me a probing stare, as if he could read my mind. I squirmed in my seat and twisted my hands like a guilty, scolded child. "Before I forget, Marcus, I might be late coming in tonight. I'm having supper with Freemont. It's possible he may be a witness for Tatum Brookins."

His dark brows lifted. "Really?"

"Yes, you'll see what I mean when you read Tatum's statement. Tatum said he saw a guy delivering laundry to Mrs. Sikes house, which would place Tatum two houses away from where Preston Campbell was shot and killed. Freemont is the only guy I know who delivers laundry. When I asked Freemont, he said yes, he was delivering to Mrs. Sikes that night. Not only that, but he remembers seeing a young black male, walking alone. If Freemont sees a picture of Tatum, he might be able to verify his story. I'm hoping Karl Silkman can give me Tatum's photo, but I don't want Silkman to know about Freemont until I'm sure of the facts."

Before Marcus could respond, Silkman returned. He handed my copies back to me and gave Marcus a duplicate stack. Marcus sifted through his copies as if he couldn't wait to read them.

Silkman sat in the swivel chair behind his desk. "Tatum's aunt described the interrogation her son endured. I've asked the D.A. and the police department for tapes. After we've transcribed them, we'll compare notes." He steepled his long fingers. "I'd like to know how you were able to obtain your information."

"I can't reveal my source, Mr. Silkman. However, our newspaper needs to publish the interviews of the suspects without incriminating my source. I was hoping that after you get the tapes from your source, I can say I received my information from you. Also, I need a picture of Tatum. I know someone who may have seen him on the night of the shooting. If so, this person could verify Tatum wasn't at the scene when Preston was killed."

Silkman pulled out the desk drawer in front of him and shuffled through it. He withdrew a grainy photo. It looked like a mug shot. "Who's the possible witness?"

I studied the photo. I couldn't believe this child was fifteen years old. His brown eyes looked wide and frightened, as if he'd seen a ghost. "I'd rather not say until after I talk to him."

Silkman pursed his lips. "I'd like to know now." He picked up a pencil and stabbed the eraser end on his desk. "In a few days, I'm expecting the D.A. to seek an indictment."

"Why do you say that if Tatum is innocent?" I asked.

"I believe he is." He slapped the papers on his desk. "I understand you need to protect your source. Why don't I leave a copy of these interrogations in the clerk's office with instructions for you to pick them up? That should protect your source. In exchange, I'll need the name of the guy you think can help prove Tatum's innocence."

"I should be able to provide that tomorrow, or Monday at the latest," I said.

Marcus stood. "We plan to publish the interviews of the suspects as soon as possible."

Silkman pushed himself up from his chair. "I expect to have them in the clerk's office this week." He squinted at me. "One other thing you need to be prepared for, Carrie Sue. If this goes to trial and the court won't allow me to present all the evidence, I may need to call you as a witness."

Marcus scowled and raised his voice. "No, we'll cooperate with you in every way we can, but Carrie can't be called as a witness. She'll be covering the trial."

Silkman nodded. "I understand. I hope it won't be necessary to subpoena her."

"You need to find a way to present all the evidence, Silkman, without calling Carrie to the stand. If she's called, and the prosecution asks her under oath to reveal her source, she'll have to refuse." Marcus motioned for me to stand and follow him. "Her penalty for protecting her source will be jail time. That's not going to happen. Not on my watch. She's shared her information with you in good faith. She believes your client is innocent. You believe your client is innocent. You're defending him pro bono, which is admirable, but I won't let you sacrifice Carrie in the process."

Chapter Nine

Snowflakes fell on the windshield of the Cadillac, as I turned into the dark circular driveway to my house Saturday evening. My body stiffened with dread at the thought of going inside.

I parked and sat for a moment, staring at the old mansion, cloaked in darkness. Without the lights on, this place looked creepy, a prewar albatross.

When Mom and Dad were alive, it buzzed with activity and warmth. I loved coming home back then. Mom would set the veranda lights to come on at dusk. She'd have a fire blazing in the living and dining room hearths when it was cold out.

She liked to have our pictures taken at Christmastime, for the cards she'd send out. She loved Christmas, though she was raised Jewish and celebrated Hanukkah and the other Jewish holidays.

I glanced at my watch. It was already five-thirty.

I zipped up my jacket and grabbed my tote full of dirty clothes. The cold, damp wind stabbed my bones as I rushed from the car.

On the veranda, I saw two rose bushes, their roots wrapped in newspapers. They were propped up against one of the Doric columns. A white envelope had been stuck inside the roses.

I grabbed the note out of the envelope and opened the front door. "Let there be light." I said as I flipped on the wall switch, lighting the teardrop chandelier Mom had bought in England.

In the brightened foyer, I was able to read the note. "Carrie Sue, thank you for your lovely article about my beloved teacher George Powell. I think it's important to let a reporter know when she's doing a great job, and you have exceeded my expectations. I'm sending these rose bushes not only to thank you, but to prove a point. I loved your humorous column about your brown thumb. I don't believe for a moment your thumb is brown, and I want you to plant these roses to prove my point. Love and best wishes, Karen Turner."

Turner was a retired teacher and principal, and one-time student of George Powell. Powell, now eighty-six, taught history on the Southside for thirty years. At a ceremony honoring him, Turner said Powell had inspired her to become a teacher. "He transported his students back in time, as they participated in history. I will never forget the day a shy student stood up and yelled 'Charge!' during a dialogue on the Civil War."

I sighed and regretted I'd written the column about my brown thumb. When would I find the time to plant rosebushes and make sure they lived?

I considered asking Freemont to plant them as I placed my soiled clothes in the washing machine, poured in detergent and turned it on.

In the master bedroom, the air reeked of perspiration and raunchy sex. Kyle's shoes and clothes were scattered over the pine floor and red throw rug. The king-sized, mahogany bed looked like an orgy victim. Sheets were tangled in the white down comforter. I inspected the mess and found red hairs, no doubt Maryann's.

I dragged my suitcase out of the closet and packed it with clothes I thought I'd need until Kyle moved out. I grabbed my black cashmere coat from its hanger and slipped it on over my leather jacket.

Next, I took out a cosmetic bag, threw in my toothbrush, toothpaste, shampoo, conditioner, cleansing cream, moisturizer, and body lotion. In the cabinet beneath the sink, I cringed when I saw Kyle's toiletry bag open, revealing a package of condoms. Kyle and I hadn't used a rubber since the day we got married. I was on the pill.

I stuffed the remaining condoms inside my jeans pocket and searched through the garbage looking for used ones. When I didn't find any, I inspected the bed.

I finally located the nasty thing on the floor and stuffed it in a plastic bag. Evidence. In another bag, I put strands of Maryann's red hair.

The old Carrie Sue would have been devastated. She may have curled up in a fetal position and cried her eyes out. The new Carrie Sue walked straight and proud with her shoulders back, soldiering to the laundry room.

I transferred my wet clothes to the tumble-dryer and set the timer. When I glanced at my watch, I gasped at the time, six-thirty. I was late for supper with Freemont.

I grabbed a phone to call him but couldn't get a dial tone. Dead.

I heard Footsteps echoing in the hallway. I'd forgotten to lock the door. I rushed to the bathroom and grabbed my cuticle scissors to use as a weapon.

"Boo." The sound reverberated through the house.

I jumped and screamed. "Damn you, Freemont Jackson."

Freemont laughed. He had on his biker's jacket, red-checkered flannel shirt, brown trousers, cowboy boots. He probably would have appeared scary to anyone who didn't know him.

"Not funny. We're not kids anymore."

"We did say six, didn't we, Carrie Sue?"

"I'm sorry. I was getting ready to call you."

"Phones aren't working. I've reported the outage. Food's ready, you hungry?"

"Starving." I walked over to slap him for scaring me and stumbled over my luggage.

He grabbed my arm to keep me from falling. "You need to put those scissors down before you get hurt." He grasped the handle on the luggage. "Why'd you leave the door open?"

I rolled my eyes at my carelessness. "I can't believe I did that. I don't know what I'm doing any more."

He shook his head and clucked his tongue. "When you're at home by yourself you need to keep the doors locked and arm yourself with a serious weapon, a gun." He pointed to the scissors. "That is not a serious weapon."

"I don't like guns. And if I had a gun, I would have killed you by now."

Freemont laughed as if he thought I was joking.

Chapter Ten

Freemont touched the yellow rose bushes on the veranda. "Where'd you get these?"

"Karen Turner." I handed him her note. "She wants me to plant them and prove I don't have a brown thumb. Will you plant them for me?"

"No, no, I saw that article you wrote. I've been meaning to talk to you about it." His chocolate eyes glared at me. "Why'd you blame me for your brown thumb?"

"I didn't blame you exactly. I realize you didn't know what you were doing. You were only six at the time."

"I have no memory of what you've accused me of, and since you've never mentioned it before, I question your veracity."

I stood with hands on hips to show my disdain. "Are you calling me a liar, Free?"

He grinned, showing his large white teeth. "I'm too polite to call you a liar."

"I remember it like it was yesterday. I was eating one of your mother's peaches. She told me to put the peach pit on the windowsill to dry, and she explained how to plant it. I did as she said and watered my peach pit religiously. Next thing I knew you were hovering. I think you were jealous. You said you were going to plant a tree next to mine and it would be bigger and better." I smirked at his smirking. "You didn't prepare your seed or soil correctly. And you forgot to water it. That's why your soil became dry and cracked. Mine was moist and produced a lovely green stem."

Freemont shook his head. "Yeah, yeah, I read what you wrote."

"You saw my green stem, and you couldn't stand it. You yanked it up and stuck it down in your dry dirt. I cried my eyes out when I saw that. I haven't been able to grow a damn thing since. You jinxed me, Free. Maybe you didn't mean to, but you did."

"Oh, bull, do you hear what you're saying? Do you honestly believe you're making sense? I have no memory of this. But let's say for the sake of argument I pulled up your little stem. Do you honestly think a six-year-old has that much power? I wish I had that kind of power, but I don't. And there's no way on God's green earth I could have jinxed you and given you a brown thumb for the rest of your life."

"I beg to differ. I think you did, and I lost confidence."

"You lost confidence and jinxed yourself. You owe me an apology and I want you to plant these roses. I'll even give you some of Mama's miracle soil." He rubbed his hands together. "If these roses live, you'll owe me a public apology in the newspaper."

"That's silly, Free. I didn't mention you by name, and if I give you a public apology, everyone will know who jinxed me."

"Dora Lee Thompson said she knew the minute she read that column you were talking about me."

I groaned. "Oh, please, I can't take this pressure. I have too much to do. I don't have time to plant these stupid roses. I need to gather enough evidence to help Tatum Brookins. If I don't, he might rot in jail for murder. Also, I need to kick Kyle out of my house, and write a marriage and divorce story."

Freemont's brown eyes questioned me. "Why are you writing a marriage and divorce story?"

"The divorce lawyer I'm meeting with on Monday gave me that assignment."

"I'm sorry, honey. I hope I didn't let you down today. I didn't get a chance to come by your office until late, and Marcus told me you'd already given the letter to Kyle. How did that go?"

"Not well. Kyle acted like a jerk. I'll give him a couple of days to get his stuff out. If he doesn't, I'll dump his crap on the driveway and have the locks changed."

"Let me know when you plan to do this, and I'll help. If I were you, I'd have an alarm system installed."

I nodded. "Good idea."

He pointed to the rose bushes. "You can plant these tomorrow. No big deal. Shouldn't take long. Are you going to plant them with the others?" He fanned his giant hand toward the rose bushes, separating my property and his. In the spring and summer, the roses bloom in a spectacular display of red, yellow, pink, white and all hues in between. Mom preferred the pink Jacque Cartier's. Granny Justice wrote about them in her journal.

"No. I think I'll plant them beside the front steps. What do you think?"

"Good choice."

"Do you remember what Granny Justice wrote in her journal about the Jacque Cartier's?"

He raised one eyebrow. "What do you mean?"

"You know. How your great, great granddaddy Simon and your great, great grandmama Georgia escaped by hiding notes in the roses?"

Freemont's eyes gleamed. "Yeah, Mama told me. Her mama told her, and so on down the line. The story may have gotten embellished through the years, but I'd like to think it's true."

"According to Granny Justice it is true, but I regret Georgia and Simon had to risk their lives to escape my ancestors' cotton plantation."

Freemont patted my shoulder like a parent reassuring a child. "Your great, great grandmother was kind, Carrie Sue. She gave Georgia her freedom and property. That was way beyond generous for that day and time."

I shook my head at Freemont's positive spin. "It didn't do Georgia any good. She couldn't legally claim her property or her freedom."

"Look on the bright side. It's a love story with a happy ending. They were smart and brave. They used the Underground Railroad to escape. Simon could have abandoned Georgia. But he didn't. He came back and left a map in the roses that led her to him. Or so the story goes."

"I used to think the Underground Railroad was an actual train traveling underground, Free, but it referred to a code they used to communicate."

"Yeah, that's what I learned. The slaves used railroad terminology to talk to one another about secret routes for escape."

I shivered from the cold as snowflakes floated through the air and melted on the veranda. "Did you believe your mama when she said my double great grandfather George was probably Georgia's father?"

Freemont laughed. "Yeah, we're related. Can't you see the resemblance, Carrie Sue?" He ruffled my blonde hair with his giant hand.

"Dad used to say we're all mixed with the exception of those who just got off the boat from Scandinavia."

Freemont nodded in agreement. "Mama said she thought George may have sired Georgia, because Georgia was light skinned and named after him."

"I'm sorry my ancestors took advantage of your ancestors, Free."

He flashed his lopsided grin. "I think you should be sorrier for defaming my six-year-old name."

I punched his arm. "Stop it. I wish I'd never written that stupid column."

He grinned. "But you did, and I'll settle for a private apology. I know you're too darn stubborn to apologize publicly." His eyes twinkled, mischievously. "Hey, I've got an idea. Why don't you ask for my forgiveness by leaving me a note in one of these rose bushes after you've planted them? I'll bet you a hundred bucks they'll survive."

I imitated his wide grin. "I refuse to take your money, Free, but I do like the idea of leaving messages here."

Freemont tilted his head and stared cockeyed at me. "But not every day. If I have something important to tell you, I'll call. Phones may not be working now, but they usually are. When they're not, I can drive or walk over. We do have modern technology and good transportation nowadays, you know."

"But you were the one who suggested leaving the notes."

He slapped his forehead. "What was I thinking?"

"I like the idea."

He groaned. "Umm, huh, you're planting them at your front steps. Convenient for you, but not for me." He smiled showing the gap between his teeth, like my gap. "Word to the wise, Carrie Sue, if you have an emergency, you'd better not depend on these roses here."

Chapter Eleven

Freemont's home, once a slave's quarters, had been enlarged and renovated many times. He'd recently replaced the porch swing with four rocking chairs.

I parked in the gravel driveway sheltered by large oak trees. Freemont pulled up beside me and parked his white van with "Jackson Laundry" in black letters on both sides. I removed the photo of fifteen-year-old Tatum from my tote and slipped it inside my jeans pocket to show to Freemont.

His lighted Christmas tree, visible through the picture window, brought back haunting memories. I no longer looked forward to the holidays.

We walked into his warm living room. A fire crackled in the hearth. "Cozy, Free." My tummy growled from the yummy aroma of home cooking. "I love what you've done here. Beautiful. I see you've bought new furniture."

Freemont helped me out of my heavy coat. He hung it inside the black armoire near the front door as I backed up to his fireplace to absorb the heat. "I like the arrangement in here. It fits your warm and welcoming personality." A brown leather couch faced two matching chairs. A red rug, bordered with diamond shapes of orange, green, blue and brown, covered most of the wood floor in his living room.

He smiled, but his half-open eyelids revealed his fatigue. He'd been doing laundry, delivering it, studying for his finals and found the time to cook supper. "I got the sofa and chairs from a furniture store that was going out of business, in Atlanta. I thought I'd get a deal. I don't know if I did, but it's all comfortable, and I'm pleased. Mama's stuff got to looking threadbare. Funny thing is, when the Salvation Army truck came, I hated to give her stuff up. Knowing Mama, she would have approved of the donation, I think. I bought the rug from a Native woman in Cherokee County. There's a small group of artists, who sell rugs, clothing, jewelry...that sort of thing. They're descendants of the Indians who were driven from that area more than a century ago."

Freemont knelt in flanker position, like when he played wide receiver in high school. He rubbed a brown hand over the rug. "The lady who made this rug said she and her family moved to Cherokee County from California because of her ancestors, and what happened to them. She said she learned the art of weaving from her mama and grandmama. This pattern has been passed down from generation to generation."

He stood, and I followed him to the kitchen, which he'd remodeled with stainless steel appliances. The maple Lazy Susan, he'd built a few years back, shone to a high gloss.

He placed a platter of fried chicken on the table. Next came bowls of peas, butterbeans, creamed corn, and a plate of cornbread. "Help yourself, Carrie Sue."

"Thank you for going to so much trouble, Free. Mm, looks and smells wonderful." I reached into my jeans pocket and pulled out the photo of Tatum Brookins. I handed it to Freemont. "Recognize him?"

While I waited for his response, I filled my plate. "No one in the world can cook fried chicken and pan cornbread and veggies like you, Free. Your Mama taught you well."

My mom grew up in Baltimore. She hated to fry. Hot grease splattered on her hands whenever she tried to fry anything. She preferred the convenience of casseroles. The Crockpot was a gift from God, she used to say, though she loved to fix spaghetti from scratch, and she collected recipes galore. She'd stored them in manila folders. I'd planned to have her recipes laminated and published one of these days.

"I once asked your mama, Mama Jackson, to write down her southern recipes, but she said, 'I never measure anything, honey. You got to watch me if you want to learn." I bit into a crispy chicken thigh and watched Freemont study the photograph of Tatum.

"Looks like the kid I saw when I delivered to Ms. Sikes. Where're they holding him?"

I chewed and swallowed. "Chief Barnum said the boys are in the juvenile detention center." I scooped some peas on top of a slice of cornbread.

Freemont filled his plate with peas, cornbread, and a chicken wing. "I'll go visit him."

"I'm glad, Free. Tatum could use the support. I've read all the boys' statements. I believe he's innocent. But please don't tell anyone that I've read the transcripts, okay? Not yet anyway."

Freemont smiled and picked up a chicken wing from his plate. "Dora Lee told me she gave you the transcripts. She made me swear not to tell anyone."

My mouth gaped in surprise. "When did you talk to Dora Lee about this?"

"She came over after work. We went for a jog. She knows she can trust me."

"I didn't know y'all were friendly. Are y'all dating?"

"We've been seeing each other. Some might call it dating."

"Free, she's a little older than you and..."

"She's white and I'm black. Is that what you were going to say?"

"No, Free. I wasn't implying that. I was thinking she's a single mother, a few years older than you. Not that age is all that significant, but do you want to take on the

97

responsibility of a family when you're graduating from college and planning to teach? And you're already busier than a one-armed paper hanger with your laundry business. Of course, it's none of my business, but you know I care about you like a brother." I huffed. "I can't believe you didn't tell me."

Freemont laughed. "I'm telling you now. Dora Lee and I aren't what you'd call serious. She comes over here to eat sometimes. Everyone needs to eat. And we go jogging. Everyone needs exercise. We've been to a couple of movies. We don't have much free time, as you pointed out. Dora Lee's mama keeps Tiffany. She's glad to do it, Dora Lee says, but she doesn't want to impose too much on her mama. Tiffany's Dad doesn't come around at all it seems."

"As long as you're happy. I think Dora Lee is a beautiful woman. I like her."

He nodded, wiped his mouth with a napkin and looked over at Mama Jackson's photo in a gold frame on top of the credenza. "Like Mama, Dora Lee works hard. She's both Mama and Daddy. She says my upbringing makes me more empathetic to her situation. I'm trying to be fair to her. I don't want to mislead her. She knows I'm not ready to commit. I need to finish college. Begin my teaching career before I make a lifetime commitment to anyone."

"Have you decided what to do about your laundry business?"

"I haven't. The community depends on me. Mama's dream was to have a separate building for the business. If I do that, I'll hire people to work and manage it, but that's in the future."

I nodded. "From what you said, I'm assuming you and Dora Lee haven't done the deed."

Freemont coughed a laugh. "Now, now, Miss Carrie Sue, that's too personal." He bowed his head as if embarrassed.

I once heard Mama Jackson tell him not to discuss sex with me. Maybe her warning was old school, but I knew she wanted to protect her son. "Are you telling me to mind my own business?"

Freemont smiled with his whole face like his mama. "No, we haven't been intimate. From the time I was old enough to realize where babies come from, Mama preached to me about being a gentleman and respecting women."

"Have you and Dora Lee played kissy face?"

Freemont roared with laughter, and I caught his funny bug. I laughed at his laughing.

"Nosy Parker. You're too nosy for your own good, Carrie Sue." He scooted his chair back and stood. "I forgot to get us something to drink. You want sweet tea or water? If you want wine, I have a bottle of chardonnay in the fridge."

"Water's fine. I need to flush out my system. I drank too much Jack Daniels last night. Marcus had a bottle, and we indulged."

Freemont raised an eyebrow. "And did y'all play kissy face?"

I laughed. "Yes, we did. I would have preferred something more, but Marcus told me he doesn't want to take advantage of my situation. And as he pointed out, I'm still married, but the marriage bond was broken when Kyle cheated. Tonight, I found a used condom and several long, red hairs in the master bedroom."

"Ugh, what a scuzzy bucket Kyle is." Freemont handed me a glass of ice-water and poured himself tea. "I like Marcus, Carrie Sue. He seems like an honest man. He says what he thinks, no B.S. But as you've told me time and again, he's a hard man to get to know. He has his guard up."

"Yes, but after a couple of shots of whiskey, he was less guarded. I thought I'd get lucky, especially after we kissed. He was obviously excited. Then Kyle showed up, drunk as a skunk, screaming at the door."

"And the romantic spell was broken..."

"Yes, unfortunately. Marcus had to go downstairs and deal with Kyle. Marcus told him I was staying with a friend. Then Marcus called a cab to take Kyle to my house."

Freemont shook his head. "One thing you need to think long and hard about. You no longer own the paper. Marcus does. And you work for him. Another thing, and this is no little thing, you've always complained about how impossible he is to please. If you get too involved and things don't work out, what do you think will happen?"

I sighed. "I don't know."

"Maybe after you divorce Kyle, you'll be able to think more clearly."

"I hope so. What about you and Dora Lee?"

"I'm too young to take on the responsibility of a wife and children. I told her that. She knows I want a teaching career. The laundry business has been good to Mama and me. But I feel the calling to teach. I want to give young people a sense of pride in themselves and their history."

"That's admirable, Free, but passion has a way of erasing logic and good intentions. Look at what happened to me. I married Kyle."

"I hate to say this, Carrie Sue, but Kyle used you. You were a basket-case after your parents died. I wasn't much help. Mama got sick and passed away not long after your folks. I wasn't thinking straight myself, but I never trusted Kyle. You told me to mind my own business. Remember?"

"Don't rub it in." I wiped my tears on a napkin. "I know I was a fool."

Freemont reached across the table and patted my hand. "You wanted to be happy. We all do. You just need to figure out how to get there. I don't think any one person can make you happy. Only you can make yourself happy and that might take a while, but one thing I'm convinced of, you'll be happier without Kyle jacking you around."

I nodded. "Are you saying Dora Lee can't make you happy?"

"I enjoy being with her, but she's not responsible for my happiness." He placed his palm flat on his chest. "She can bring me moments of joy, sure, but as to being content long-term, that has to come from within."

"Dora Lee works for Chief Barnum. Doesn't that worry you?"

Freemont shook his head. "Not one bit."

"It worries me, though."

"I don't care what Barnum thinks. What Dora Lee does in her off hours is none of his business. She's a grown woman, and I'm a grown man. She's free, and I'm free."

"I know. Your Mama didn't call you Free for nothing, but I want you to at least consider this. You're planning to talk to Tatum, make a statement to his lawyer. On top of that, you're seeing Chief Barnum's secretary and rattling some powerful cages of folks who have proven they're not always fair. They arrested Tatum even though the other boys said he had nothing to do with the shooting. What does that tell you?"

"Tatum is being railroaded."

"And Chief Barnum told me Tatum is a member of a black gang. I don't believe that for one second, and my gut tells me, you need to be careful."

"As I said, I'm not worried, and I don't want you to be, Carrie Sue. You're going to do what's right, and so am I. Damn the consequences."

Chapter Twelve

December 10

Freemont invited me to spend the night in his guest bedroom. "It's late and the roads might be iced over, better safe than sorry."

I thought about his offer. "Tempting, but our phones aren't working, and I told Marcus I'd be back tonight. If I can't call him to let him know I'm staying here, he might think I've had an accident. Or he might conclude I've reunited with Kyle. I don't want him thinking that."

"Suit yourself, but I believe your safety is more important than what someone thinks." He held my coat for me to slip into. "Are you going to plant the roses tomorrow? It's kind of cold to plant them, but roses are hardy. They should make it." He returned Tatum's photo.

I backed up to the crackling hearth. I wanted one last burst of warmth before facing the cold night. "I need to, but what if Kyle's home? He usually is on Sundays, and I'd like to avoid him if possible."

"You can't go on avoiding him forever, Carrie Sue. That's your house, not his. Also, I'll be there if you need me."

"Okay, Free. I'll call you tomorrow morning, and we'll arrange a time. That is, if your phone's working."

I walked toward the front door. "Supper was delicious. I had to stop myself from licking my plate. When my life settles down, I'll return the favor."

"I'll count on it." Always the gentleman, Freemont opened his front door for me, followed me out and opened my car door. "Be safe. Take it slow." He waited in the driveway and waved goodbye as I backed out.

I returned his wave and pulled onto Freedom Lane. The sky looked black. Clouds blocked the moon and stars. Spooky.

I drove slower than usual, to avoid skidding on black ice, and popped in an Elvis cassette to brighten my mood. Mom loved Elvis. When he died, she cried like she'd lost a family member. I was a teenager at the time, and thought Elvis was a hunk, but I mostly listened to the Bee Gees, Fleetwood Mac and the Beatles. Listening to Elvis now makes me feel closer to Mom, and this cassette contained some of her favorite songs. I sang at the top of my lungs all the way back to the office.

The Southern Journal looked like a giant gingerbread house with all the Christmas lights on. I parked in my usual spot, grabbed my duffle and suitcase out of the car.

Fatigue had weakened me. I huffed and puffed up the stairs to the front door. My muscles ached with each step. I felt "rode hard and put up wet" as Mama Jackson used to say.

I sniffed my underarms, grimy and in need of a shower. I half-dragged, half-carried my luggage up three flights to the apartment and almost fainted when Marcus came out of the bathroom with a towel wrapped around his waist and another around his neck. I gasped at the sight of his bare chest, muscular arms, tight abs.

His eyes widened when he saw me. I couldn't read his expression through his bearded face. Embarrassed or happy to see me. Hard to tell.

My face burned as I stared. I got a whiff of his aftershave. "Hi," was all I could manage to say.

Using the towel around his neck, he patted his damp head. His arm-pit hair was a shade darker than the chestnut hair on his head. "Glad you made it here okay, Carrie. How was your night?"

My heart battered my chest, and I couldn't gather my thoughts to speak in a complete sentence. "Long."

Marcus gave me one of his penetrating stares. "Did Freemont recognize Tatum's photo?"

"Yes, he believes Tatum is the same guy he saw the night of the shooting."

"Which places him well away from the scene when the shots were fired, right?"

"Right."

"Freemont came by today. Did he tell you?"

"Yes."

"Everything worked out okay?"

"Yes." My voice sounded hoarse, probably from my heart pounding in my throat. "But we need to discuss some things."

His steely eyes locked with mine. "Okay. Sure, Carrie, but you look beat. Why don't we talk tomorrow? No rush. Sleep late if you feel like it. I'll tread softly in the morning. Bathroom's all yours." He glanced at my luggage. "Can I help you with that?" He pointed toward my bags.

"No thanks, I'm fine." I glanced through his open bedroom door. On the table next to the bed was a half-full bottle of Jack and a shot glass.

"Alright, let me know if you need anything, Carrie." His voice was firm and businesslike, even though he was naked, except for the towel wrapped around his middle.

"I will."

As he turned, I stared at his butt with an overwhelming desire to snatch his towel off. I wanted to make him feel as vulnerable as I felt.

"Sleep well, Carrie."

To regain control over myself, I squeezed my eyes shut. "Jesus, what's wrong with me?" I blurted out, without thinking.

He turned. His dark eyebrows knitted in a frown. "What did you say?"

My face burned. "I was talking to myself. I wouldn't call you Jesus, although you look like Jesus...only hot...I mean... ignore me. I'm not making any sense."

I thought I saw an amused spark in his dark eyes. "That's okay. Get some rest. You'll feel better tomorrow."

Before I could humiliate myself even more, he closed his door.

I ran into my bedroom and fell back on the coral bedspread, clutching my chest. A wild, uninhibited woman had seized control of my heart and soul, I thought.

Chapter Thirteen

At 8:00 a.m., I dragged my sad self out of bed. I'd made a wreck of the sheets. I'd tossed and turned all night. My mind kept revisiting my life with Kyle, and all the times I'd suspected him of cheating. Did his betrayal justify my behavior with Marcus? I thought so, but Marcus seemed determined to keep our relationship as chaste as possible.

He'd left coffee brewing and another note on the kitchen table: "I'm at home working," he wrote. He scribbled his home number again as if he'd forgotten I had it. "Call me if you wish, and we'll talk. Try to relax and enjoy your day." I liked this caring side of him, though his note was a little too impersonal.

To force him out of my brain, I concentrated on getting dressed. I put on blue sweats and running shoes and pulled my hair into a ponytail.

I gulped coffee like it was going out of style, and dialed Freemont's number. The staccato busy signal told me the phones were still dead.

On my second cup of coffee, I began a "to do" list with the premise of tackling the most difficult task first. 1. Write a marriage and divorce story.

I grabbed my word processor out of my tote and wrote about the death of my parents. This felt equivalent to cutting a vein and letting it bleed.

At some point, I got around to the marriage story. "When I lost Mom and Dad, Kyle seemed to be hanging around all the time. You might say I fell in lust, not in love, not in the way my parents loved each other. The truth is I married Kyle without getting to know him. I made a bad choice. He'd been married twice before."

"As soon as we married, passion went out the window. I now realize Kyle enjoys the challenge of conquest. Once he's victorious, he moves on."

Anger engulfed me as I wrote. "After we married, Kyle no longer looked at me with love or lust. He lusted after other women. Whenever we entertained, he flirted shamelessly with the beautiful young actresses and the female students he invited to the house. He loved to throw parties. During those parties, he'd sneak away with one of the women while I played hostess. I questioned him about his disappearances, but he always seemed to have a logical excuse. If I continued to question him, he'd become defensive and angry. I don't know why I put up with his disrespect. I could blame it on my naiveté, but let's face it - I was foolish, and didn't want to admit I'd made a monumental mistake. Otherwise, why would I want to stay married to a man who cheats, who rarely washes a dish and who never picks up after himself? Why would I want to stay married to a man who doesn't notice me or desire me anymore?"

I described in detail the morning I caught Kyle with Maryann, and how I found the stray hairs and the used condom. "I brought evidence of his cheating," I typed. "If I hadn't caught him, I might still be in denial. Kyle is aware I want him out of my house. I told him in a letter. Mom and Dad willed the house to me with the stipulation that I keep it in the family. If we have to hire a private detective to prove he's cheating and stop him from claiming anything of mine, let's do it."

As I typed I remembered Mom's wise advice. *"Always keep your money, your possessions, and your bank accounts in your name. Your Dad is a wonderful man, and I love him dearly, but I wish we'd kept everything separate from the beginning. We could have avoided a great deal of conflict."*

Mom gave me this advice after she and Dad had an argument about money. She'd taken draperies to Sunshine City, a new drycleaning company, specializing in draperies. She wrote a check on the joint account to pay for the cleaning but neglected to record the check. When Dad couldn't balance the account, he asked the bank to send him all cancelled checks then confronted her about the one she made out to Sunshine City.

"Did you go to the nudist colony?"

"Don't use that tone of voice with me, and don't question me like that," she yelled. *"I'm not one of your employees. I'm your wife."*

A few days later, she drove by the dry cleaners and remembered. Mom demanded an apology from Dad, but he refused and proceeded to attach a large manila envelope to the side of the fridge. He wrote in black marker, *"Put Receipts in Here."*

That's when Mom separated her account from his. They rarely argued about money after that, and I learned a valuable lesson.

When Kyle and I married, I didn't add him to my accounts or put his name on anything I owned. Thanks to Mom's advice, Kyle couldn't get his hands on my inheritance.

After I printed out my epistle, I placed the pages inside a file folder and stuffed it in my tote. It felt good to scratch this painful task off my list.

Next, I needed to talk to Ms. Sikes. Too bad I didn't ask Freemont for her number and address last night when I had the chance. I dialed his number again but got the same rapid busy signal as before.

Without Freemont's help, I had no choice but to search through the unwieldy Atlanta phone book. Only one "Sikes", listed on Virginia Avenue in College Station. Tatum said he was walking by there when he heard the gunshot that killed Preston.

I copied down the address and dialed the number. It rang and rang. No answer, and no machine to leave a message on.

My gut, sensing urgency, told me to drive over there. I stuffed my Tandy inside my tote, slipped on my heavy coat.

The freezing wind almost blew me over. If not for the cold wind, it would have been a tolerable day. The sun was shining. A lone white cloud, shaped like a clover leaf, adorned a blue topaz sky.

I turned the caddy's heater on full blast and attempted to live in the moment. People who enjoy each moment, rather than project into the future or dredge up the past, are much happier, I'd read.

I glanced at my list. 2. Talk to Ms. Sikes. 3. Plant the rose bushes in a place where they'll get the morning sun. 4. Go to grocery store and buy ingredients for Mom's spaghetti, foolproof and yummy. 5. Maybe call Tyrone Johnson about my Spitfire.

Tyrone loved to work on the Triumph spitfire cars. He parked them in a circle, as if they could communicate. He'd offered to buy mine from me. Why not sell it to him?

I pondered that question as I drove, searching for Ms. Sikes house. I'd memorized the address and soon spotted the white numbers on a black mailbox - at the corner of Virginia and Highland.

I pulled into the concrete driveway beside a black Chevy van. The one-story stone house, beige with green shutters, looked immaculate. The grass had been neatly mowed and the hedges trimmed. Yellow chrysanthemums encircled a giant oak tree in the center of the front yard. A nativity scene decorated a window box beside the main door. Smoke rose from the chimney.

No doorbell, only a brass-ring knocker. I clanged it three times.

When no one answered, I yelled, "Hello, anybody home?"

The door open and I faced a young black woman. She looked to be about my age, attractive, tall, and thin, in a red wool suit.

I smiled to appear nonthreatening. "Hi, I'm Carrie Sue Justice. I'm looking for Ms. Sikes."

"I know who you are," the woman said.

I didn't remember meeting this woman, but I assumed she must have recognized me from the picture on my column. "I hope this is the correct address for Ms. Sikes."

The woman's brown eyes widened. "I don't mean to be rude. We're on our way to church. Why you need to talk to Mama?"

I glanced at my watch, ten-fifteen. "I'm sorry if I've caught you at a bad time, but this is very important. I won't delay her very long. Could I come in for a sec?"

The young woman shook her head no, frowned and stepped outside. "Mama's not well," she whispered. "Can I help you with something?"

From my tote, I pulled out the photo of Tatum and handed it to her. "Do you recognize him? Police arrested him and three other boys for the murder of Preston Campbell."

"I don't know. What's his name?"

"Tatum Brookins. He told police he wasn't at the scene when Preston was killed. He heard the shot, but he wasn't there. He also said he saw Ms. Sikes that night and greeted her. I'm hoping she can verify his story. If he knows her, she probably knows him and remembers that night."

The young woman touched her forehead with a slender brown index finger. "Mama has Alzheimer's. Her memory's no good. She won't make a good interview if that's what you're looking for."

I sighed. "I was hoping she could help verify what Tatum told police."

"I been trying to get her ready for church and she's arguing with me. She don't know what day it is." She gave the photo back.

I heard a banging noise behind her. An elderly woman appeared in the foyer. Her hands clutched the wheels of her rolling chair. She wore pajamas, dotted with red hearts. Her curly grey hair framed her dark brown face like a halo. "Where're your manners, Lillie Bell? Ask this young lady to come in."

Lillie Bell wagged her finger like a mother scolding a child. "Mama, we need to get you dressed or we gonna be late."

"Oh, poo, where's your manners? Please, come on in, honey." She rolled her wheelchair back and spun around. I followed her to a rectangular living area, crowded with overstuffed furniture, fringed lamps, crocheted doilies and knickknacks. A decorated Christmas tree with multi-colored lights dominated one corner of the room.

I held out my hand. "Hello, Ms. Sikes, I'm Carrie Sue Justice. I won't take much of your time, but I need to show you a photo of someone and see if you know him or remember seeing him a few nights ago. It was the same night Freemont Jackson delivered your laundry."

Rather than shake my hand, she wheeled her chair close to a beige sofa. "Sit down, honey. I got time. You not taking it."

I showed Ms. Sikes the photo of Tatum. "Do you know him?"

She squinted at the picture. "I do. He a good boy, he helps me. He come by here sometimes. He helps me get in and out the house. He a good boy, yes, he is. Lord, Lord, I know this boy. He's a good boy." She tapped the photo with an arthritic finger.

"Do you remember his name?" I sat down on the couch across from her.

Her yellow-brown eyes stared as if lost in her thoughts. "Lord, I can't call it up. I know him. Lord, help me, my mind's no good."

"Does the name Tatum Brookins ring a bell?" I asked.

She smiled and pointed to the photo in my hand. "It sure does."

"Ms. Sikes, I don't know if you've read or heard the news lately, but Tatum's been arrested in connection with the shooting death of Preston Campbell. Do you remember seeing him last Wednesday night?"

She squinted and put a finger in her mouth. "Let me think."

I leaned toward her. "That was the same night Preston was killed. Also, the night Freemont Jackson delivered your laundry."

Ms. Sikes nodded but didn't respond.

I tried another tactic. "By chance did you hear a gun shot or a noise that sounded like a gun shot that night? Tatum claimed he said, 'Hi' to you about the time Preston was killed, which would place him away from the scene of the crime."

Ms. Sikes's mouth dropped open. "He's a good boy, he won't hurt a fly. He says I saw him. I saw him. Yes, I saw him." She started twisting her hands, a sign of agitation.

Lillie Bell stepped beside her mother and whispered in her ear. "You don't need to be getting upset, Mama. You need to get dressed for church."

Ms. Sikes slapped the wheels of her chair and frowned. "I told you. I wanna stay here. I's talking to this nice lady." She waved her hand as if dismissing her daughter. "You go on, Lillie Bell. Leave me be."

"Mama, I'm not gone leave without you. This lady's gone leave soon."

"I like being in my home. You wanna put me in some place I don't wanna be."

Tears flooded Lillie Bell's eyes as she plopped on the red and yellow striped chair across from me. "Mama, I want what's best for you."

My stomach knotted in distress. If Ms. Sikes had Alzheimer's, she wouldn't make a reliable witness for Tatum. "Thank you for your time, Ms. Sikes. I didn't mean to upset you." I patted her gnarled fists. "I have to go now, but I'd like to come back and see you again if that's okay."

I offered my hand to Lillie Bell. "Thank you, too." She gave my hand a soft shake.

As I walked out, I heard Ms. Sikes say, "He's a good boy, he's a real good boy. I help him if I can. He helps me."

Chapter Fourteen

A lump lodged in my throat as my home came into view. The magnolia trees in the front yard seemed to be reaching out in welcome. The large pillars glistened in the sunlight. The sun beaming through made freckled light dance on the veranda, reminding me of a Monet painting.

Thank God, Kyle's car was gone. A large bag of dirt had been positioned beside the rose bushes. A shovel was propped against a column nearby.

I pulled out a sheet of paper stuck between one of the branches and recognized Freemont's precise handwriting. "I'll be back shortly. I'm doing laundry, as usual. I didn't know your schedule. Our phones are still dead. I brought you a shovel and Mama's miracle soil. I've given a lot of thought to what we discussed regarding your brown thumb. You need to plant these roses to prove I didn't jinx you. They'll do better if you dig deep holes and use every bit of this bag of soil. On the bag are planting instructions. I passed Kyle leaving. If he comes back before I do, and you don't want to deal with him, come over to my house.

Your favorite green-thumbed, black brother."

After I studied the planting instructions on the bag, I unlocked the front door and maneuvered around the boxes, evidence of Kyle's preparing to move out. I examined the big box near the stairway. Packed inside were theatrical costumes, swords, framed photos of his performances, and his acting and directing awards. For him, this stuff had sentimental value, unlike our marriage.

I jumped up and cringed when I heard the door open, Kyle sauntered in, smiling, as if he'd been crowned King of the Universe, in his torn jeans, plaid flannel shirt and brown leather jacket. He ran his fingers through his copper hair and stroked the stubble on his face.

"Hi Carrie Sue, great to see you." He held up his hands as if surrendering. "I come in peace." He snickered.

I wanted to slap him, but I thought it was more important to make a quick getaway. I rushed toward the door. "I was just leaving, Kyle. I'm glad you're packing. Looks like you'll be out of here soon."

He grabbed my arm, spun me around and slammed me against the door. My head hit the hard wood. "We need to talk," he growled.

I slapped his face with all the strength I could muster. "Get your hands off me. I want nothing to do with you. The sooner you get out of here, the better." I reached for the doorknob.

Kyle pressed the full force of his body against mine. "You're going to listen, Carrie Sue." His nostrils flared. His copper eyes looked like the depths of hell. He grabbed my wrists and forced them up over my head against the door.

I churned and twisted but couldn't get away. His brute force scared me. My mind flashed back to an article I'd written about a local high school girl, who'd been beaten and raped. Her face looked like raw meat. "My ex-boyfriend did this, because I broke up with him," she'd said.

Kyle ground his body into mine and forcefully kissed my lips, no doubt to leave a bruise, his mark.

I bit his mouth.

"Goddamn you, Carrie Sue."

I shoved my knee up between his legs.

Blood gushed from his lips as he grabbed his jewels. "Shit."

I opened the door, rushed out, and collided with Freemont. He placed his large hands on my shoulders and studied my face. "What's wrong, Carrie Sue?"

I turned to spit out Kyle's blood. "I'm feeling sick and need to leave." I could hear my voice trembling. "We'll plant the roses later." I reached up and touched his face to reassure him. "Don't worry. I'm fine. Go home. Don't get involved with this." I didn't want Freemont fighting with Kyle. Kyle would lose the battle but knowing him, he'd press charges against Freemont.

I grabbed one of his arms to pull him off the veranda, but he stood firm, unbudgeable. I didn't see his van. He must have walked over. "Do you want me to take you home, Free?"

Freemont scowled. "No, that won't be necessary."

"Okay but go home. We'll talk about this later." I ran down the steps, jumped into the car and sped away.

I couldn't remember driving to the grocery store. Thankfully, I'd made a list, or I may have forgotten what to buy.

I placed my items on the counter, and greeted Shanna, the checker, an attractive woman with skin the shade of golden wheat and short black hair.

"Hi, Carrie Sue, how are you?"

I grabbed my billfold and pulled out my checkbook. "I could be better, Shanna."

She began ringing up the groceries. "I know what you mean. It's been crazy around here since that boy was killed. Cops have been swarming around asking questions. I was afraid I'd get fired."

I cocked my eyebrows in surprise. I couldn't imagine anyone firing competent, dependable, hardworking Shanna. "I don't understand. Why would you get fired?"

"Police said two of the boys stole cigarettes from here. Another boy stole a teddy bear. I was working that night and didn't catch them. I wish I had eyes in the back of my head, but I don't." She totaled my items.

I took out a pen, wrote out a check and handed it to her. "Did you know any of the boys?"

"Not really. The white boy who got killed worked at the church. He came in here sometimes. He was nice and polite. The boys arrested for killing him came in often. They liked to hang out. If you know what I mean." She placed my check in the cash register and handed me the receipt.

As she bagged my groceries, I withdrew Tatum's photo from my tote and showed it to her. "What can you tell me about him? He was arrested with the others, but he was spotted two houses away when Preston Campbell was shot and killed."

"I was surprised he got arrested."

"Why were you surprised, Shanna?"

"He never hung out. I didn't see him with the others. He's kind of a loner. If you know what I mean."

"Did you see anyone carrying a gun that night, Shanna?"

"No. I wish I'd paid more attention." She massaged her forehead. "If I'd seen a gun, I would have called for help." She pointed to the button on the side of the counter. "I have a ringer here. I would have mashed it if I'd seen anyone with a gun, and maybe that sweet boy wouldn't have gotten killed." She shook her head. "I was worn to a frazzle that night. I don't usually work nights. Jimmy had the flu and I filled in for him." She bit her bottom lip. "I shouldn't be talking to you about this, Carrie Sue. Please don't quote me. If you do, I'll get fired."

Chapter Fifteen

I parked behind Marcus' jeep. His car was there, but that didn't mean he was. He often jogged or walked to his house and left his jeep parked. I thought about our encounter last night. My face burned, partly from embarrassment, but mostly from the memory of seeing him half-naked.

The cold wind shook me back to reality as I stepped from the Caddy with the bag of groceries. I stumbled on the curb but managed to hold onto the bag without spilling anything.

I trudged up the stairs and unlocked the door. The outside Christmas lights shone to high heaven, but on the inside, it looked appallingly dark. An aching loneliness hit me as I flipped on the wall switch.

I dumped the groceries on the entrance table, and dialed Freemont's number. "Please God, let the phones be working this time."

"Jackson's Laundry," he answered.

I forced a smile. "I want to apologize for the way I acted this afternoon. Are you okay?"

"I'm okay. What about you? And don't lie. You were bleeding when you left."

"Oh no, Free. It wasn't my blood. It was Kyle's. He pushed me against the door, and I bit him."

"Oh..." Freemont paused. "Good, he deserved it. He and I got into it, had a little clash."

I cringed. "What happened?"

"I told Kyle to try me if he wanted to beat up somebody."

"I'm sure he told you everything was my fault."

"Yeah, he said this was the second time you've attacked him. I told him I've known you since childhood, and I've never known you to attack anyone."

"Thank you, Free, but I'm sorry you got involved."

"I thought the asshole needed a warning."

"You and Kyle didn't get into a fight, did you?"

"No. I just scared him a little. He'll probably say I threatened him, but there were no fisticuffs."

"I'm sorry you got caught in the middle, Free. I should have explained what happened."

"Listen to yourself, Carrie Sue. It wasn't your fault. You said Kyle pushed you. That's abuse."

"I'm hoping to be rid of him soon." I exhaled loudly, trying to expel my anger and heartache. "Let's not waste any more time talking about him. I'd like to forget." I glanced at the bag of groceries. "I'm fixing spaghetti tonight. You're welcome to join me and maybe Marcus if he can come, but I haven't asked him yet."

"I would ordinarily, but I've got an early day tomorrow. Let me take a rain check."

"Sure, I understand. Soon as I get back home. I'll have you over."

"When do you think that'll be?"

"In a few days."

"Okay, I'll check on the roses in the meantime. We don't want them dying before you get a chance to plant them, do we?" He chuckled.

"Ha, ha, yeah right. Thanks, Free. See you soon."

Chapter Sixteen

I called Marcus. I'd memorized his phone number.

His answering machine came on with his gruff, unwelcoming, recorded voice: "Give your name, purpose and number." All business.

I waited for the beep. "Hi...it's Carrie Sue, I have a lot of stuff to talk to you about, though I know I shouldn't say 'a lot', because the last time I used that in a news story, you said it's a no-no, because a lot means property. Oh, well, to be more specific, I need to talk to you about Tatum Brookins and other things. I'm at the office now. I'm making spaghetti tonight. It's one of Mom's recipes, and I'm sure you'll love it. Supper will be served around six-thirty or sevenish. See you then...if you can make it. Oh, and if you'd like to bring wine that would be lovely. I bought a bottle of burgundy. I'm using some of it in the spaghetti sauce."

After I hung up the phone, I shook my head in disgust at my rambling, awkward message, and climbed the stairs with my tote and bag of groceries.

I searched the cabinets for cooking utensils and found two heavy iron pots and a flat pan for heating the bread, but no cutting board.

I used a stone plate for dicing up the onion, garlic, green pepper, mushrooms, and parsley. The onion made my eyes smart, and I had a good cry. Mom used to store onions in the refrigerator. She said if onions were cold, they wouldn't sting your eyes as much.

I sautéed the meat and drained off the excess grease before I tossed in the veggies and some spices. As the yummy aroma filled the kitchen, my stomach started growling.

Mama Jackson used to say all good cooks must taste what they make before it's served, but I went overboard. I ate half a bowl and had to force myself to stop.

Next, I tossed in two cans of diced tomatoes, a small can of tomato sauce, sprinkled in more cayenne, added oregano, six bay leaves, and additional parsley sprigs. After I tasted it, I added a slosh of burgundy wine.

While the sauce simmered, I sliced the loaf of Italian bread and stuffed slivers of butter in between the slices.

Marcus hadn't called, and I'd resigned myself to eating alone when the wall-phone rang. I rushed over and grabbed it. "Southern Journal."

"I like the way you answer the phone."

My knees weakened as I heard his voice. I stretched the phone cord out so I could sit on one of the chairs at the kitchen table. "My boss insists I answer like that."

"Are you referring to your perfectionist boss, the one who resembles Jesus?"

My face burned, remembering what I'd said last night. "Like Jesus, in appearance only."

"Is your invitation still open?"

My breath caught in my throat, and I couldn't speak for a moment. I had to bite my tongue to keep from saying I was open to anything he wanted.

"The sauce is simmering as we speak." I was on the verge of saying I'm simmering, too.

"Thanks for the invitation. I'll be there shortly. Do you like Merlot?"

My body tingled. "Yes, I do. It should go well with the spaghetti."

"Okay, I'll bring a bottle. Anything else you need?"

"No just bring yourself."

"See you soon, Carrie."

After he hung up, I boiled water and threw in the spaghetti. While it cooked, I slid the Italian bread in the preheated oven and set the table, using the stone plates I'd found in the cabinet. Since I'd forgotten to buy napkins, I folded individual paper towels in half and placed the forks on top of them.

I was draining the pasta in the colander when Marcus walked in. I gasped at the sight of him. He wore jeans, a crisp white shirt and leather jacket, and oh, my God, he'd shaved off his beard and mustache. I touched his face. "Smooth! You look great."

His hair seemed shorter, neatly combed back, barely skimming his shirt collar. He took out a bottle of California Merlot from a paper bag. For the first time since I'd known him, I had a full view of his shapely mouth, dimpled chin and only one dimple on his left cheek. Wow.

He pulled out the drawer, where I'd found the wooden spoon earlier. His long fingers withdrew a corkscrew, and with the ease of a wine steward, he popped open the Merlot. "Spaghetti smells delicious."

I could have said the same about him, squeaky clean with a hint of spicy aftershave and his own unique manly scent. "I've already been sampling, and if I do say so myself, it's good." I smiled goofily. "I like being able to see your whole face. Where did you find someone to cut your hair on a Sunday?"

"My next-door neighbor is a barber. He offered to make me more presentable. I thought it was time for a change." He grabbed the stems of two wine glasses from the cabinet, set the glasses on the counter and poured the Merlot. He handed me a glass and leaned against the counter.

I tasted the wine. "Lovely."

"Can I help you with anything, Carrie?"

All sorts of lusty thoughts invaded my mind. "No, everything's ready." I removed the warm bread from the oven and arranged it on a platter.

He turned off the oven. "Carrie, you want us to serve ourselves from here?" He waved a hand over the sauce pot, Italian bread, and pasta.

My eyelashes fluttered. "Yes."

"What about music? I brought a cassette that I think you'll like, and there's a boom box in the bedroom."

"Music would be nice." I watched him take long strides down the hall.

He returned carrying a black Sony music box. He placed it on the kitchen counter, plugged it in and pressed "play." A soulful, chanting choir filled the room.

He handed me a plate from the table and motioned for me to go first. "This is the Chorus of Prisoners, from Beethoven's opera Fidelio."

I forked out a scoop of pasta on my plate. "I like it, but it's very sad." I used a wooden spoon to scoop out the sauce on top of the pasta and then grabbed a slice of Italian bread. "I didn't know Beethoven had written an opera. What's it about?"

Marcus forked the pasta on his plate, spooned spaghetti sauce over it, skipped the bread, but grabbed a container of grated Parmesan out of the fridge. He sprinkled cheese on his spaghetti and handed the container to me. "The main character, Florestan, is locked in an underground cell, sentenced to die from starvation."

I carried my wine and food to the table. "Why was he sentenced to die?" I sat in the same spot where I had kissed him two nights before.

He sat in the chair opposite mine. "Florestan had criticized the governor's illegal activities."

I wrapped the pasta and sauce around my fork. "How does it end?"

"His wife dresses as a man and saves him. It's a story of bravery and heroism."

"Sounds interesting, I love stories about strong women."

Marcus nodded. "So do I."

We ate in silence listening to the opera. He filled my empty wine glass and poured himself another. "Great spaghetti." He swirled the last of his pasta and sauce around his fork then gave me a breathtaking smile.

"Thank you. It was Mom's recipe," my throat cracked. "Would you like water? I forgot to put it on the table." I scooted my chair back and stood.

He put his fork down and motioned for me to sit. "I'll get it." He grabbed two glasses from the cabinet and filled each to the brim from the waterspout attached to the fridge. He handed me one.

I took a sip. "Thank you." I drank the rest of my wine.

Marcus directed his piercing navy eyes at me. "How was your day, Carrie? What did you do?"

I shared my conversations with Mrs. Sikes and the grocery checker Shanna. I left out my encounter with Kyle.

As I spoke, he poured me another glass of wine and listened without interrupting me. We'd drained the bottle of Merlot by the time I'd finished my spiel.

Marcus leaned back in his chair, spreading his long, powerful legs out and sighed. "One of my sources said the Klan is planning a demonstration to protest the killing of Preston Campbell. If my source is correct, a representative from the Klan will appear at the Council meeting this week."

I could feel a dark curtain of pain around him. "Are you sure?"

He nodded. "My source is pretty reliable."

"Okay, I'll follow up at the Council meeting tomorrow night, but I have that appointment with the divorce lawyer tomorrow morning, and I won't be able to make the staff meeting."

"If anything happens you need to know, I'll inform you." He ran a hand over his face "If the Klan marches here, it'll polarize the community. It could get out of control if there's not enough security." He shook his head. "Other than covering the Council meeting and following up on Campbell's death, you should think about the best way to publish those statements from the suspects. Silkman said he will have his own copy of the tapes soon. After he gives them to us, we'll compare. If they match up, we can use Silkman as a source rather than implicate Dora Lee." He took a sip of water.

"Also, Marcus, I'll have a story about a homeless man, the guy who walks to the libraries every day. One of the librarians said she was concerned about him. She's wondering where he'll go when they close the libraries to computerize." The libraries in South Atlanta had always used the card-filing system, but with the advancement of technology, librarians needed to transfer the information from those cards into a computer program.

He nodded. "Okay, good, and get the crime report as usual. Do you think you'll have time to write your column?" His dark eyes captured mine. "We often receive calls from readers, who say they enjoy it."

"You probably get negative calls too, but you don't tell me about those." When I first started writing my column, Marcus encouraged me to speak from my heart. He never censored my words. My column was my own opinion and came with a disclaimer, unlike my news stories, which had to be factual or "heads will roll" Marcus had said.

He shook his head. "If I heard anything negative, I'd tell you." He smiled and I thought I saw a happy twinkle in his eyes. "You have quite a bit to tackle this week. If you need help, let me know."

I flashed him a smile. "I think I can handle it all. I need to be busy. Takes my mind off things."

Marcus stood. "I know what you mean. I feel the same." He reached for my empty plate. "Finished?"

I nodded. "Yes."

He took my plate, placed it on top of his. "You cooked. I'll clean up. Go rest. Enjoy yourself."

Chapter Seventeen

I walked to the bathroom, thinking how easily he'd dismissed me when I wanted to stay and talk to him. But I couldn't dwell on it. I needed to concentrate on investigating a murder, helping a teenager prove his innocence. I had enough on my plate without allowing my thoughts of Marcus to interfere, and after my crazy day and nasty encounter with Kyle, I needed to wash all the crud off.

I adjusted the shower water to as hot as I could stand it. The heavenly, pounding spray massaged my tight neck and shoulders.

I stayed in the shower longer than usual, shampooing and conditioning my hair. I gave the conditioner plenty of time to soak in and hopefully work magic, or I wouldn't be able to comb my unruly mane.

While the conditioner soaked in, I shaved my under arms and legs, and wondered why so many people recommended a cold shower to relieve frustration. A hot shower felt much more relaxing, I thought.

After I rinsed out the conditioner and turned off the shower, I dried my hair using a diffuser. Without the attachment on the blow dryer, I'd look like an electrocuted Rapunzel. Mom used to say she loved my hair, but I knew she wanted to make me feel better about my appearance.

I often captured my hair in a ponytail, chignon, or bun, even though Lanie Lowery at Lanie's Locks said I should wear it down, "Big and free. That's the style now." I took Lanie's advice and when I looked in the mirror, a wild-looking woman stared back at me.

I doused myself with lotion, wrapped my body in a towel, creaked open the door and peeked out. I didn't see Marcus. The door to his bedroom was closed. He'd probably secluded himself, I thought.

As I stepped out and headed to my designated bedroom, he walked down the hall.

I froze when I saw him.

He stopped. His eyes widened as if shocked. "Sorry."

I expected him to escape inside his bedroom, but he stood there, looking at me. I couldn't think of anything clever to say.

He sucked in a breath and continued to gape. I usually hate it when men stared or focused on my breast and legs, but in this situation, I wanted Marcus to appreciate my body and think of me as a desirable woman. I trusted him.

As I stood there like a statue, my towel slipped off and fell to my feet. I could feel my face burning while standing completely nude in front of him. Felt like one of those nightmares where you're walking around nude and everyone else has clothes on.

"Whoops," I said and reached down to retrieve the fallen towel.

He walked over and placed the towel in front of my nakedness, as if he wanted to preserve my modesty. At this point, I had none.

As he gently tucked the towel around my chest to secure it, I grabbed his head and kissed him squarely on the lips. The wild, wanton hussy inside me had taken charge.

His eyes widened, and I thought he might reject me again, but I was prepared to take that risk. He was like an electromagnet, and I was captured in his hypnotic field.

I dug my fingers into his hair. He moaned and smothered my mouth in a deep kiss. I heard myself moaning, too, and the next thing I knew my towel came undone again. I didn't care. He didn't seem to care either. He growled, as if he shared my lust.

I tried to remove his jacket, but I couldn't get the sleeves over his muscular arms. My fingers fumbled with the buttons on his shirt as he trailed moist kisses down my neck.

I unzipped his jeans and touched his erection.

He placed his hands on my arms and pushed me back. "Baby, no, we need to talk."

I loved the fact that he called me baby. But why would anyone want to talk at a time like this?

He leaned over and touched my forehead with his. "I don't want you to take this the wrong way, Carrie, but I can't allow myself to lose control. I'm your supervisor and your dad entrusted me to teach and guide you. I would be breaking his trust and violating my own personal beliefs if I took advantage of you. Also, you're still married."

I huffed impatiently. "Kyle broke the marriage bond when he cheated on me. I don't consider myself married to him anymore. In a few weeks I won't be."

He wrapped me in his arms. "I think he's a damn fool for what he did, but I'd be foolish as well, if I let myself hurt you."

I didn't know what to say. Was I confusing sex with love? Regardless, I felt not a single pang of guilt.

After my parents died, I'd tried to behave in a way I thought they'd be proud of, even though they were no longer on this earth to approve or disapprove. I worked hard and tried to follow the golden rule.

When I married Kyle, I convinced myself he loved me, even though our lovemaking seemed mechanical and shallow, not at all loving. There was always this empty void in our relationship. We never spooned or cuddled, and I yearned to be held, to be loved. I wanted to tell Marcus this, but I didn't know how.

"Marcus, there are no guarantees in life, but I think it's important to seize the moment when something feels right."

He stared into my eyes, as if he understood, and led me into his room. I sat on his bed. He sat next to me.

His eyes looked feverish. "I respected your parents, Carrie, and I respect you. I want what's best for you. You're very talented and I want you to reach your full potential both as a woman and as a journalist. I don't want to interfere with your growth. And I can't become an unnecessary distraction." He smiled, but his eyes were sad, vulnerable, and fearful.

The hussy in me would not be deterred. She took charge, climbed onto his lap, and wrapped her legs around his waist. "I've become a much better reporter and writer under your guidance. You've taught me so much. I admire you, and I'll always admire you, even though you've pushed me away."

I pressed my naked breast against him. "Hold me. Make love to me." I kissed his neck.

He blew out hot breaths, as if he were on the verge of losing control. "Ah, Carrie, you're very beautiful. I'm not worthy of you. If you knew everything about me, you wouldn't want me."

"Marcus, please don't tell me what I want or don't want. I know what I want. Don't you think my feelings are important?" I stroked his face.

"Yes, of course," he sighed.

I nibbled his ear and whispered. "Share yourself with me. I know you're hurting. I'm hurting too. We need each other. We need this."

He sighed and smothered my mouth in his in the most passionate kiss I've ever known, but too soon, he stopped and pulled back like a soldier at attention. "Carrie, we need to wait and think about this."

"I don't want to wait, Marcus."

Against his will, I managed to take hold of his erection and moments later it was buried inside me. Not knowing how long he'd give me to find my pleasure, I moved swiftly, back, and forth, feeling every inch of him.

"I'm there," I sighed.

He moaned at his release, and I realized I loved this man. I'd always loved him.

He held me and stroked my back for several minutes before he stood to undress. He folded his clothes neatly on top of his duffle and climbed back into bed nude.

He ran his hands over my body and kissed me tenderly. His mouth worked its way downward. He kissed my neck, my breast, my tummy, and the inside of my thighs. "Are you okay with this?" he whispered.

"Yes," I said, hoarsely.

His mouth and tongue made love to me in ways I'd only dreamed about. I cried out, but he showed no mercy, and in my delirium, I lost track of the number of times I climaxed.

Chapter Eighteen

After we made love, he stared into my eyes as if they held the secrets to the universe. "Do you want to sleep in here with me, Carrie?"

I smiled at his invitation. "Yes, I don't have the energy to walk across the hall, Marcus. I'd love to sleep in here with you tonight."

"It's more morning than night."

"Are you correcting me, Marcus?"

He gave me a serious squint. "Carrie, I hope you know I probably won't change." He lifted a strand of my hair from my face. "I'm a control freak who lost control with you."

I pouted my lower lip. "Are you sorry you lost control?"

He sucked in a breath. "No, but it wasn't smart. My priorities have been work and more work. I can't bear the thought of hurting you. I want to help you, not hurt you. I want the newspaper to succeed and continue the tradition your dad started. And I don't want to impede your progress. You're a solid journalist, Carrie." He kissed my forehead. "I don't deserve you. And you're not free to be with me, even if I did deserve you."

"Is that what you wanted to say before I threw myself at you?"

He groaned a sigh. "Obviously, I wanted you. Who wouldn't? You're beautiful and talented." He placed his index finger inside my mouth and touched the gap between my teeth. "I love your smile, your passion, everything about you. But for a very long time, I've been one of the walking dead. I'm closed due to what happened in my past, and I think you deserve more than an unavailable man. If you knew the whole truth about me, you wouldn't want me."

I tried to decipher what he was saying. He was telling me he loved everything about me, but he felt incapable of providing what I needed. Yet he had satisfied me beyond what I thought possible. Had I satisfied him? If so, why did he look sad? I tried to decipher the answers as I stared at his handsome face.

"What is the whole truth about you, Marcus?"

He let out a long sigh. "You need to sleep."

I opened my eyes wide. "I'll sleep after you tell me."

He shook his head as if exasperated. "What was I thinking, getting involved with a nosy journalist?"

I laughed, though I didn't appreciate the nosy journalist comment; it was too impersonal. "You said, I need to know about you. Tell me what I need to know."

"I drink too much. I need a few shots of whiskey before I can sleep or hope to sleep. And I'm a workaholic, but you know that already."

I groaned. "Why do you think you're an unavailable workaholic?"

He hissed through his teeth. "When I work, I escape from guilt, but we need to talk about this some other time. I'm exhausted, and I know you are."

"I have two more questions."

"What are they?"

"Other than the wine we shared did you drink any alcohol today?"

"No."

"Do you think you'll need whiskey now in order to sleep?"

He grunted a laugh. "No, I won't have any problem sleeping now."

"I have one more question."

He frowned. "You said only two questions."

"Just one more," I said, sweetly. "Why do you feel guilty?"

He squinted as if in pain. "We don't have enough time to go into that now, Carrie. You need to sleep."

"I'll sleep after you answer me. If you don't, I won't be able to sleep."

He scowled and ran a hand through his dark hair. "Alright, you asked for it, but after I tell you, I don't want to talk about this ever again and if you decide to get up and leave this bed after you hear what I have to say, I'll understand."

My heart hammered, not knowing what to expect and perhaps afraid to know the truth about him. "Okay."

He sucked in a breath. "I don't know what your dad may have told you about me, but during the Vietnam War I flew B-52s. And when you drop bombs from B-52s you carpet bomb."

I touched his mouth to stop him. "What exactly is carpet bombing?"

"It's when you drop napalm at a target, but you actually bomb a much larger area." He closed his eyes, and I thought for a moment he was drifting off to sleep.

"Is that all you wanted to say, Marcus?"

He opened his eyes. "For now, yes, get some sleep."

"There's more to this. I know it. You're not telling me the whole truth." I frowned at him.

He sighed and rolled his eyes. "I joined the Air Force after I graduated from college. In the Air Force, I learned to fly."

I saw the pain in his dark eyes and felt a pang of guilt for asking him to delve into his past.

"Before I was sent to Vietnam, I married my childhood sweetheart Susan. Her dream was to become a war correspondent. She became one of the best. She loved her work.

She and I were both risk takers. We thought we were indestructible."

He stared at the ceiling. "In Vietnam, I flew various aircraft before I was assigned to B-52s. I took pride in what I did. I followed orders as precisely as possible, though, as I mentioned, there's no way to carpet bomb precisely." He inhaled a slow, deep breath. "I didn't consider the death and destruction I caused. Flying anesthetized me to all of that. From the air, you don't see the bodies or body bags on the ground. But in one day that all changed."

"What caused the change?"

"My napalm hit a hospital." He groaned at the memory. "My wife was flying in a helicopter not far from there. If I'd known she was in the path of my napalm, there's no way in hell I would gone near there."

I gasped. "Oh, Marcus, no, you can stop now if you want to."

"You asked me, and you need to know." He put a hand over his eyes. "My bombs hit the 'copter Susan was riding in. The copter went down, and she died in the crash." He sighed loudly. "I killed my own wife, Carrie." He stared at me, his eyes glistening with his tears.

I knew his guilt must be overwhelming, but to what extent, I couldn't begin to imagine. I suffered survivor's guilt when my parents died, but his guilt was worse, way beyond anything I'd experienced. No mere words could adequately soothe him, but I needed to try. "Marcus, I'm so sorry. But you weren't responsible for her death. You can't be sure your bombs hit the copter she was riding in."

He moaned. "There was no doubt."

"But what evidence do you have? Isn't it possible that enemy forces shot down the helicopter?" I hugged him, tightly.

"Don't you think I've tried to prove to myself I didn't kill her? But eventually, I had to face the truth."

I blinked away my tears. "Even if it's true, Marcus, it was a horrible accident. You can't blame yourself. You were following orders. And, as you said, you had no way of knowing she was over there."

He turned slightly and punched the headboard. "Following orders is no excuse. Even the damn Nazis claimed they were following Hitler's orders."

"That's not the same thing, and you know it. There's no comparison," I wondered if he'd shared all of this with Dad. Dad wasn't a psychiatrist, but he was an empathetic listener. He and Marcus were close. "Did Dad know?"

He wiped his face. "Yes. I thought I needed to tell him before he hired me. He was a great man, Carrie. I miss him very much."

"I miss him, too," I licked my tears.

He wrapped his arms around me. "I wish I could change the past, Carrie. I'd give anything if I could. But I can't. All I can do is strive to survive and follow the principles your dad espoused. He used to say his last name forced him to seek justice. I'm honored to continue his cause. Taking over the newspaper has been cathartic for me. I may never be able to forgive myself for what I've done, but this newspaper gives me hope for redemption. Life teaches hard lessons. I've learned not to blindly follow someone in authority. And I've learned never to settle for mediocrity. I think the problems in our society are exacerbated when we do. We must always strive for perfection."

"Marcus, other than Dad, you are the most honorable man I've ever known. I love you."

Marcus stroked my hair. "I want you to love yourself, Carrie. You can't love anyone unless you love yourself first. As for me, I have serious problems that you don't need to concern yourself with. I may never be able to offer you the kind of love you need and deserve. I'm a haunted man who can't let go of the past. You're a beautiful, intelligent, talented young woman. You deserve better. You deserve the best."

"I think you are the best, Marcus."

Chapter Nineteen

December 11

I jolted awake with Marcus calling my name. He stood beside the bed with a towel around his waist. His hair looked wet. His lips smiled. "How much time do you need to get to your appointment?"

I sat up, startled. It took me a moment to process what he'd said. I glanced at the clock on the bed stand. "Oh, no, is it seven already?"

He nodded. "Do you have time to make your appointment with the lawyer?"

"I have time. Debbie Jasper is at Sam's firm, not too far away. I'm surprised I slept this late on a Monday."

He leaned over and kissed me lightly. His mouth tasted of mint. His body smelled of soap. "It's raining. Temps are falling. Why don't you take my jeep? It has four-wheel drive and winter tires. I'll leave the keys on the kitchen table. I made coffee."

I swung my legs over the side of the bed and wrapped my arms around him. "Thank you."

As he pulled me up, I noticed his erection under the towel and touched it. "And a very good morning to you, Marcus."

He slapped my butt. "You'd better get going. I don't want you speeding in this weather."

I snatched his towel off and wrapped my legs around his waist.

His eyes widened in surprise. "What am I going to do with you?"

I placed my arms around his neck to balance myself. "I can think of one thing you can do."

He held up my thighs and butt with his strong hands and arms to keep me from falling. "I wish we had more time, baby, but we don't, you don't."

I beamed at my new assertiveness. "Um, let me calculate." I planted my mouth next to his ear and whispered, "I think we have time for a quickie." I kissed him passionately and maneuvered my hips to take him in.

We thrust wildly at each other and fell back on the bed, moaning when we'd finished. He stroked my hair.

I sighed. "I wish I didn't have to go, but I do."

His mouth curved wickedly. "Is that how it's going to be now? You have your way with me and leave?"

I loved this playful side of him. "Don't worry, Marcus. I'll call you."

His eyes darkened. "You'd better. Now get going. And don't drive like a maniac. Let me know you've arrived safely."

Chapter Twenty

I showered in a flash, toweled off and moisturized. No time for makeup, only lip gloss.

I slipped into a white silk blouse, black suit, and black boots. I had an abundance of black in my wardrobe. I'd been in mourning too long.

With no time to style my hair, I let it hang down to reflect my new mood. I rushed to the kitchen where I gulped down coffee and grabbed the keys Marcus had left on the table. He'd written me a note that said, "Call me when you get there."

I put on my black coat and placed the folder with the marriage and divorce story in my tote.

When I reached the offices downstairs, I waved to Marcus. He was in his office with the door open, talking on the phone. At the sight of him, a warm rush flowed through me. I smiled. His face reddened and his mouth dropped open as he waved back.

The staff meeting would begin soon, and I wanted to be out of here before everyone arrived. I'd been called an open book, never good at hiding my feelings. Marcus, on the other hand, had always been inscrutable. Would that change now that we'd become intimate? Or would he remain the "unavailable man" he claimed to be? I pondered these questions as I drove to see the divorce lawyer.

Chapter Twenty-One

Grinning like the proverbial Cheshire Cat, I walked into Debbie Jasper's reception area with five minutes to spare. I'd driven like a fiend, despite Marcus's warning.

An attractive brunette in the red power suit sat behind a shiny mahogany desk. She greeted me with a wide smile and "Good morning."

"Yes, it is a good morning. I'm Carrie Sue Justice. I have an appointment with Debbie Jasper."

"Ms. Jasper is expecting you. She's on the phone now. She'll be with you shortly. Would you like a cup of coffee?"

"No, thank you, I've already had some, but I'd like to use your phone if that's okay." My stomach fluttered at the thought of calling Marcus.

Betty pointed to the black telephone on the table beside one of the leather chairs in the waiting area. "You're welcome to use that one." Her voice sounded soothing, appropriate for someone who worked for a lawyer with stressed-out clients. "Do you require privacy, Ms. Justice?"

"No, this is fine. Thank you." I sat in the chair next to the phone and dialed the office.

I expected Lisa to answer. She usually did, Monday through Friday.

"Marcus Handley," he said in his sexy baritone.

My toes curled and my heart thundered. "Hi, it's Carrie Sue. You'll be pleased to know I didn't get a speeding ticket."

He exhaled loudly into the phone. "So even though you broke the law, you arrived safely."

"More or less. How's the meeting going?" I sounded breathy.

"It's going. I'll tell you about it later. Thanks for calling. Good luck. I'll see you soon." From his businesslike tone, no one would have guessed we'd shared the hottest sex of my life.

"Okay, bye, Marcus."

I heard a hollow click and realized he'd hung up without saying goodbye. My heart thudded with a sore ache, but I told myself it wasn't personal. He was at the office, conducting a staff meeting. What did I expect?

I placed the phone back in its cradle as a tall blonde woman with a buzz cut walked toward me. She was smartly dressed in a pin-striped pants suit and heels. She smiled warmly. "Hello, Carrie Sue, I'm Debbie Jasper. It's a pleasure to meet you." Her holly-green eyes beamed.

I stood and shook her hand firmly. She was more than six feet tall. Her face, body and hair screamed dominatrix. The perfect ball-busting lawyer to handle my divorce, I thought. "Hi, Debbie, it's nice to meet you." She smiled wider, revealing her white teeth and prominent molars.

I followed her down the hall to a lush burgundy and gold office. She sat on her massive sofa and motioned for me to sit beside her. All four walls held tapestries of butterflies. Butterflies? Really? Not something I'd expected from Dominatrix Debbie.

"I love the butterflies," I said.

She glanced at them. "Yes, I'm rather fond of them, too. They represent the four stages of life, and how we must appreciate every moment of our lives. Did you know that butterflies have none of the genetic material of the caterpillars and chrysalis from which they emerged?"

"Wow, that's a true metamorphosis, isn't it?"

Debbie nodded. "It is."

From my tote, I withdrew the folder containing my marriage and divorce stories. "I did my homework." I handed the folder to her.

She removed the typed pages. Her green eyes raced over what I'd typed.

I tried to read her expression. "I was in a zone when I wrote that. Hope I've given enough detail."

"Is there anything else you'd like to add, Carrie Sue?"

"I think I've already described in my divorce story how I found the strands of red hair and the used condom. But did I mention I brought those things with me as evidence of Kyle's cheating?"

She twisted her lips in a weird smile, as I handed the plastic bags to her. "Good, Carrie Sue. Thank you."

After she placed the evidence on her massive, mahogany desk, we discussed her fee, which was reasonable. "Since you're a client of Sam's, you're on the honor system. You pay after the divorce is finalized. I don't expect any problems. There are no children involved. You don't want alimony. However, we need to make sure he doesn't take anything from you, as you mentioned in your divorce story." She tapped the file with her neatly manicured index finger. "Sam mentioned in confidence you inherited quite a few assets. Kyle shouldn't be able to touch that, but Sam said you made money when you sold the newspaper business, and I want to make sure those assets are secure and untouchable. If you wish, I'll hire a private investigator to follow your husband."

"Okay."

"Is there anything else you want to say, Carrie Sue?"

I described how Kyle followed me to Karl Silkman's office Saturday and how he attacked me yesterday.

159

She grimaced. "Let's get a restraining order against him."

"Okay. I've told him I want him out of my house, and he's been packing and preparing to get out. Once he leaves, I'll change the locks and get a security system in place."

She gave me a reassuring hug. "Do everything you need to do to protect yourself, Carrie Sue. Are you staying at your house now?"

"No and I won't feel safe there until after he moves out. I've been sleeping in one of the bedrooms above my office. Kyle doesn't know I'm there."

"Good. And if you have a couple of close friends you trust, inform them of your comings and goings. Tell them Kyle scares you. If they ever suspect you're in danger, tell them to notify the authorities immediately." Debbie grabbed a giant silky pillow, shaped like a baseball bat. "Many of my clients need to express their anger. Feel free." She stood and held the bat like a big-league hitter.

I gasped and jumped when she pounded the arm of the sofa with it. Did my divorce lawyer have anger issues or was she merely giving me a demonstration?

Chapter Twenty-Two

After meeting with Debbie, I rode the elevator up to Karl Silkman's office. As I walked in, he was walking out. "Hi, Karl, I had a meeting downstairs and thought I'd stop by."

His hands brushed the lapels of his charcoal-grey suit and then straightened his red-and-grey striped tie. "Come on back. I can spare a minute."

As soon as we reached his office, I said, "I talked to the man who delivered laundry to Ms. Sikes the night Preston Campbell was shot and killed. He verified what Tatum said in his interview with police."

He rubbed his forehead as if it hurt. "What's the name of the witness?"

"Freemont Jackson."

"And is Jackson positive he saw Tatum?"

"I showed him Tatum's picture. He said he believes he saw Tatum and remembers saying hello to him the night of the shooting."

Silkman grabbed a pen and pad from his desk. "How can I get in touch with him?"

I recited Freemont's phone number and address. Silkman scribbled them on the pad.

"And I spoke to Ms. Sikes." I grabbed my address book and read off her contact information. "Unfortunately, she may not be much help to Tatum. She's in a wheelchair and has Alzheimer's, but she seems to remember him. She says he's a good boy. You could possibly use her as a character witness if she's considered competent."

Silkman stroked his mustache. "Thank you. The district attorney's office is seeking a Grand Jury indictment."

"Do you think all the boys, including Tatum, will be indicted?"

"DA seems confident all the boys will be prosecuted as adults."

I gasped in surprise. "But how can they be tried as adults when they're not adults?"

"Ultimately the Grand Jury will decide whether there's probable cause to prosecute for murder. Keep in mind they'll hear only one side. When the D.A., or one of his assistants, asks for an indictment, the Grand Jury generally grants it. Defense attorneys have no say in the matter. We aren't even allowed in the same room." He sighed as if frustrated. "I still haven't gotten the tapes I requested from the police department. When I do, we'll transcribe them and give you a copy. But I have one request. When you publish, don't say I gave them to you."

"But you said you'd leave them for me in the clerk's office, and I could say I got them from there?"

"I'd rather you use your by-line in the article or publish without a by-line."

I nodded, though I couldn't agree without discussing this with Marcus. I didn't want us to publish the transcripts until I felt certain Dora Lee was in the clear. "Let me know when you plan to leave the transcripts in the clerk's office, okay?" When he didn't respond, I fidgeted nervously, combing my fingers through my hair. "Do you mind if I use your phone to make a quick call?"

He extended his hand toward his desk. "Be my guest." He withdrew a gold pocket watch from the inside of his suit coat and glanced at it. "I need to go. If you require anything, ask Josie, my secretary. Oh, and one more thing, regardless of the wishes of your publisher Handley, I may need to subpoena you if we go to trial. My client's life is at stake."

Chapter Twenty-Three

When I dialed the office, this time Lisa answered.

"Hi Lisa, it's me, Carrie Sue. How're you?"

"Hi Carrie Sue, I'm feeling great, I had a lovely weekend, went Christmas shopping. I'm about done. What about you?"

I opened my mouth to answer, but she continued talking. "We missed you at the meeting. Marcus said you had an appointment."

"That's right. Is there anything I need to know?"

"Not really, except be prepared for Marcus's new look. He's shaved off his beard and mustache and had his hair cut."

Unsure of how to answer, I hesitated before I spoke. "How does he look?"

"I've always thought he was a handsome man, even with the beard, but now, oh my. Not only that, but he was in a great mood. He didn't bark at anyone today, not once. So far, so good, but don't get your hopes up. He's still as demanding as ever, only nicer about it."

"Is he around, Lisa? I need to tell him something." My heart hammered in anticipation.

"He left here right after the meeting. Can I give him a message?

"No, just tell him I called, and I'll catch him later."

Chapter Twenty-Four

As I stretched back in Marcus' jeep, I thought about the many times I'd cried in this parking garage after meeting with Sam about Mom and Dad's estate. I'd lie in a fetal position and bawl until I found the strength to drive out.

In comparing then and now, I realized I'd finally made peace with my grief. I was like one of those butterflies in Debbie's office. I'd had a complete metamorphosis. Marcus was a vital part of that transformation, and for the first time in my life, I was in love. I had no doubt and rather than mourn here as I have in the past, I relived my intimate moments with Marcus. Unfortunately, I lost track of time, and when I glanced at my watch, I discovered an hour had passed since I left Karl Silkman's office.

Not ready to drive back yet, I withdrew a notebook and started writing another "to do" list.

1. Tell Marcus about meeting with Silkman. Can we use him as a source, even though he doesn't want to be used? If he leaves transcripts in the clerk's office, will that solve the source issue? He said the

Grand Jury will meet soon and decide if there's probable cause for prosecution. D.A. wants to try all the boys as adults. Is there anything we can do to stop this injustice? Silkman still wants to subpoena me.

2, Cover Council meeting tonight. Learn about possible Klan march.

3. Plant rosebushes.

4. Buy sexy lingerie

5. Call Tyrone about Spitfire.

6. Have the locks changed and the security system installed.

I jumped when I heard a knock on my window. I turned to see the armed guard I'd met yesterday.

"Everything okay?" he asked.

"Yes, I'm just sitting here, making a 'to do' list."

He shook his head. "It's never safe for a woman or anyone to sit alone in a parked car while she writes checks, reads, make lists, or naps."

"You sound like my dad." As I said this, I could almost feel Dad's spirit, warning me via this guy.

Chapter Twenty-Five

I felt a wave of panic when I drove up to the Southern Journal and discovered Mom's Cadillac had vanished. It wasn't on the street where I'd parked it. I couldn't remember if I'd locked it or not. Mom stored spare keys inside her vehicle, and I hadn't taken the time to find all of them.

I leaped from the jeep and raced up the stairs to the office. Who would be stupid enough to steal a car parked in front of a newspaper building in broad daylight? Would Kyle be that stupid? Probably.

I pulled open the heavy front doors. Lisa smiled from behind the reception desk. She looked calm and collected. I wanted to shake her. Make her feel my panic.

"Mom's Cadillac is gone, Lisa. I didn't drive it to my meeting this morning. I drove Marcus' Jeep." I jabbed a finger toward the side window. "It was out there when I left. Did you see anything? Do you know anything about it?"

She chewed on her red mouth, stood, and walked over to me. "Marcus has it. He left a note on your desk."

I gulped deep breaths to calm my racing heart. "Why did Marcus take Mom's car without telling me?"

Lisa tilted her blonde head to one side, as if confused. "His note mentioned something about having your car serviced. I thought you knew." As she said this, I glanced though the window and saw Marcus jumping out of the Cadillac.

I gasped at the sight of him, running up the stairs. He wore a tailored, tan corduroy suit. His white shirt was unbuttoned at the neck, no tie, and no heavy coat, though it was cold out.

My heart flip flopped as he opened the door. I tried to speak, but no words came.

Thankfully Lisa intervened. "I was just telling Carrie Sue you took her car to get it serviced." She twisted her red lips into an odd smile and hugged me. "Bless her heart. She thought someone had stolen it."

I nodded, confused as to why Marcus had Mom's car serviced without asking my permission. "Marcus, we need to talk." My voice sounded child-like.

He licked his lips. "Sure, Carrie. Any messages, Lisa?"

Lisa glanced from me to Marcus, as if expecting an explosion. "Yes, I put them on your desk."

I walked ahead of him to his office. He closed the door behind us and pulled out a desk chair. He offered it to me like a maestro directing an orchestra to play softer and propped his butt on the edge of his desk. His smoldering eyes met mine, and my resolve weakened, but not enough to back down. I needed to make him understand. He was my lover, not my caretaker. "I panicked when I didn't see Mom's car outside. If you had to make a trip somewhere, that's fine, of course. After all, I had your jeep, but why did you take it upon yourself to have Mom's car serviced?" It occurred to me I still referred to the Cadillac as Mom's car even though she was dead.

He ran a hand through his dark hair. "Your tires were bald, and you needed an oil change, but you're right, I should have asked your permission first. Did you realize you didn't lock your car?"

Before I could answer, he said. "I found a key without a problem. Your dad used to say your mom stored keys inside her car like a squirrel hording nuts, and he was right." He raked his fingers through his hair again, as if agitated. "Nothing prevented me from getting inside and starting it." He sighed loudly. "And another thing, your tank was on empty, and I needed to fill it."

I coughed to clear the lump from my throat. "You filled my tank, too."

He nodded.

"Marcus, I appreciate your thoughtfulness, but I'm not a child and you have enough to do without taking care of stuff I should have handled myself."

He rubbed a hand over his face. "You're definitely not a child, Carrie, but I wanted to help you out, and frankly I like to know you're driving a safer vehicle." He smiled. "I know you've been swamped with work and everything that's going on in your personal life."

I started to tell him he was my personal life, but I clammed up.

"I'm sorry if I've upset you, Carrie. I acted impulsively. I'm not normally that impulsive. You must be rubbing off on me." He flashed a glorious smile.

My face burned. "I certainly rubbed off on you last night and this morning."

His trousers winged out in front. He slapped the side of his desk. "Not fair. I have a meeting with a bunch of Rotarians soon, and my body is responding like a teenager's."

I smiled, pleased with his spontaneous reaction. "I feel like a teenager in love."

"Not that long ago, you were a teenager."

"It's been seven years since I was eighteen. I first met you then and started working here as a reporter."

He nodded and his eyes beamed, as if he found my comments amusing.

"I'm only ten years younger than you, Marcus. Even though I may not act my age or seem responsible half the time." I withdrew my checkbook from my tote. "And speaking of being responsible, what was the total bill for servicing the Cadillac? I insist on paying you back."

He held his hands up. "No, no, I wanted to do this for you."

I groaned in protest. "I can't let you buy my gas and pay for servicing my car. What exactly did you have done?"

Marcus massaged his chin. "Larry, my mechanic, gave you four new tires, a tune up, changed the oil, oil filter and air filter. He'll rotate and balance the tires every three-thousand miles and that's when you should have your oil changed." He shifted his commanding body and gripped the edge of his desk like he was flying in turbulence. "When I noticed your car was in bad shape, I was worried about you and wanted to make sure you're safe. Consider this my gift to you."

I studied the floor and the scuff marks imbedded in the hard pine. I often found images in carpet or wood. This time I saw a heart, as my own heart swelled. Marcus felt responsible for his late wife's death, but I couldn't allow him to worry excessively about me and cripple him emotionally, even more than he'd been crippled. I loved this man. No way in hell would I debilitate him. "Thank you, but as I said, you have many more important things to do than taking care of something I should have done."

He sighed, a quiet moan. "Carrie, I can't imagine anything more important than your safety. I may have overstepped a boundary today, but I hope you understand I meant well." He placed his hand over his heart.

I gave him what I hoped was a tender smile. "I understand, Marcus, but next time, ask me first, please, before you do something like this."

He looked down as if searching for the right words. "You've been preoccupied lately. You're going through a divorce. You work nonstop. You and I are involved in an intimate relationship when our business relationship requires us to hide our feelings. I know this creates new problems for you." He twirled a pen on his desk. "This was my way of trying to make your life a little easier."

In his dark eyes was a combination of kindness and fear. I wanted to hug him. Relieve his fears and guilt. Tell him not to be afraid. There are no guarantees in life.

"Marcus, being with you has made me happier than I've ever been."

He smiled, seductively. "I feel the same."

Wow, what a powerful concession from this private man. I didn't quite believe him, of course, but I loved hearing him say those words. "I need to figure out a way to reimburse you."

He frowned. "You've already given me more than I could ever repay, Carrie." He glanced at his aviator watch and sighed. "I have to leave soon, but first, tell me about your meeting with the divorce attorney."

I gave him a quick summary. He listened without interrupting.

To lighten the mood, I described the pillow baseball bat Debbie kept in her office. "Fortunately, I didn't need to use it."

He laughed and continued to give me his full attention.

"Debbie says the divorce should go through without a problem."

"That's great news, Carrie. I hope she's right."

I didn't tell Marcus about the restraining order against Kyle, nor what Debbie said about keeping two friends informed of my whereabouts. I usually kept Marcus informed, but he shouldn't demand to know my every move and obsess about my safety.

As I looked at this incredibly sexy man, my mind blanked. To spark my brain, I referred to my "to do" list.

"After my appointment with Debbie, I went to see Karl Silkman. He said the D.A. is planning to ask a Grand Jury to indict Tatum and the others for Preston Campbell's murder. Karl promised to let me know when the Grand Jury convenes. In addition, the D.A. wants to try these boys as adults. Can you believe that?"

Marcus closed his eyes and shook his head. "We need to publish those transcripts in the next edition."

"I expect Karl to place a copy in the clerk's office. If he does, we can say we got them from there. I don't want anyone to point fingers at Dora Lee."

He nodded. "Great work, I'm proud of you, Carrie."

I wanted to kiss him, but I knew I couldn't. Not here, not now. "Thank you, Marcus."

He pointed to the list in my hand. "Anything else we need to talk about?"

"I'd like to change some of the locks to my house. I have a deadbolt on the front door, so that's no problem, but I'm thinking I need a more secure system."

Marcus nodded. "Jeff Daniels can help. He sweeps this place to make sure the phones aren't tapped. He's developed safety systems more advanced than anything I've seen. Jeff used to be with the CIA. He retired a few years ago. He can do just about anything electronic. He's installing something for me at my house now. I'll drop by and talk to him."

"Don't go out of your way, Marcus. I can call him myself later. No rush."

His brow furrowed. "I know you're covering the Council meeting tonight, but what are your plans today?"

"I need to plant some rosebushes at my house and make sure Kyle has moved out."

Marcus nodded. "If you're going home, maybe Jeff can drive over there and meet with you. I'll ask him." He narrowed his questioning eyes. "And you said you were planting roses?"

"Karen Turner sent me rosebushes recently. Remember the column I wrote about my brown thumb?"

He nodded but said nothing.

"She wants me to plant them to prove to myself I don't kill every living thing I stick in the ground. I feel obligated to make sure they live. That's why I need to plant them today. I know it's cold, but Freemont thinks they'll live."

He ran his tongue over his lips, walked over and tilted my chin up with his right index finger. Our eyes locked. He sucked in a breath. "Can I expect to see you tonight after the Council meeting?"

My body flushed hot. "I'm planning to sleep here...with you."

He exhaled slowly. His warm breath caressed my face. "I'll be looking forward to tonight then."

Chapter Twenty-Six

As I walked out of Marcus' office, I said "Hi" to Lindsey.

"We missed you at the staff meeting, Carrie Sue." She sashayed toward me looking like a runway model in her emerald, green suit. She wore her sleek, black hair in a French twist.

Marcus walked briskly past us. Over his shoulder he announced, "I put the Christmas parade information on your desk, Lindsey. College Station resident Victor Hightower will be the Grand Marshal. Hightower fought in the Olympics and won the World Boxing Association's Cruiserweight title. I've heard he's training to become a heavyweight. Interview Hightower as soon as possible and get the details."

"Will do, Marcus," she said to his back.

As he walked out, she whispered. "Don't you think Marcus looks amazing without all that facial hair?"

"Yes, he does." I tried to sound indifferent, though my heart hammered.

She beamed a smile. "When I told him how great he looks, he didn't even acknowledge the compliment." She laughed. "He's a handsome devil and doesn't know it."

I cringed as my green-eyed monster emerged. I couldn't bear the thought of women like Lindsey gushing over him, but I had to face facts. He was irresistible and eligible, and I was still married. "Sorry I missed the meeting, but I'm glad it went well."

Lindsey's brown eyes danced. "You're positively glowing, Carrie Sue."

I smiled at the compliment. "I am?"

Her smile widened, revealing her perfect white teeth. "I've never seen you look this va-va-vavoom sexy."

She placed her hand on my head like a holy-roller preacher trying to heal me. "I should hate you for being so beautiful. Kyle had better watch out." She winked. "Speaking of Kyle, what's going on with you two? When he came in here Saturday, I got the feeling y'all weren't getting along."

I pretended to be surprised. "What do you mean?"

She tapped me on the arm. "You know. Something was off. I saw daggers in your eyes, girl, and when Marcus rushed out of here, I got the impression he had to break up a fight. Did you and Kyle argue about something?"

"It's a long story, Lindsey."

"I asked Marcus what happened, but he just shook his head and ran upstairs. I know

I'm a busybody and shouldn't talk. I've felt like killing my husband more than once."

I chewed on my bottom lip. I had to be careful with Lindsey, the newspaper's answer to Barbara Walters, notorious for drawing out secrets. If Lindsey knew Kyle and I were divorcing, she might repeat it and it'd be all over South Atlanta before tomorrow. "I was in a rotten mood Saturday. That's all."

Her long lashes fluttered, as if processing information. "You've never been moody without good reason, Carrie Sue. I wish we could do lunch and have girl-time, but I promised Stan I'd meet him." She was referring to her husband Stan Jernigan, whom she often described as "the ambulance-chasing barrister I married."

I exhaled a thankful sigh when Lisa walked in and interrupted Lindsey's inquisition. "Carrie Sue, Marcus is on the phone. He needs to talk to you."

"Thanks, Lisa. See you later Lindsey. Enjoy lunch. Tell Stan, hi from me."

"Will do." She glanced at her watch. "Oh gosh, I'm running late. He's waiting for me at his office." She draped the strap of her black tote over her shoulder and dashed out.

I watched her leave before I punched the blinking button on the phone at my desk. "Hi, Marcus."

"I talked to Jeff. He'll meet you at your house around two if that's convenient."

"I'll be there. Thanks." As I said this, I noticed Lisa staring at me. Her thin eyebrows hovered over inquisitive eyes.

"My pleasure," he whispered. "See you tonight." He hung up before I could respond.

As I placed the phone back in its cradle, Lisa was still staring at me, as if she knew all my secrets. "Carrie Sue, I brought some spaghetti from home. Would you like to share it with me?"

"Thank you, but I had spaghetti last night." I bit my tongue to keep from telling her who I dined with. "Let's plan to have lunch another time, okay?"

She smiled. "I'd like that." She walked over and hugged me. "Are you feeling better? You were very upset when you came in."

"I kind of freaked out, didn't I?"

She nodded. "With good reason, Marcus shouldn't have taken your car without asking. But don't tell him I said that."

"I won't, Lisa. Don't worry, but I do need to get going."

"Will you be back in today?"

"Yes, ah, I mean, no. I have a Council meeting tonight, but I'll see you tomorrow." I grabbed my tote and rushed out the door before incriminating myself further.

As I climbed in the Cadillac, I noticed its body looked clean and shiny, the interior immaculate, dusted, and vacuumed. My heart swelled with gratitude. Why would Marcus do all this?

On the passenger's seat, I noticed an envelope and a pad. Clipped to the envelope was a note in Marcus' scrawl. "Carrie, you forgot to fill out your last expense report. I put some forms inside the envelope for your convenience and included Larry's information. Contact him to continue servicing your car. I usually keep track of mileage on a pad and put expense receipts for gas, etc. inside an envelope. You can use this system if you think it'll work for you."

I sighed, frustrated with myself. I'd been floundering and forgetting things. No surprise my Spitfire conked out on me. I couldn't remember the last time I'd had that thing serviced.

"I'm sorry if I've been such a disappointment," I whispered as if Mom and Dad could hear. They'd raised me to be responsible and independent, but I'd failed to measure up.

I sat for a moment, moping, studying my hands. I couldn't believe I was still wearing my wedding band.

I yanked it off and threw the ring in the glove compartment. I switched Mom's diamond solitaire, the one I'd used for an engagement ring, to my right ring finger.

After I finished moping, I drove to the nearest mall. On the way, I tried to remember the last time I'd worn sexy lingerie. I'd never purchased any for myself, but Lindsey had given me a black teddy as a wedding gift. I wore it on our honeymoon, but Kyle got drunk and fell asleep while I was in the bathroom. Now the thought of wearing the ill-fated teddy turned my stomach.

When I entered the shopping area, it looked crowded. A line of children waited to see Santa.

As I walked into Frederick's, a recording of Eartha Kitt singing Santa Baby greeted me. A blonde salesclerk in a gold, mini dress asked, "Can I help you?"

"Yes, I hope so. I'm looking for lingerie."

She showed me a red see-through bra, matching panties, and garter belt. One glance and I decided it would fit. No need to try it on. "Looks good, I'll take that."

To complete the ensemble, she grabbed some thigh-high black nylons and held up a long, red velour robe. "The wrapping for the present inside." She flashed a wide smile allowing me to see every tooth in her mouth.

After I bought the robe, she pointed to a see-through body suit in purple. "This would look fab on you." Trusting her judgment, I bought that, too.

When I walked out of the store with my shopping bag, I glanced at my watch and gasped. I couldn't believe the time.

I raced like Dale Earnhardt to get home, but I was late. Thankfully Jeff Daniels was still there, standing beside his Harley motorcycle when I drove up. He was tall and thin. His grey hair framed his stern face like a bathing cap.

I jumped out of my car and apologized.

"I've already checked the perimeter," he said. "But I need to take a look inside."

I unlocked the front door as Freemont drove up. He hopped out of his van and eyed the Harley. He looked daunting in blue jeans, cowboy boots and a brown leather jacket the color of his skin. "Hi Carrie Sue, are you planting roses today?"

I laughed and hugged him. "I am."

I introduced Jeff to Freemont. "Jeff is an expert on security systems. Remember, Free, I told you I was thinking of having one installed? I think you were the one who suggested it." Freemont and Jeff shook hands.

"I might be interested in having something at my place, if you've got the time." Freemont pointed in the direction of his house. "I live only a mile away."

I walked ahead of them. "Y'all talk security. I've got rose bushes to put in the ground."

Jeff examined the interior of my house as Freemont asked questions. I tuned them out, ate a peanut butter sandwich and confirmed Kyle had taken the boxes he'd packed. The chest of drawers he'd used was empty. None of his clothes were in the closets. Thank the Lord.

I started humming the Chorus of Prisoners from Beethoven's opera Fidelio that Marcus and I had listened to the night before. The tune stayed in my head as I peeled off my business clothes and dressed casually in jeans and a blue turtleneck sweater.

I searched through my closet for something colorful to wear to the council meeting later and located my purple knit dress.

Next to the dress, I spotted my Thriller jacket, like the one Michael Jackson wore in his popular video. I slipped into the jacket and heard Freemont's voice booming from the hallway. He sounded enthusiastic about getting security at his house. He'd never been robbed, but I wondered if he felt threatened now that I'd drawn him into helping Tatum.

Chapter Twenty-Seven

The Christmas tree in Town Square brought back memories of when Mom, Dad and I came here to celebrate the lighting of the tree. I parked in front of the red-brick College Station City Hall building and reminisced until it was time to attend the Council meeting.

Before I went in, I checked my tote to make sure I had my tape recorder. I usually tape these meetings. My concentration lagged at night, especially when politicians rambled on and on.

I walked up the concrete steps with a dreadful feeling, as if I'd entered a field of negative energy. I wanted to turn away and leave, but I had a job to do. I forced a smile and greeted one of the policemen.

Mayor Bill Burnett waved at me when I entered the council chamber room.

I returned his wave. He and four Council members sat behind the horseshoe-shaped platform in the back of the room.

I picked up a copy of the agenda from the speaker's podium and read through it. Klan attorney Robert Landingham was scheduled to speak first.

I'd never met him, but as I glanced around the room, I thought I should be able to spot a KKK attorney. Trust your instincts, Dad used to say. "The more you trust them, the stronger they'll become."

My instincts told me Landingham might be the man in the blue suit with the medium-brown hair, sitting in a front pew, near the podium. I sat beside him and punched the "record" button on the tape machine.

"Hi, I'm Carrie Sue Justice with the Southern Journal."

He smiled warmly. "Robert Landingham, a pleasure to meet you."

I wondered how this affable man could represent a terrorist organization of murderers and rapists. Granny Justice wrote about the Klan in her Journal, and I'm ashamed to admit that plantation owners and former slaveholders like my ancestors tolerated its members.

"I see you're on the agenda tonight, Mr. Landingham. Can you give me a heads up on what you plan to discuss?"

"Absolutely. I'm the attorney representing the Ku Klux Klan. As you may or may not know, the City Manager turned down our petition to march. That's a clear violation of the first amendment. I'm here tonight to inform the Council that U.S. District Judge Bill Kelly has ruled in our favor."

"When you say the court has ruled in your favor, what does that ruling mean exactly, Mr. Landingham?"

"It means the City's ordinance cannot stop the Klan from marching as planned on Saturday, December nineteenth." Landingham handed me a copy of the Judge's ruling.

"What city ordinance are you referring to?"

"The ordinance that requires the Klan to pay in advance for additional law enforcement."

"Do you object to having extra security to prevent violence during the march?"

"We don't object to the additional security. We simply feel we shouldn't have to pay for it."

"How much did the city ask the Klan to pay?"

"Three-thousand dollars."

"Does the Klan have the money to pay it?"

"That's beside the point, but to answer your question, no, we don't have the funds to pay that amount."

"I've heard the lack of funds might have something to do with the lawsuit filed by the Southern Poverty Law Center." I remembered The SPLC sued the Klan after KKK members lynched a young black man. The lawsuit was filed on behalf of the victim's mother.

Landingham gave me a thin smile. "The Klan is not rich, if that's what you're asking."

"Would you say the lack of money means the Klan is dying?"

"No, I wouldn't say that."

"How many Klan members do you predict will march December nineteenth in College Station?"

"Grand Dragon Kern Stevens expects to attract one thousand members from all over the country, in light of the recent murder of Preston Campbell at the hands of a black gang."

My face burned with anger. I took a deep breath to keep my temper in check. "A jury hasn't convicted the teens charged with that crime, and there's no proof they were members of a black gang."

He hiked up an eyebrow but said nothing.

"Is the Klan planning to use the death of Preston Campbell to gain membership and boost funds, Mr. Landingham?"

He smirked, making his mustache crooked. "There's a Klan rally tomorrow on the steps of city hall. You're invited to come and take pictures."

No way in hell would I cover this rally and give the Klan free publicity to raise money. Surely Marcus would agree.

* * *

As I drove up to the Southern Journal building, I noticed Marcus' jeep was gone.

A wave of worry and disappointment swept over me. I thought he'd be here.

A cold, fierce wind hindered my route from the car to the front door. I unlocked the office and walked into darkness. The outside Christmas lights burned brightly, but the inside looked gloomy.

I flicked on the lights and trudged upstairs with my bags. When I reached the third floor, I found his note on the kitchen table. "Carrie, I had to run a few errands. Marcus." His note didn't say what time he'd left or when he'd return.

I walked to the bathroom, undressed, showered, brushed my teeth, and rubbed on the vanilla lotion I'd bought from Fredrick's. I put on the red, see-through bra and panties. It took my fingers a while to hook up the black stockings to the garter belt.

As soon as I tied the sash of the robe, "the wrapping for the gift inside," I heard echoing footfalls on the stairs. I took a deep breath and walked out in my stockinged feet to wait at the landing.

Marcus looked yummy in a blue pullover sweater, black leather jacket and jeans. "Hi," he whispered. His eyes gave me the once over. "Lovely." He carried two paper bags, one in each hand.

I reached up and touched his hair. It felt cold and damp as if he'd recently taken a shower. I stood on my tiptoes to kiss him. His lips were soft and surprisingly warm, despite the chill outside.

"Your Dad used to like the Green Nile restaurant, and I thought you might enjoy something from there. I also picked up a bottle of their Chardonnay." He tilted his head toward the kitchen.

I followed him in. "That was sweet of you, Marcus."

He flashed a sexy smile. "You're using that 'sweet' word I'm not used to hearing."

I laughed. "The very first time I ate Ethiopian food was at The Green Nile. Mom and Dad took me. I was about fourteen or fifteen."

He set the bags on the table, pulled out a chair and motioned for me to sit. "Let me serve you, Carrie." He grabbed plates from the cabinet then arranged the flatbread. "This bread is called injera, and the vegetables and meats are called tibs."

I nodded. "I told Mom and Dad I knew why the Ethiopians were starving. They couldn't eat the spicy food..."

Marcus popped the cork on the Chardonnay. He poured a glass for each of us. "I'm assuming your taste buds have changed since then." He placed two drinking glasses under the waterspout on the outside of the fridge, filled them, and handed one to me.

"I think so. My taste buds are older, if not wiser."

He sipped his wine. "How was the Council meeting?"

I told him about the interview with Landingham.

As I talked, he nodded and expertly rolled up a portion of the tibs inside the bread with his right hand. He offered it to me. I took a bite.

"Carrie, I despise the Klan, but they do have a right to march. We'll have to hold our noses when we cover it, but let's ignore the rally. We don't want to give a hate group free publicity."

"I agree."

His brow furrowed. "I almost forgot. I brought music." He stood, withdrew a cassette from the pocket of his leather jacket and walked to the boom box.

After he clicked in the cassette and pressed "play," Karen Carpenter's lovely voice began to sing, *Close to You*. She died the same year I lost my parents, but I decided not to mention that. I didn't want to ruin the evening with tragedy.

"I love this song." I drank my wine.

He refilled my wine glass. "I've been listening to this tape lately, trying to plunk out the songs on the piano."

"Dad told me you play beautifully."

"I practice at it. It's good therapy."

"I'd like to hear you sometime."

He nodded. "Okay." He stretched out his legs. "What happened with Jeff Daniels this afternoon?"

"He inspected my house. He's working up a security plan and preparing an estimate. If I agree, he said he can install it sometime this week. "Freemont wants to get a security system installed at his house, too. He came by while Jeff was there, and they talked."

His eyes pierced mine, triggering my desire. "What else did you do today?" I realized he hadn't said squat about what he'd been doing himself. Typical of him, but rather than mention this, I told him about planting the roses. He listened as if fascinated.

As Karen Carpenter sang *Top of the World*, I untied my robe. "Also, I went shopping." I stood and pulled back the robe to show off my lingerie. "I bought this. What do you think?" My face burned while waiting for his response.

He stood and moved toward me. His fingers raked through my hair. "Beautiful, very beautiful." He smothered my mouth in a hungry kiss while exploring my body with his hands. He found the hole in the crotch of my panties.

"Ah," he moaned.

My body shuddered from the feel of his fingers. He seemed to know exactly how and where to touch me. In seconds, I climaxed and collapsed against him.

He scooped me up in his arms, carried me to his bedroom, removed my robe and laid me on the bed. His eyes seemed to darken, as he removed his clothes and freed me of mine. His mouth kissed every inch of my body, sending shock waves.

When he finally eased himself inside, he asked, "Am I hurting you?"

"No, you feel amazing," I said, "I love you."

He didn't say he loved me back, unfortunately, but he made sure I climaxed again before he found his release. When he finally came, he moaned as if I'd wounded him.

Chapter Twenty-Eight

Marcus' eyes looked almost black, his hair ruffled and sexy. His dark stare pierced mine, as if he could read my mind, my soul. I wished I could read his.

He tucked a wayward strand of my hair behind my left ear. "How are you feeling, Carrie?"

I struggled to define my jumbled emotions. "Happy and satisfied. How are you feeling?"

His beautiful mouth smiled as if my words pleased him. "Terrific." His eyes narrowed. "Are you sure I didn't hurt you?"

"I feel wonderful."

"I'm relieved. I'd never want to hurt you. I was afraid I may have."

"Why would you think you'd hurt me?"

He exhaled a sigh. "You're tight and I'm big. I lost control and wasn't careful...And I was afraid I may have been too rough and torn you."

His use of the word torn sounded strange. "Have you ever torn anyone before?"

He frowned. "Yes, but I don't want to talk about that, Carrie."

I huffed. "You mean you don't want to tell me."

He closed his eyes. "That's right."

"Why?"

"Because it involves my late wife, and it's personal."

My stomach clinched. "I feel as if you're shutting me out, Marcus."

He stroked my arm. "I don't mean to." He squinted as if in pain. "Please, understand. I don't want to go there. So don't badger me. I'm not one of your interviews."

I poked him hard in the chest. "No, you're not one of my interviews, Marcus. You're my personal life."

He chewed on his bottom lip. "I respect your feelings, and I'd like for you to respect mine."

"I do respect your feelings, Marcus. I've respected your privacy for seven years, but when you said you were afraid you may have hurt me, I'd like to know what that means, exactly."

He groaned, and I didn't expect him to answer me. Maybe he was right. This was none of my business. If he refused to talk about it, so be it. He had a right to his privacy, and if he didn't want to share certain things with me, that was his choice. I looked into his eyes but didn't speak.

He closed his eyes, as if he wanted to hide. "When Susan and I first made love, we were young, eighteen and inexperienced.

She was petite, only five feet tall. I was the same size as now, six-five. When we attempted intercourse, I tore her. It turned out to be severe."

"Oh, no, Marcus, that's terrible. I'm sorry, but I'm sure you didn't mean to."

His eyes remained closed. "I took her to the emergency room. A surgeon was able to repair the damage, but Susan was hurting, embarrassed and afraid. I was afraid, too. After she healed, I learned to please her and we enjoyed a good sex life, but I had to be very gentle, and we used a lubricant to make it easier on her." He exhaled a sigh. "From now on, Carrie, I'd rather not talk about the past. I don't want to open old wounds."

I snuggled up to him. "Forgive me for being so nosy."

"I suppose it's an occupational hazard."

"I'm glad you feel comfortable enough to share personal things with me."

He kissed my hair. "I've shared more with you than I have with anyone."

I wanted to climb inside and feel the full measure of his warm body. "I love you, Marcus, but I realize you may not be ready to love me or anyone yet."

His eyes looked sad. "I've tried to express how I feel, Carrie. If this isn't love, I don't know what is."

Chapter Twenty-Nine

I snapped awake when I heard screaming. Marcus looked like a shadow in the darkness as he whipped his body from side to side. "No, no, no." he yelled.

I shook him. "Marcus, Marcus, wake up. You're having a nightmare."

He stared, wide-eyed at me, as if I'd threatened to kill him. "Jesus," he groaned and sat up on his side of the bed, his back to me. "Sorry I woke you up, Carrie. Go back to sleep." He buried his head in his hands.

I got on my knees behind him and began to massage his shoulders. He moved away, as if rejecting my touch, and walked naked out of the bedroom.

I called after him. "Marcus, where're you going?"

"I need a moment alone. Go back to sleep," he ordered.

My stomach tightened from his rebuff. Was he blaming me for his nightmare? Yes, probably. I'd opened old wounds from his past.

I waited in the darkness, listening. My heart raced. I heard the hallway creaking. It sounded like he was pacing back and forth.

The toilet flushed.

I heard clanging in the kitchen. Was he cleaning up the mess we'd left last night or banging pots and pans to relieve his frustration?

After what seemed like an eternity, he walked back into the bedroom and slipped under the covers. I turned to face him. "Are you okay?" I gently touched his chest.

"Better now. Sorry I woke you, Carrie." When his lips touched mine, I smelled his whiskey breath. "Try to sleep, now and please don't ask me any questions. Okay?"

I slid my arms around him. "Is there anything I can do?"

"Your being here is enough."

When I felt his penis stiffening against my leg, I slid down under the covers and talked to it. "Obviously, you don't want to sleep."

Chapter Thirty

December 12

When I awoke, Marcus was staring at me. A pink sunrise seeped through the blinds behind him, framing his head like a halo.

I rubbed the sleep out of my eyes. "Good morning,"

He played with a strand of my hair. "Did you sleep okay in spite of me?"

"I slept great, but I'm sorry about your nightmare."

"I'm the one who should be sorry, Carrie."

Until recently, since we'd become intimate, I'd never known Marcus to apologize, but now he seemed to be apologizing for things beyond his control. I thought this might be due to the tremendous guilt he'd been carrying from the tragic death of his wife. "Do you have nightmares often?"

He frowned and I knew he didn't want to answer. "Less and less, but I don't want to talk about them."

I ran my hand over his swirl of dark chest hair. "What time is it?"

"About six thirty." His eyes looked the color of the cobalt vase on my dining room table. He smiled. "I enjoyed watching you sleep, but don't tell me that's sweet."

I giggled. "But it is sweet."

He gave me a crooked smile. Without the beard I could admire the full beauty of his lips. They reminded me of Elvis Presley's, and I remembered when Elvis came to the Atlanta Omni in 1973, Mom took me to see him. I was about twelve at the time. The moment I saw Elvis perform I knew I'd reached pubescence.

No fantasy or sexual experience could compare to the lovemaking with Marcus, but at this moment, I couldn't quite believe the man stroking my arm and sending tingles was the same grouch who'd mentored me for seven years.

His fingers were magical feathers on my skin. "I wish we had more time alone, Carrie. There's so much going on right now. But after everything settles down, and after your divorce is final, I'd like to take you on a trip, a vacation. I'll need to hire an additional reporter, of course, and ask Thomas to join the newspaper full time." Thomas was Lisa's husband, a retired journalism professor in his sixties and at least twenty years older than Lisa, though he looked fit and fiftyish.

"Retirement doesn't seem to suit Thomas, does it?"

"No, he's restless. He's mentioned several times he'd like to work more."

My heart raced at the thought of taking a trip with Marcus, just the two of us. The last time I took a vacation, Kyle and I went on a three-day honeymoon cruise to the Bahamas. Kyle drank too much and got seasick. "I wish we could get away together, Marcus. But I have a confession to make."

He frowned. "A confession?"

"I'm afraid to fly."

He kissed my shoulder. "After what happened to your folks, I completely understand." He licked his lips. "We could drive out west if you'd like. Stop along the way. See the sights. We'll need at least two, three weeks for that though."

"Sounds lovely. Maybe we could visit your family in California. Don't they live in Irvine?"

"My mother, sister and her twin boys are there, yes. My father died not long after I returned from Vietnam."

I stroked his chest. "I'm sorry. How did he die?"

"Heart attack."

"How old was he?"

His face contorted, as if my question wounded him. "Fifty-six."

"That's young." I thought of my parents. They were younger when I lost them. Mom was forty-six and Dad was fifty, but I didn't want to belittle Marcus's loss by mentioning their ages.

"I wish he'd taken better care of himself. He'd been complaining about a backache. He looked tired. We were pasting up and proofing copy when it happened. I don't think I've mentioned this before, but Dad owned a string of newspapers. I learned the business from him. In many ways he was like your dad." His voice cracked with emotion. "One minute Dad was talking to me. The next minute he was on the floor." He sighed. "We couldn't revive him. He was pronounced dead on the way to the hospital. Ninety percent of his coronary arteries were blocked. That's what the autopsy said. Mom is a nurse. So is my sister. They were constantly nagging him about his diet and the importance of regular checkups. I tried to get him to go to the gym with me, but he never found the time."

"When did you last see your family?"

He stared up at the ceiling. "Last December, around this time."

"I remember now. Thomas covered for you. I missed you, even though Thomas was not nearly as grumpy and demanding as you are."

He hiked an eyebrow. "Is that so?"

I laughed. "Are you planning to see your folks this Christmas?"

He closed his eyes and shook his head. "No."

"Why not?"

"Oh, God, Carrie, you have no mercy. You won't be satisfied till I bare my soul, and I'm not sure I can do that. But to briefly answer your question, I can't get away. I have responsibilities here. Also, last year Mom accused me of being a sad sack. She wanted me to be more carefree and feel the Christmas spirit. I couldn't seem to accomplish that to her satisfaction. And I felt a little guilty for putting a damper on the holidays. She's not responsible for my happiness, I told her, but she exhausted herself trying to make me and everyone else cheerful. When I talk to her over the phone, which I try to do at least once a week, I can usually convince her I'm okay and things are going well, but in person I can't fool her."

I snuggled up to him. "I must have the same desire as your mother."

He pulled away and gave me a confused stare. "Oh, is that so?"

I jumped on top of him, pushed his muscular arms over his head and against the bed. "I want to make you cheerful. What about now? Are you feeling happier?"

He smiled. "I'm feeling pretty darn good. Why wouldn't I? I have this beautiful woman on top of me."

I loved the feeling of being in control of this powerful man and bringing him pleasure. I could have made love to him all day, but the phone rang in the kitchen and rudely interrupted us.

I rose from my comfy position, lying on top of him. "Who could be calling this early?"

He frowned. "Aw, Christ. Let's ignore it."

When the racket stopped, I relaxed on top of him. He stroked and kissed my hair until the phone started ringing again.

I sighed. "Do you think it's an emergency, Marcus?"

He groaned. "I'd better get it." He rose from the bed.

Unwilling to leave my nest, I stayed in bed and strained to listen to Marcus as he talked on the phone, but I couldn't hear what he said to the caller.

When he walked back inside the room, I propped myself up on my elbows to get an eyeful of his naked body. "Who was it?"

He sat next to me. "Karl Silkman. He called to let us know about the bond and Grand Jury hearings. They're both scheduled for this morning at nine."

"God, Marcus, they're really rushing this along, aren't they?"

He frowned and nodded. "I'd like to think the Grand Jury won't return a 'true bill,' which would mean an indictment, but nowadays Grand Juries agree with the prosecutor. Not what our Founding Fathers intended when they wrote the Grand Jury Clause as part of the Fifth Amendment."

Marcus, my mentor, was speaking, and I knew not to interrupt unless I needed clarification.

He smiled and pulled me up. "As you probably know, the Grand Jury process has changed drastically since it was first established. In the beginning it was supposed to protect the accused." He paused to give me a chance to react. I nodded my understanding, and he continued.

"Before the Grand July Clause became a part of the Fifth Amendment, though, there was an important case that paved the way for it."

"Which case was that?"

"John Peter Zenger in 1734."

I smiled my admiration at his encyclopedic information. "Why was that case so important?"

"Zenger was a newspaper publisher. He published articles criticizing the Royal Government of New York. The Government tried to prosecute him for libel, but three times Grand Juries refused to indict. They ruled that he should be free to speak. As a result of the ruling, the colonists realized they had the power to protect themselves from oppression."

He ran his hand up and down my back, and I realized I didn't feel at all self-conscious listening to my mentor while we were both nude.

"We can discuss this case later, Carrie, when we have more time. But I think it's an important one. The outcome supported Freedom of the Press in Colonial America. It was also a precursor of the Fifth Amendment, which includes the Grand Jury Clause. As you may know, the Fifth Amendment mentions Due Process of Law that was later included in the Fourteenth

Amendment, ratified in 1868. The Fourteenth Amendment says no person can be deprived of life, liberty, or property without due process of law. This law supported the early civil rights act of 1866. Equal protection under the law to all citizens was meant to protect former slaves after the Civil War."

He paused, his eyes searching mine for a sign I understood.

I nodded, and he continued.

"As to the Grand Jury Clause in the Fifth Amendment, it's one of the only parts of the Bill of Rights the states are not required to enforce. That means states don't have to hold Grand Jury hearings, but when a state requires a Grand Jury hearing, prosecutors can make up their own rules. They can allow hearsay, which is not allowed in a jury trial, and they can leave out important evidence."

After I digested what Marcus was saying, I said, "If I didn't know better, I'd think you were a law professor in another life."

He smiled. "In this life, I can't get the newspaper business out of my blood." He kissed my forehead. "Before I forget, Silkman said he'll leave a file with your name on it on a table in the clerk's office. It's basically a copy of what you gave him, I think. We'll check it out to be sure before we publish it in the next issue. And we'll need to decide how to reference everything. We can say that the statements came from the clerk. That will relieve you of having to protect your source and should free Dora Lee of suspicion." He gave me a quick hug. "Now hit the shower. I'll make coffee."

I winked. "You want to join me in the shower?"

He sighed. "Then I wouldn't be able to let you go."

Chapter Thirty-One

Tatum Brookins, Jeremy Andrews, Calvin Newson, and Leroy Cortez appeared at the bond hearing looking like frightened, lost children. I took out my camera and snapped their pictures as they stood side-by-side, wearing grey sweatshirts, jeans, and black tennis shoes without laces.

Fulton County Juvenile Court Referee Sam Bailey, a short bespectacled man in a dark blue suit said, "Bond denied. These youths have records ranging from truancy to burglary and aggravated sodomy. The well-being of the community is at stake if they are released."

Tatum had been under supervision for truancy, Bailey said. It burned me to hear that truancy was his only offense. I didn't know anyone who hadn't skipped school a time or two.

Leroy had the most extensive record, Bailey said, "From the age of ten, he has been charged with burglary, criminal trespass, theft by taking, aggravated sodomy, child molestation and shoplifting."

Jeremy had a simple battery charge, shoplifting and criminal trespass on his record, according to Bailey. Calvin had a robbery by snatch, a pending trespass charge and burglary charge.

Karl Silkman requested bail for Tatum. "Truancy is not a sufficient reason to deny bail. My client is not a danger to society."

"Bail is denied, Mr. Silkman," Bailey said.

Jeremy's lawyer Lovett Boucher stood and requested bail for his client.

Bailey denied him bail and appointed public defenders for Leroy and Calvin.

I snapped a few more pictures then rushed to the clerk's office. I asked the lady behind the counter if someone had left a file for me.

She pointed toward an alcove and the round table inside it. "Not with me. Look over there." Resting on the table I found a folder with my name on it.

I thanked her and examined the contents. They appeared to be a duplicate of what I'd given to Karl.

After leaving the clerk's office, I returned to the waiting area near the Grand Jury Room. Karl was sitting outside, his brow furrowed.

I told him I found the file and thanked him for leaving it. "Know anything yet?"

He said Assistant D.A. Vernon Abbott was presenting the prosecution's case against Tatum, Calvin, Leroy, and Jeremy to the Grand Jury.

I couldn't believe I was the only press represented. The other media outlets would have to call up the prosecutor's office for the outcome. Sloppy reporting, Marcus would say.

District Attorney Wallace Sheppard, a tall, stout man with salt and pepper hair, walked briskly by.

I caught up to him. "Hi, Mr. Sheppard, I'm Carrie Sue Justice with the Southern Journal."

"Yes, Ms. Justice, I know. How can I help you?"

"Would you comment on the Grand Jury hearing of the teens accused of killing Preston Campbell."

"We expect an indictment, and they'll stand trial as adults."

I frowned. "Why try them as adults when they aren't adults?"

His lips formed a thin line. "They've already fallen through the cracks of the juvenile court system, and they're criminally inclined. They haven't been taught discipline and therefore must face the consequences of their actions. Their families didn't teach them. The school system didn't teach them."

I huffed and wanted to ask him if he'd read the transcripts, but I couldn't open that can of worms, not yet. "Tatum Brookins has truancy on his record, but nothing criminal. Yet he was denied bail. Why?"

"I'm not at liberty to discuss individual suspects at this time."

"Mr. Sheppard, I'm told the teenage suspects are being held at the Juvenile Detention Center, but now that bail has been denied, will they still be retained there?"

He nodded. "Yes, until a jury convicts them."

I snapped a photo of Sheppard and walked toward Karl who sat in a straight-back, uncomfortable looking chair outside the Grand Jury Room. "Karl, I noticed the four suspects wore similar clothes. Who provided those clothes?"

"Someone in Juvenile probably bought four outfits of the same kind, but I'm not sure. It could have been the easiest thing to do, but I believe it must have been intentional, to make them look like a gang. They weren't wearing similar clothing when they were arrested."

I told Karl I needed to make a phone call. He directed me to a payphone in a hallway alcove. I plunked in a quarter and punched in the office number.

Lisa answered.

"Hi Lisa, it's Carrie Sue. How's it going there? Anything I should know?"

"You had a call from Jeff Daniels." She recited his number. "And another from Kevin Jones with the Atlanta Police Department. He said you can go with the undercover officers Saturday night. I assume you know what he's talking about."

"Yes, thanks." I couldn't tell Lisa I'd planned to do a story about prostitution and drugs. I needed to tell Marcus first. "Is Marcus in? I need to talk to him."

"I expect him back any minute. He's been trying to escape Neeley Nelson all morning."

My stomach knotted, as my green-eyed monster appeared. Neeley was an attractive and shapely redhead, the local Chamber of Commerce director, with an obvious crush on him. He seemed unaware of her obsession. She wrote a monthly column called Chamber Contact. Marcus was on the Chamber board as Dad had been.

When the Chamber first hired Neeley, Lindsey wrote a feature article about her. In the article, Neeley said she'd posed nude for Penthouse until she had a "come to Jesus moment," and decided to return to college and earn a degree in business.

Plus, she was somewhat of a Betty Crocker. She was always baking cakes and cookies to give to Marcus, even though he'd rather eat an apple than a cookie. Whenever Neeley delivered her goodies, he'd place them on the table in the break room for all of us to share. Once she brought in a Lane Cake spiked with enough whiskey to give us all a buzz.

"What's he doing with Neeley?"

"Oh, honey, don't get me started. She and Marcus had a nine o'clock appointment here to talk about the banquet Saturday night. He's the keynote speaker, as you know. He's planning to talk about the need for insurance reform, not tort reform, and I don't think that's sitting well with some of the chamber members."

I stretched the metal phone cord to peer down the hallway. No action outside the Grand Jury Room. "I knew the Chamber was pushing for tort reform in the General Assembly, but I'd forgotten Marcus was speaking at the banquet. What happened at the meeting with Neeley? Did they have a disagreement?"

Lisa sighed into the phone. "Not exactly, but let me just say, Neeley came in here with her own agenda. She was wearing pink tights and a low-cut sweater and pink running shoes. Her breasts can't be real. They're huge. Her tights were so snug, you could see her camel-toe. Neeley claimed she was dressed like that to work out later. Which is her business...I don't care what she wears, but I don't like it when she orders me to take her calls while she's in a meeting with Marcus. Why would anyone call her here in the first place?"

"That's weird, Lisa. Has that ever happened before?"

"No, thank God, and fortunately their meeting didn't last long, but get this, when she came out, she proceeded to use your desk and phone to return calls."

My face burned with anger. Not only was she chasing after my man, but she'd also taken over my personal space. "Did Marcus agree to that?"

"He was in his office with his door closed, working. I don't think he had any idea what she was up to until he walked out and saw her there. I heard him say, 'I thought you'd left, Neeley.' She told him she had urgent calls to return. He assumed she'd be leaving soon, I think. Marcus walked upstairs. While he was up there, she told me she'd always wanted to take a tour of the building and see the upstairs part. I told her that was private and not open to the public."

"That was a good answer, Lisa." Lisa preferred to be the only one to organize and access the archives on the second and third floors. She thought of that as her territory. If someone asked to look at back issues of the newspaper, she'd lug down the giant folder needed.

After normal business hours, Marcus didn't want anyone up there, not even Lisa, without his approval.

"What did Neeley say to that?"

"She wanted to know what Marcus was doing up there. I told her it wasn't any of my business to know what he was doing. I figured he was changing into his running clothes, and I was right. This time of year, he usually runs in the middle of the day, unless he's too busy or has an appointment. I was hoping Neeley would leave before he came down, though my instincts told me she knew his schedule. I swear I think that woman stalks him, and sure enough she insisted on jogging with him today."

I gulped. "And he agreed to that?"

"No, but before he could get out the door, Neeley said she needed to talk to him. She said some of her members were in a tizzy about his stance on insurance reform, and she said they were concerned about what he was going to say in his speech. He said he'd talk to her later about it, but he wouldn't change his speech no matter what, and if she objected, he'd step aside, and she could get someone else to speak."

Neeley wouldn't be able to find anyone to replace Marcus, a dynamic and charismatic speaker, or at least not at this late date, I thought. "Wow, Lisa. What did Neeley say?"

"She still wanted Marcus to speak, she said, but she needed to tell him what some of her members were saying, and she insisted on jogging along with Marcus and filling him in on everything they'd said."

"What did Marcus say?"

Lisa sighed into the phone. "Marcus said he'd rather talk to her later. You would have thought she'd back away and leave, but not Neeley. She wants what she wants and doesn't care what anyone else wants."

"Are you saying she went running with Marcus?"

"That was her plan all along, and the reason she wore that workout getup. But not long after they left, Marcus called me from the City Café."

My heart leaped into my throat. "Why did he call you from there?"

"Neeley suffered a migraine while she was running," he said, and didn't have her medicine, because she'd left her purse here. But get this. Marcus asked me if I'd drive her car to the City Café and bring her purse. He said she'd drive me back in her car. But when I got there, she took her pills and said she'd rather go back with Marcus, because she had a few more things to discuss."

I took a deep breath. "Why wasn't he more assertive with her? Marcus is usually outspoken."

"I think he underestimated her determination to be with him."

"And they haven't gotten back yet?"

"I see them now, Carrie Sue. They're walking up the steps. Please don't breathe a word of what I told you." She gasped. "Oh Lord, you won't believe what she just did."

"What?"

"She jumped up and kissed him."

I slammed my hand against the wall. "How did he react?"

"He's wiping off her lipstick."

My heart sank, but I couldn't show my jealousy. Lisa didn't know I'd been intimate with Marcus.

Lisa cleared her throat. "Carrie Sue's on the phone, Marcus."

"Carrie?" Marcus whispered, as if out of breath.

My heart pounded. I started to tell him to go to hell, but then remembered Lisa asked me not to breathe a word of what she'd told me. "I need to go, Marcus. I'll call you later."

I slammed the phone back in its cradle and stared at the wall. My frustration and unexpressed feelings had lodged in my lungs, threatening to choke me.

I inhaled deep breaths and wondered if my jealousy might be misplaced due to Kyle's cheating. Maybe, but my heart hurt, and I was beginning to think no man on earth could be trusted.

I picked up the phone again, plunked in another quarter and called Jeff Daniels. Jeff answered on the second ring. I listened as he described in exhaustive detail the security system he planned to install in my house. I interrupted to ask him how much this would cost. He gave me a breakdown. It sounded reasonable, even though my distraught mind couldn't grasp the details. "Okay, Jeff, you're the expert. I want to make sure my home is safe. When can you get started?"

"Whenever it's convenient."

"I'll call you when I get to my office, and maybe we can arrange a time this afternoon, okay?"

"Great."

After I hung the phone up, I walked back down the hallway to the Grand Jury Room. I nodded to Karl and sat next to him in one of the uncomfortable chairs.

In the silence that followed, I opened my computer and tried to write, but thoughts of Marcus and Neeley invaded my mind. I wanted to tell Neeley to keep her hands and lips off my man, but considering I was going through a divorce, I couldn't.

The doors to the Grand Jury Room swung open and slammed me back to the moment. I stood and watched Assistant D.A. Vernon Abbott walk out. He looked almost as tall as Marcus, but with shorter brown hair and horn-rimmed glasses, magnifying his hazel eyes.

"What did the Grand Jury decide?" I asked him.

"Jeremy Andrews, Tatum Brookins, Leroy Cortez and Calvin Newson have been indicted for the burglary and murder of Preston Campbell."

His words hit me like a stomach punch, and from the look on Karl's face, he felt a similar shock. I knew the Grand Jury's judgment had nothing to do with facts, but my sense of doom seemed almost unbearable.

"Did you talk with Freemont Jackson?" I asked Karl.

He nodded. "Yes. We have his statement."

"Is there a chance the charges against Tatum will be dropped?"

"We'll ask for dismissal of all charges against him during pretrial, though it's doubtful the Superior Court Judge will rule in our favor since the Grand Jury has stated there's cause for a jury trial."

I shook Karl's hand. "Keep us informed, okay?"

"Sure."

Walking back to my car, I felt deflated and fatigued. All my efforts to help Tatum have failed, I thought.

I wanted to believe he had a chance in our judicial system, but unfortunately justice hadn't worked for him so far, and I had a terrible foreboding that something tragic was about to happen.

My hands wouldn't stop shaking. I thought I might be suffering from low blood sugar and grabbed a candy bar out of my tote.

Once inside the Cadillac, I gobbled down the candy bar and started making another "to do" list to keep my mind from focusing on negative stuff. "1. Take another photo of homeless man Damon Cardoza. He needs to glance at the book he's reading, not at the camera."

I stopped writing to glance at my watch. I didn't have much time if I wanted to catch Damon at the College Station Library. On his walks, he usually kept the same schedule Monday through Friday.

Librarian Louise Samson informed me of Damon two weeks ago. She'd called the newspaper to say the Southside libraries would close temporarily, due to computerization. As an afterthought, she mentioned Damon. Louise said she thought the closings might upset him.

I'd told Marcus this story would make a great sidebar next to the article about the closings. He agreed.

The first time I tried to interview Damon he scurried away like a scared cat, but eventually I won his trust and learned the details of his life. His parents had owned a ranch in Wyoming until his dad died. His mom sold the ranch, though Damon begged her not to, and for that reason they had a falling out, he said.

He found another ranch to work on, and hoped to buy his own spread one day, but his plans changed when he fell from a horse, broke his leg and hurt his back. His injuries prevented him from riding and roping. Searching for less strenuous work, he saw in a newspaper ad that contractors in Atlanta were looking for carpenters. Damon had learned woodworking on the ranch, and he thought he could do the carpentry jobs without a problem, he said.

Five years ago, he caught a bus to Atlanta from Laramie and worked on some of the most luxurious townhouses in the city. Unfortunately, the carpentry jobs ran out, and he couldn't find work anywhere. Eventually, he became homeless and homesick. In the libraries he could read books about the west and feel closer to his beloved Wyoming.

"He never sleeps while he's here," Louise said. "He's always reading, but I worry about where he sleeps at night when it's cold out."

"The libraries are quiet, and I like quiet," Damon said. "I don't like the city noise and in here, I get a chance to read about cowboys and such. Then I don't miss my home as much. I look for work every day. If I can't find any, I start walking to the libraries."

"Contractors won't hire Damon now because he's homeless," Louise said.

As I thought about Damon, a wave of urgency filled me. I wanted to get his story written and published pronto. He needed a permanent place to work and live and save money so he could fulfill his dream of going back home and owning a ranch.

"I've recovered from my injuries," he said the day I interviewed him. "All this walking has helped. I'm in better shape than ever."

I couldn't imagine walking fifteen miles each day and being homeless in this weather. The cold wind showed no mercy. It pushed against my car and blew snowflakes on the windshield as I broke all speed limits driving to the library.

With no time to spare, I parked haphazardly, grabbed my camera, and rushed inside.

The library's warmth embraced me as I walked in. I waved to Louise. She smiled and pointed to the back, where I found Damon at his usual table, surrounded on three sides by bookshelves.

He seemed engrossed in a hardback entitled The American West. His long brown hair fell below his shoulder. His beard had gotten longer since the last time I saw him. He wore a grey flannel shirt and jeans that Louise and the other librarians had gifted him.

"Are you worried about having to rearrange your schedule due to the library closings?" I asked Damon.

"No," he whispered. "I saw the schedule. They won't close all the libraries at once. One library will always be open during the day."

I focused my camera. "Damon, I'd like to take a photo of you while you're reading your book, if you don't mind."

Following my instruction, he stared at the photograph of a cowboy riding a bucking horse.

I snapped his picture. "Thanks, Damon. Good luck."

"Good luck to you," he whispered.

From the library I drove to the Southern Journal. I cringed when I didn't see Marcus' Jeep. Was he with Neeley again? I couldn't help but wonder as I grabbed my tote and trudged up the stairs.

Lisa met me at the door. "If you're hungry, why don't you join me? I just warmed up some chicken cacciatore. There's plenty."

I thanked Lisa and followed her to the break room.

She dished out a large portion of the chicken dish onto a paper plate and handed me a plastic fork. I poured two glasses of water from the spout outside the fridge and handed her one.

Lisa sat across from me at the table with her own plate of cacciatore. "Marcus went to his house to work. He's called a couple of times asking for you."

I nodded and ate a bite of the chicken. "Mm, this is tasty, Lisa."

She covered her mouth with her hand as she chewed and swallowed. "I made a big casserole dish of it. Thomas doesn't like meat. He prefers vegetables." She squinted at me. "Are you okay, Carrie Sue?"

"I'm a little tired."

Her red lipstick still looked fresh, even though she was eating. "Marcus looked tired, too."

I thought she might be fishing for information and didn't know how to respond. What if she'd snooped in the bedrooms upstairs? If she'd snooped, she'd have seen my suitcase, clothes, and lingerie.

"I tell you, Carrie Sue, that Neeley is crazy about Marcus. When they got back, he went upstairs to shower and change, and she pried me with questions."

"What kind of questions?"

"She asked if I'd ever heard of him dating anyone. I said, 'no,' but Marcus keeps his private life private. Then she started talking crazy."

"What do you mean by crazy?"

"She thinks she and Marcus were destined to meet and be together. Crazy stuff like that." Lisa pointed to the side of her head and made a circle with her index finger. "That woman is nuts."

I took a sip of water, hoping to relax the lump in my throat and the queasiness in my stomach. "Thank you for the delicious food, Lisa. You're a wonderful cook, but I had a candy bar earlier, and I'm not as hungry as I thought. Please don't be offended."

She smiled, as if she understood. "Not at all."

Back at my desk, I called Jeff Daniels and told him to meet me at my house. After I hung up, Lisa walked toward me. "Marcus is on the phone."

I punched in the flashing button and answered with a cool, "Yes?"

"Hi, Carrie, what did the grand jury decide?"

"All four boys were indicted for murder and robbery. They were all denied bail, even though Tatum has only truancy on his record. I can't go into the details now. I'm meeting Jeff at my house soon. He's installing the security system."

Marcus sighed. "Did you pick up what Silkman left at the clerk's office?"

"Yes, and they appear to be a replica of what Dora Lee gave me."

"We'll publish them in the next issue."
He paused for a moment. "Are you okay?"

I bit my tongue. "I'm just in a rush. I'll talk to you later, Marcus."

Chapter Thirty-Two

Jeff walked in and informed me he'd finished setting up my security system. I stopped writing to give him my full attention. He explained how the system worked, and we did a run through.

Afterwards I gave him a check for his services, and he left. The grandfather clock chimed five times.

I stretched to relieve the tightness in my body. I'd been sitting for too long and I needed to stretch or do some form of exercise.

I walked out onto the veranda and plopped in one of the rockers. The moon looked like half of a honey-dew melon, beautiful, but damn cold. I thought about poor Damon and wondered where he'd sleep tonight as I shivered and stared up at the stars blanketing the sky.

I started to count my blessings, but my blue funk stopped me. I decided I needed to go for a run and work my way out of my depression. In high school I ran cross-country and won first place in our district. Mom had framed the blue ribbon and hung it in my room, but Kyle took it down and I had no idea where he'd put it.

I slipped into my Thriller jacket, laced up my running shoes and jogged down the circular drive to pitch black Freedom Road. I should have carried a flashlight to help identify the eerie sounds coming from the dense trees and bushes.

Mom once hit a bear on this road. It was a foggy early morning, and she'd thought she'd hit a cow until the bear stood up.

My lungs burned by the time I reached Freemont's house. His van was gone, or I would have stopped. Not knowing when he'd get back from making his deliveries, I turned around and started jogging back to my house.

When I was halfway home headlights blinded me. I couldn't see the vehicle, but the headlight indicated the vehicle traveled on the wrong side of the road, veering over to my side. Speeding.

I jumped from the road to the grass verge to avoid getting hit. My right foot landed in a hole, and I lost my balance. I tumbled down the steep embankment and collided with the concrete drainage ditch.

The fall had knocked the breath out of me. I was lying flat on my back, trying to determine if I'd broken anything. I had a sick feeling, and maybe I was being paranoid, but I suspected someone had tried to run me over. Fear froze my spine as I lay there, feeling numb and paralyzed, listening to the night sounds. I heard what sounded like a growl. *God, help me.*

My knees and hands stung like fire. I struggled to push myself up and shake the pine straw off. My ankles and legs felt stiff and sore, as I hobbled back to my house, aching with each step.

When I finally made it in, I swallowed two aspirins and inspected my injuries. My knees and hands bled. I washed them and staunched the bleeding with antibiotic ointment.

The message light on the kitchen phone blinked. I hit Play.

"Hi Carrie, it's Marcus. I'd like to take you to dinner tonight. I'll pick you up around six-thirty if that's okay. If not, call me at home. Otherwise, I'll see you soon."

I started dialing his number, but stopped when I noticed the time. It was already six-fifteen. He would have left by now. He should have given me more notice and waited for my reply.

I sighed, wrote him a note, telling him to come in, "door's open."

I didn't want to leave the door unlocked, but what choice did I have? The running water would make it impossible for me to hear the doorbell.

I limped to the bathroom, sponged off, dressed in jeans and a beaded black sweater. I was fluffing my hair when the doorbell rang. I expected him to come in, as my note had instructed, but when the doorbell rang a second and third time I began to wonder. What if it wasn't Marcus?

I walked to the bedroom, pressed my ear against the door until I heard footsteps in the hallway. The kitchen was on the other side of the house, or I would have grabbed a knife.

When I finally peeked out, I saw Marcus standing there, looking handsome in a camel-hair sports coat, white shirt, and jeans.

When I came out of the bedroom, he waved my note in his hand. "I'm surprised you left your door open, Carrie. You want to be safe, don't you? Isn't that why you had Jeff install the security system?"

I groaned at his chastising. "You didn't give me much notice, Marcus. I didn't get back until a few minutes ago."

He smiled. "I'm sorry, but I'd rather you stay safe. I would have waited." He lifted his right arm, carrying the black overcoat. "I came prepared."

He kissed my lips softly. "What's wrong, Carrie?"

I bit my lip to keep from telling him about my accident. He'd probably worry excessively, I thought.

"I tripped and fell while I was jogging. It was dark, and I didn't bring a flashlight."

He frowned. "Do you feel like going to dinner?"

I nodded. "Yes, where are we eating?"

"I thought we'd try the new French restaurant. It's not far from here. Do you like French food?"

My body ached all over, but I forced a smile. "I do."

After I locked up the house as Jeff had instructed, Marcus led me out, opened the passenger's door and helped me in. "Are you sure you're okay?"

I nodded and he cranked up the jeep. Orchestral music flowed from the stereo. I rested my head against the seat and listened.

"This is a medley of Tchaikovsky; Romeo & Juliet and Fantasy Overture," Marcus said. "The next one is George Gershwin's Rhapsody in Blue, followed by a Rachmaninoff's Rhapsody, and then Schubert's Serenade and Debussy's Clair De Lune."

"What a lovely selection." I took deep breaths and willed the music to relax me. Soon I drifted off to sleep.

I snapped awake when Marcus pulled over on a grassy knoll and parked. We were out in the middle of nowhere. No restaurant in sight.

He leaned across the bucket seats, took my face in his hands and kissed me. A moment later, he pulled away and glanced out his rearview window.

"What's wrong, Marcus?"

"I think I made a mistake."

"What do you mean by mistake?" I braced myself, expecting him to tell me he regretted our relationship. I wondered if he might be feeling guilty about what he and Neeley did today. What exactly did they do? The question haunted me as I waited for his response.

"I shouldn't have allowed myself to be so impulsive. See that Yellow Cab behind us?"

I turned to look. The cab's headlights were about two car lengths away.

"On the drive over to your house, I saw a cab like that tailing me, and it's now parked behind us."

I grimaced, recalling the car that almost ran me over. I didn't think it was a yellow cab, but I wasn't sure. The headlights had blinded me. "Maybe it's a coincidence, Marcus. It can't be Kyle. He should be at the theatre by now."

He shrugged and cranked his jeep. "I hope I haven't created more problems for you, Carrie."

I reached over and touched his face. "Don't worry, Marcus. It's dark out. How could anyone see us? And even if someone saw us, a kiss can be interpreted any number of ways." I thought about how Kyle forced himself on me and what Lisa said about Neeley kissing Marcus. Had she forced herself on him? Or had he enjoyed it? I decided this might be the perfect opportunity to ask. "Someone can kiss a person on the sly without that person wanting to be kissed."

He steered his Jeep onto the road. The cab waited a moment then pulled out behind us. "Didn't you want me to kiss you? Although I admit now, it may have been careless of me."

"I love kissing you. That's obvious, isn't it? I was thinking of another scenario."

He frowned as if confused. "What scenario?"

I chewed the inside of my cheek, trying to hide my feelings. I didn't want to release a flood of emotion. I wanted to appear calm. "When I called the office today and asked to speak to you, Lisa said you and Neeley were walking up the stairs. Then Lisa said something like, oh no, like she was shocked, and when I asked her why, she said Neeley had kissed you."

His brows hovered low over his dark eyes. "You must have gotten an earful." He shook his head. "Carrie, I'm not interested in Neeley. Is that what you're asking?" He turned to glance at me.

"I guess you think I'm stupid for feeling jealous."

"No, I don't think that. Your feelings are what they are."

I studied this incredibly handsome man. He could have any woman he wanted, why me? "Neeley is single, and you're single. And when we first got together, I was the aggressive one, and now Neeley is being aggressive, and you're no longer a member of 'the walking dead' as you have referred to yourself." I paused. "Or at least parts of you are more alive."

His mouth curved into an amused smile, but he remained silent. Typical of Marcus, he'd rather I talk. Then he doesn't have to explain himself.

He waited, as if he wanted me to elaborate, but when I grew silent, he said, "Carrie, I don't know what else to say. I've told you I'm not interested in her. If I were, I would have asked her out or accepted her invitations."

"What kind of invitations?"

He sighed. "I'll be happy to talk to you about this if you need me to, but as I said, I'm not interested in her. I don't enjoy being with her."

I watched him, trying to detect any signs of insincerity. "Do you enjoy being with me?"

He turned my way and squinted. "I wouldn't be here if I didn't, but my feelings are complex."

"What do you mean by complex?"

"When your dad hired me and asked me to tutor you, I considered you off limits. "When a person in authority takes advantage of someone he or she is supervising or teaching, I think that's wrong." He sighed. "It's true you approached me, but I lost control and I'm ultimately to blame."

He exhaled loudly. "I never intended to put you in a difficult position. I know it's damn near impossible for you to hide your feelings and as it is, we can't be open about our relationship. You're going through a divorce, and I know that's tough on you. The last thing I want to do is make you feel vulnerable and complicate your life. I want you to feel powerful. You are powerful."

I doubted his words. "You really think I'm powerful, Marcus?"

"Yes, Carrie, I do. My wife Susan was a feminist. She often talked about the limitations society places on women, but she also said women place limitations on themselves. Susan had a unique perspective as to why, even regarding the sex act. She said the man had the advantage of entering the female and this can make her feel vulnerable. For that reason and others, she said women must be diligent to retain their power and identity."

"Susan sounds like a true pioneer." I wondered if I'd ever measure up to her.

He nodded. "Our relationship - yours and mine - is complicated, but I hope you know I want the best for you. I don't want you to lose sight of the wonderful person you are. I certainly don't want you to feel threatened by Neeley Nelson. You need to focus on yourself, and never lose your passion and power. You are an amazing reporter. You don't give up. You continue to dig for the truth. Tatum Brookins' case is a prime example. You managed to get the transcripts of those interviews with the four black teens, and you're determined to prove Tatum is innocent. Your experience with

Kyle has created distrust and rightfully so." He paused, as if measuring his words. "I don't intend to betray your trust, Carrie, but I think you need to examine your relationship with me and decide if you want to be involved with a man like me, who can't seem to let go of the past. I don't know if I'll ever be able to offer you what you need."

Marcus kept glancing in the rearview mirror at the Yellow Cab behind us. He stopped gazing when the cab sped around us and out of sight.

Chapter Thirty-Three

When I saw the name Pot Aux Roses in red above the entrance to the restaurant, I remembered the full-page ad in our newspaper, announcing its grand opening. I pointed to the name on the marquee. "What does Pot Aux Roses mean?"

Marcus opened my door and offered his hand to help me out. Dad used to open doors for Mom. She said she loved his chivalry, and I appreciated this courtesy from Marcus, especially now. My aching muscles needed all the help they could get.

"It means the pot of roses, but colloquially it means secret." He placed his hand on the small of my back and led me toward the rose-covered archway entrance.

"Reminds me of the roses I planted, and guess what? I saw a new bud on them this afternoon."

He smiled. "That's good. You no longer have a brown thumb?"

I laughed. "If the roses live, yes, and that means I wasn't jinxed. Freemont was right. He said it was all in my head. I need to leave a message in the roses telling him I'm sorry for blaming him. We've decided to continue the tradition our ancestors started. Freemont's double great-grandfather, a slave, left a map in the roses that allowed his double great-grandmother, also a slave, to escape my ancestors' plantation. Or at least that's what my grandmother wrote in her journal."

"How did your grandmother verify this?"

"She was a teacher, and she loved genealogy and found a copy of the deed to the property my great-great grandmother left Freemont's great-great grandmother. After she found the deed, she searched for his ancestors, and eventually located them."

Marcus guided me into the restaurant. "Perhaps we should publish portions of your grandmother's journal in our history section."

A tall, dark, tuxedoed man greeted us with "Bonsoir."

"Bonsoir," Marcus replied and gave the maître d' his name.

The maître d' led us to our table, with its white cloth, candle, and single red rose. Romantic. The restaurant looked crowded, for a Tuesday night.

Marcus assisted me with my coat and pulled the chair out for me. After he scooted me in and took his seat across from mine, the maître d' handed us rose-embossed leather menus. Marcus opened his and studied it.

His handsome face and eyes glowed in the candlelight.

"We could publish portions of your grandmother's journal, or you could write a column about the unique history. Does that appeal to you?"

I opened my menu and tried to decipher it. "I don't know, Marcus. I'm thinking we should keep it our secret. I don't want to get weird notes from strangers. Right now, Freemont and I are the only ones leaving notes there." I laughed, remembering the last note he'd left me.

He looked up from his menu. "What's so funny?"

"You probably won't find it amusing, but Freemont left a note saying his security system will be better than mine. We've had this playful rivalry going since childhood."

A blonde woman in a French maid's costume came to our table. "Hi, I'm Renée. I'll be serving you tonight." She recited the specials. "What can I get you to drink?"

Marcus glanced at me, and thankfully not at the scantily clad Renée. Kyle would have visually undressed her by now.

"Do you know what you want to drink, Carrie?"

"Water, and a glass of chardonnay, please."

Marcus ordered a bottle of Sonoma Coast Chardonnay.

She smiled, her eyelashes batting. "Excellent choice, Monsieur."

After Renée left, I spotted Neeley Nelson entering the restaurant. She wore a form-fitting, red sequined dress. Her red hair billowed over her shoulders. One might have thought the red dress and red hair - the color of a carrot - would clash, but she looked like she could pose for a Vogue spread.

I gasped. "Oh, God, no, please tell me I'm imagining her."

She wiggled her way toward our table, as if we'd invited her. I watched in horror as she leaned over Marcus and pressed her cheek to his. "Hi, handsome. What a coincidence to see you here."

Marcus pushed his chair back and stood up, towering over Neeley. I couldn't read his face and didn't know if he was expecting her, surprised to see her, or happy she'd arrived. "The owner is running an ad in our paper." He glanced at me, and I thought I saw discomfort in his eyes. "We're returning the favor. A quid pro quo."

She looked up at him and winked. "Maybe you can convince the owner to become a Chamber member."

"I've never met him. Darla signed him up." Darla Denton was the Southern Journal's super saleswoman.

Neeley gave me a tight-lipped smile. "Is this a special occasion, or may I join you two?"

His eyes locked with mine. "Carrie and I have business to discuss, Neeley. Why don't you go corner the owner and convince him to join the Chamber? He must be here. It's opening night."

Neeley's green eyes widened. "Where's your hubby tonight, Carrie Sue?"

"At Stage Atlanta."

"Oh well, that's convenient, isn't it?"

I didn't respond to her sarcasm, though I had to bite my tongue to keep from saying, get lost. Didn't she sense she wasn't welcome?

Apparently not. She lingered and at one point, slid her hand up and down Marcus' arm. "You'll be interested to know that Saturday's banquet is completely sold out. You are quite the draw, big guy."

My face burned. It must have looked as red as the rose on the table. Why didn't he tell her to stop touching him? I pushed myself away from the table, getting ready to make an exit, when Marcus sat and scooted his chair up to the table.

Renée presented the bottle of wine and expertly opened it with a corkscrew. She poured a sample into Marcus' glass. He swirled it around in the glass, smelled it, then took a sip. "Good."

Neeley patted Marcus on the shoulder. "Well, I'll leave you two to whatever."

Chapter Thirty-Four

On the drive back to my house, I listened to the soothing music and felt the warmth of Marcus' hand in mine. He'd already apologized for Neeley's intrusion. He had no idea she'd be at the restaurant, he said, and I believed him.

After he pulled into my circular driveway and parked, he turned toward me and cradled my hands. He flipped them over and examined my injuries. He kissed them as gently as Mom used to kiss my hurts to make them feel better. "You must have taken quite a spill."

I nodded but saw no reason to explain the circumstances of my fall.

He stared into my eyes, as if he thought he could read my mind. Love tingles ran through me.

His lips covered mine in a warm, urgent kiss. Our tongues wrestled, and we made out like pubescent teenagers. The windows fogged over. I didn't want to stop, but he pulled away when I unzipped his pants.

He exhaled a sigh. "I'd like to stay, but I don't want to cause you a problem, Carrie. I'd better go."

Was he serious about leaving? I didn't want to be alone after what had happened on my run. With the security system Jeff had installed, I should have felt more at ease, but fear prickled up and down my spine at the thought of spending the night alone in this big old house. I considered telling Marcus about my fears, but I was afraid he'd overreact. I might not be in danger at all, only scared.

"Why don't you pull your jeep into the carport and close the doors? No one will know you're here."

In the 1800s when this house was originally built, it had a carriage house and stables. Mom redesigned the area into a garage, but she kept the original doors. Most garage doors slide up and down, but this heavy door opened and closed from the side. I preferred to leave the garage open due to the difficulty in closing it, but in this situation, we needed to hide Marcus' jeep.

He jumped out, walked around to my side, and opened my door. "Go in and get warm, Carrie."

I bundled my coat around me to fend off the icy wind. The security lights flashed on as I approached the veranda.

At the front door, I noticed a folded piece of paper wedged in the crack near the knob. I gasped when I read it. "You will be sorry, bitch." The letters in the note had been cut from newspaper headlines, all different sizes, like a collage a child would create.

My heart jackhammered as I unlocked the door and typed in the security code to disable the alarm system. I rushed inside and hid the note in the junk drawer of the hunt board. Did Kyle do this? My gut told me he wouldn't pull this kind of stunt.

I wondered if I should tell Marcus about the note, but I knew if I told him, he'd obsess about my safety.

"Calm down," I said to steady my nerves. "Don't get spooked. You're safe. You're not alone. Marcus is here. He's parking the car."

I walked into the living room and sat in one of the love seats. The large wool rug in the living room inspired Mom to decorate it in reds and browns, I remembered. The cozy grouping of furniture around the stone fireplace reflected her inspiration.

I stared at the built-in shelves on the back wall. They held books and a stereo system.

I heard footfalls in the hallway. "Carrie?"

"I'm in here, Marcus."

He sat beside me on the loveseat. "What's wrong? Why are you sitting in the dark?" He reached over and turned on the Tiffany lamp.

Tears coursed down my cheeks. I wiped my face as Marcus pulled me into his arms. "You're shivering." He released me and walked to the fireplace. I watched him build a pyramid of logs. He found the lighter on the mantel. I wondered how he knew it was there. The first and only time Kyle built a fire in that fireplace I had to help him locate the lighter.

I pointed to the stereo system. "If you'd like some music, there are cassettes in that case beside the stereo."

Marcus searched through the tapes. He held up a cassette and smiled like a little boy with a guilty secret. "Barry White?"

"Why not?"

He inserted the cassette. *Oh, what a Night for Dancing* filled the room.

Marcus walked over and pulled me to my feet. The aspirin I'd taken earlier, combined with the wine, had numbed my pain enough for me to dance with him. I followed his lead, with my head on his chest, as we moved in a slow two-step.

We danced until Barry started singing, *Never, Never Gonna Give you up*. Marcus guided me to the loveseat, removed his black overcoat and folded it over the back.

As we sat, he pulled me into his arms, holding me close as if he sensed I needed comfort. "How are you feeling?"

"Better now."

As Barry sang *It's Ecstasy When You Lay Down Next to Me*, Marcus began massaging my neck and shoulders. "You're tight."

I sighed. "Yes, I am, but you're loosening me up. Thanks for dinner tonight. The food was delicious." I didn't dare mention Neeley Nelson again, though she invaded my thoughts. I'd looked for Neeley's hot pink

Porsche in the parking lot but didn't see it. I shuddered thinking, she may have followed us in the yellow cab.

Marcus pulled me into his lap, and I let my hands travel over him. He felt hard.

"Mm," he hummed and gently pulled my face to his. "I never thought I could feel this way again." He sucked in a breath, repositioned me in his lap and slipped off his camel-hair jacket.

His magnificent face glowed in the firelight. "Are you warm enough, Carrie?"

"I'm on fire, Marcus."

He pulled my sweater over my head. "Me, too. God, you're beautiful," he whispered.

I unbuttoned his shirt as Barry White sang *Hung up in Your Love*.

Marcus laid me back on the loveseat and undressed me. I felt like a bubbling volcano by the time he took me. I didn't recognize my own voice groaning.

He scooped me up in his arms and carried me to the master bedroom. "I want to make love to you all night, Carrie."

Marcus made good on his promise. Daylight peeked through the curtains before he allowed himself release.

Chapter Thirty-Five

December 13

The ringing phone woke me. I grabbed the receiver from the bed stand. "Hello."

"Carrie Sue?"

My sleepy mind couldn't identify the woman's voice. "Speaking."

"This is Debbie Jasper."

"Hi Debbie."

"We need to talk as soon as possible. Can you come to my office today? I have an eleven o'clock and a two-thirty available. What time is better for you?"

I stretched. My body ached all over from last night's fall and the gymnastics with Marcus in the bedroom. "Two-thirty is probably good."

"I'll see you at my office this afternoon then." She hung up without saying goodbye.

I fell back on the bed. Why would she want to meet again so soon? And why couldn't she tell me over the phone what we needed to discuss?

I pondered the questions as I lolled around in bed. The house sounded empty. Marcus had left, but I had no idea when.

The pillow next to me smelled of him. I hugged it and felt a piece of paper, a note, written in his right-slanted scrawl.

"Carrie, my sleeping angel, I couldn't bear to wake you. I have an early appointment at the office. Try to relax and recover. I'll call you later or you can call me. I made coffee. Your security system looks like mine. I'll lock the door when I leave. Love, Marcus."

The grandfather clock chimed ten times. The last time I'd slept this late I had the flu. I threw back the covers and shivered. The heat was on, but the high ceilings sucked up the warmth.

I slipped on my flannel robe, shoved my feet into my furry slippers and headed to the kitchen for coffee. Marcus had given me this coffee maker as a wedding present. Kyle never made coffee. He preferred tea, meaning Marcus was the first man to make coffee in the machine he'd given me.

I carried my cup of coffee to the dining room and sat in one of the cushioned chairs around the mahogany table. It was a gorgeous piece, an antique from England, Mom had snapped it up at a garage sale.

She had the walls painted the color of my eyes, baby blue, she'd said. She and Dad made me feel like the most special daughter in the world. God, I missed them.

I sipped my coffee and tried to shake off the loneliness and sick feeling lodged in my gut. The words, "You will be sorry, bitch," kept haunting me. I wanted to solve the puzzle of who wrote the note in my door. I wasn't raised to be scared. I was raised to be brave, and if I let this person control my emotions, he or she would win. I refused to allow that and decided to break the pall by making a "to do" list.

l. Ride with undercover cops Saturday night, but don't tell Marcus until afterwards. If he asks why I failed to inform him, I'll say I didn't want him to worry, and I knew I'd be safe and wanted to get a great story with photos.

The doorbell rang, interrupting my list making. I wasn't expecting anyone.

I glanced through the peephole Jeff had installed in the front door. A dark-haired woman stood on the veranda. She held a bouquet of roses. The peephole had misshaped her face.

I watched her and allowed my imagination to take hold. I thought of the fairytale Snow White, and the poisonous apple the evil queen/witch gave Snow White.

I peered through one of the side windows. A van with "Flowers for You," printed in hot pink, had parked in the driveway. When I saw the van, I snapped back to reality, disengaged the security code, and opened the door. Face-to-face the woman looked harmless, not at all like my scary vision through the peephole.

She greeted me with a wide smile. "For you." She handed me the roses.

I thanked her and offered her a tip.

She said, "My tip was included."

I rushed inside to read the card. "Je t'aime, from your undeserving admirer, Marcus."

My heart swelled as I contemplated the drastic changes in Marcus' life and mine. Marcus had transformed from a stern, perfectionist supervisor to an exciting and romantic lover. Dad greatly admired Marcus, and I thought he and Mom would be pleased to know we were together.

I placed the roses inside a Cobalt vase and set them on the dining room table. They brightened the room and I wanted to thank Marcus for his thoughtful gesture.

I picked up the kitchen phone and dialed the office number.

"Southern Journal, Lisa speaking."

"Hi Lisa, it's Carrie Sue. May I speak to Marcus?"

"Hi Carrie Sue, he's in a meeting. Let me see if he can talk."

My heart leaped in my throat as I waited.

"Hi," he whispered.

"Thank you for the beautiful roses, Marcus, and for...everything. I loved your message, too."

"I'm glad. Are you coming in today?"

This wasn't the time to mention my afternoon meeting with Debbie Jasper. "I'll be in later, hopefully before five. Is that okay?"

"Of course, I'll look forward to seeing you." He hung up without saying goodbye.

I cradled the receiver to my chest. I wished we could have talked longer, but I knew he couldn't whisper sweet nothings during a business meeting.

I admired the roses and daydreamed about him, until I heard footfalls in the hallway. I'd forgotten to lock the door and set the alarm. Not smart.

I grabbed a knife from the kitchen. "Who's there?"

The house sounded quiet, too quiet. No more footsteps.

"Boo!"

I screamed and dropped the knife. "Damn you, Freemont Jackson." I wanted to slap him.

He doubled over in laughter. He had on blue jeans, western boots, a grey sweater, and a black bomber jacket.

When he stopped guffawing, he flashed a smug smile. "I came by to see your security system. Jeff's installing a state-of-the art system for me today."

"Pay-back will be hell, Freemont. Wait and see."

"Yeah, I hear you." He poured himself a cup of coffee, sat across from me at the dining table and proceeded to explain what

Jeff was installing for him. "I'll have cameras in the back and front of my house. Security lighting and everything you've got, plus." Freemont talked with his hands, showing his enthusiasm. "Jeff is going to put a monitor on the inside that will allow me to see everything that's going on outside. Not only that, but I can record in slow motion and won't have to change the VHS that often. When the tape needs changing, a red light comes on telling me it's time to put in a new tape. Isn't that something?"

"Why on God's green earth do you need all that, Free?"

His eyebrows shot up. "I keep cash, and I don't want anyone stealing it."

"Yes, but you've told me you hide the money under your floor in a safe. Don't you think a security system like mine would be sufficient for you?"

He shook his head. "Your pitiful little alarm didn't even go off."

I huffed. "That's because I forgot to set it."

He hiked an eyebrow. "Not only that, but you forgot to lock the door. You need to start remembering. With my system, I'll have a camera that'll take a video of whoever's messing around who shouldn't be."

"Well as long as you're happy with it, Free. That's all that matters. I want you to be safe. Did you get a chance to talk to Tatum Brookins?"

"I was just about to tell you. Yes, I talked to Tatum. He seems like a good kid."

"I'm glad. Karl Silkman said you gave a statement and agreed to testify for Tatum."

He nodded. "I'm hoping I can help him. I can't say I heard a gunshot, but I saw Tatum when I was delivering to Ms. Sikes that night."

"A Grand Jury indicted all four boys yesterday."

"I know. It's a travesty." He squinted at the roses. "Where'd you get these?" He pulled on his lower lip. "I know you didn't get them from the yard." He flashed a sly, Cheshire cat smile.

I stared at my hands. "Marcus sent them."

"Red roses mean passion and love."

"That's what they say."

"You and Marcus got something going on, don't you?"

"Kind of."

He laughed. "Kind of? I think you two been doing more than kissy face."

"We didn't get involved until after I caught Kyle cheating."

Freemont shook his head. "Uh, uh, uh, Carrie Sue, you need to be careful. I like Marcus. I do. He seems like a straight-up guy, but you've told me more than once he can be unpredictable and impossible to work for."

"I know, Free, but that was before I understood him and before he opened up to me."

He frowned, as if disapproving. "From the sound of it, you're the one who's opened up to him."

I punched his shoulder. "Not funny."

He chuckled. "Are you're saying you've discovered a new Marcus, a completely different Marcus from the one you've known for years?"

"I have. He's been amazing."

"Yeah, uh huh, but a word of warning, Carrie Sue, you're on the rebound. You need to think about this long and hard. Didn't you tell me not to let my emotions rule? Well, I'm giving you your advice back."

As Freemont cautioned me against getting too involved with Marcus, I thought of the threatening note I'd found and decided to tell Freemont, my confidant from childhood. "Wait right here, Free. I need your advice on something." I walked to the hunt board to fetch the note.

When I returned to the table and handed it to him, he squinted as if he couldn't believe what he was seeing. "Where did this come from?"

"It was on my front door last night. Marcus and I went out to dinner and when we returned, I found the note. Marcus was parking his car in the garage and didn't see it. I decided not to tell him about it."

"Why wouldn't you want him to know?"

"I didn't want him to worry, and I didn't want to wreck our evening by giving this more importance than it deserves."

Freemont laid the note on the table and continued to stare at it. "Do you think Kyle did this?"

"I don't know, Free. It's possible. It doesn't seem like something he'd do, but I have an appointment with the divorce lawyer this afternoon. I'll show it to her. Get her opinion."

Freemont nodded. "Have it fingerprinted. I've touched it now and so have you, but there could be other prints on here." He shook his head as if disgusted. "I have a bad feeling about this, Carrie Sue. My first guess would be Kyle, for obvious reasons. I'll keep a look-out and drive by your place as often as I can. I'm glad you've got that security system. Now you need to remember to use it." He pointed to the note. "There's an angry sicko out there trying to scare you, and angry sickos are dangerous."

Chapter Thirty-Six

Debbie Jasper paced back and forth in her burgundy business suit that matched her sofa. The top of her short blonde hair was spiked as if she'd been pulling on it. "We have a serious problem, Carrie Sue." Her unblinking green eyes confronted me. "Kyle has engaged a money-grubbing lawyer named Lucas Swindal, a fitting name for what he is. He called me early this morning and said Kyle has discovered you're having an affair."

My chest tightened. I got up from her sofa and reached for her soft baseball bat. "Son of a bitch."

Debbie nodded. "My thoughts exactly. We've already served Kyle with divorce papers, citing irreconcilable differences. It's the fastest and least complicated way to proceed. Adultery is a misdemeanor. Kyle would probably contest the divorce if we charged him with adultery. When Swindal made his ridiculous accusation against you, I countered with the fact that Kyle is the one who's been cheating on you, and we have evidence to prove his infidelity. If he wants to play hardball, we will." She inhaled a long breath. "Your reputation is beyond reproach, I know." Debbie patted my hand. "And from now on until Kyle signs your divorce papers, I need you to behave like a cloistered virginal nun. Understand?"

I nodded, though my burning face must have revealed my guilt.

"We have a private eye following Kyle. We'll get the down and dirty on him soon."

"Kyle is a cheater and a taker, Debbie. He lived in my house, a house I inherited from my parents, a house I've lived in all my life. He provided very little money. He sponged off me. Tell him I'll gladly give his ring back along with this thing." I pointed at the watch. "This was his anniversary gift - although I paid for it -but he can have it back." I gave Debbie a doleful stare. "But he can't touch my house or my inheritance, can he?"

"Anything you've inherited, which is still non-marital property, he can't touch."

I sighed my relief. "He rarely bought groceries. Once in a blue moon, he'd reimburse me for the power and phone bills. Damn, what an asshole." I pounded the bat against the floor. "I was an idiot to marry him. I should have known he couldn't keep his dick in his pants. He's been cheating on me from day one."

Debbie hugged me. "I'm checking into his last divorce. If we can prove his divorce wasn't final when he married you, we'll file for an annulment."

I studied the floor. "That won't work. I saw his divorce papers before we got married."

"But there might be a technicality you're unaware of. I'm working on that angle. Also, didn't you say Kyle was abusive? He shoved you into a door and stalked you, and followed you to an appointment and scared you?"

I didn't dare mention how I tried to stab him with a letter opener. "Yes."

"And if we can prove he intentionally misled you and cheated on you from the beginning, this will give us yet another angle. However, it's my duty to tell you, the fastest way to get this divorce over with, and get on with your life is for Kyle to agree that the two of you have irreconcilable differences. Otherwise, this could drag on and on."

"I don't want it to drag on and on, Debbie. I want it over."

"I know, Carrie Sue, but Swindal has a reputation for going after the money, and Kyle doesn't have any. I've seen a copy of his financials. He's had two divorces, and he's paying alimony to the second wife."

I gasped in surprise. "He is? I had no idea."

"Yes, Carrie Sue, and if he kept that fact from you, we have another angle we can use."

"He did keep it from me."

"That's fraud; but I don't know if we can make it stick. One good thing is, Kyle is employed. He's teaching part-time and directing plays. But he's financially strapped, which means he may ask for money." Debbie paused. "Swindal said Kyle would like to meet with you. My guess is he wants to get back together."

I stomped my foot on the floor. "No way in hell will I agree to reconcile with that asshole. I wish I'd never met him."

Debbie patted my arm. "It might speed things along if you'd at least meet with him, Carrie Sue. We can arrange a conference here in my office Monday morning, if that's agreeable with you."

I sighed, feeling trapped. "The last thing on earth I want to do is meet with Kyle, but if you think I should, I'll try to stomach it. But as far as paying him, he's the one who should be paying me for all the bills he didn't pay, and for wasting a year of my life." I took off my platinum watch and handed it to her. "Put this damn watch in an envelope and give it to him. Tell him he can have it. I don't want it."

She smiled sympathetically. "You said you wanted to end the marriage as quickly as possible. I'm willing to go to court if need be, but as I said, knowing Swindal, he'll urge Kyle to ask for money."

We stared at each other for a moment. "How much money do you think he'll want, Debbie?"

"There are no children involved, and you two were married only a short time. But if we can get Kyle to sign the divorce papers pronto by offering, say, five or ten thousand, would you be willing to do that?"

"No, I don't want to give the son of a bitch a cent, other than the watch and wedding band."

"The other option would be to fight to the bitter end, but in the meantime, your private life will be on hold. And without a financial incentive, he could drag this on until he's ready to marry again."

I groaned. "Do what you think is best, Debbie. Sam has confidence in you, and I trust your judgment. You know I want out of this marriage, but I don't want it to cost me an arm and a leg."

She patted my arm. "I'll arrange a meeting with Kyle in my office Monday morning at nine."

"I'd rather walk through fire, but okay, I'll meet with him." I withdrew the nasty note from my tote and held it up for her to see. "I found this stuck in my front door last night. I've touched it and a friend of mine has touched it, but there could be another set of prints on here."

Debbie frowned at the note. "Do you think it's from Kyle?"

"I honestly don't know, but I was thinking you could get it checked out."

She stood, walked to her desk, and pulled out a tissue from the box. She wrapped the tissue around the note before she handled it. "My guess is whoever took the time to do this wore gloves, Carrie Sue, but I'll have the detective investigate. In the meantime, you need to be careful, be vigilant. If you notice anything suspicious, or see anyone following you, get a complete description. Report it to the authorities. And I'd like to know as well."

I thought about the yellow cab that followed Marcus and me last night but decided not to tell Debbie. She wanted me to act like a chaste nun. If she knew I was with Marcus, she'd suspect I'd been dishonest with her.

Should I tell her about the car that ran me off the road? I pondered this, but then decided I might be overreacting. Freedom Road was narrow. It had been dark. I wasn't carrying a flashlight. Was it my fault, or had the driver intended to hurt me? The question troubled me as I left Debbie's office.

Chapter Thirty-Seven

I parallel parked in my usual spot in front of the Southern Journal and sat for a minute, glancing in the mirror to check myself. My eyes looked red from crying. Marcus was sure to notice, but I couldn't tell him about my meeting with Debbie. He'd insist on getting involved, and I didn't want to place him in jeopardy.

I debated what to do. I wasn't a legal expert, but I'd read about a statute called Alienation of Affection, which permitted the third party, who would have allegedly caused the breakup of a marriage, to be sued. Marcus didn't break up my marriage, but that didn't mean Marcus couldn't be sued under this statute. I couldn't let him become a target and lose his financial security. He had enough capital to buy the newspaper and the building housing it. He owned a home and part of a California vineyard.

Debbie had assured me Kyle couldn't touch my house and my inheritance, but what if he went after Marcus?

I grabbed the eye drops out of my tote, dribbled some in my eyes and glanced in the visor mirror. They still looked puffy and irritated, but not as red.

I raced up the concrete steps. I was shivering by the time I walked in. Lisa waved as I entered. She was occupied on the phone thankfully, and I was spared a lengthy conversation with her.

I rushed to my desk, plopped my tote on top of it and waved to Lindsey. She was typing on her word processor while on the phone. The receiver was propped between her left ear and shoulder.

She smiled and waved back.

I knocked lightly on Marcus' office door to give him the roll of film I'd shot. He opened his door and his face seemed to light up. I saw love and tenderness in his smiling eyes. He had a phone pressed to his ear, but motioned for me to come in.

I watched him. He was a wonderful man. He strove to do his best and bring out the best in others. He'd suffered unbearable loss, and yet managed to endure and succeed. This afternoon, he looked fetching in a steel-grey suit and white dress shirt.

"You're busy, Marcus," I whispered, not wanting to interrupt his business call. "I'll talk to you later."

He shook his head, pulled his chair around for me to sit and propped his butt on the side of his desk. His cobalt eyes peered into mine.

I broke eye contact, took a deep breath to gain control and noticed an open drawer with a handgun inside. Marcus usually kept this drawer locked and now I realized why.

As he hung up the phone, I pointed to the pistol. "Why do you have a gun in there?"

His eyebrows lifted. "Other than exercising my second amendment right, I own guns for security and sport. I go to the shooting range occasionally." He slammed the drawer closed. "I have two more at home, plus the Colt Cobra thirty-eight your dad gave me. I think it would be a good idea if you owned a gun. I'll give you one and teach you how to use it."

"No. I hate guns." I thought about what he'd said. "I'd wondered what happened to Dad's gun. Now I know. He gave it to you?"

"Yes, and I value it greatly."

"Dad said it was the same kind of gun Jack Ruby used to kill Lee Harvey Oswald. I couldn't find it the morning I caught Kyle cheating, thank God, or I might have killed him. I was that angry."

Marcus smiled. "Your dad said your mother hated firearms, and I suppose that's why he decided to give his gun to me."

My head swam with this new knowledge. "Yes, I remember Mom wanted him to get rid of it."

"I treasure that gun more than any of my others and..."

Someone knocked on his door, interrupting. He frowned. "Who is it?"

"Lisa."

Scowling, Marcus stood and swung the door open.

Lisa strolled in and closed the door behind her. "Neeley Nelson is here. She says she needs to talk to you, Marcus. I told her you were in a meeting and couldn't be disturbed, but you know how persistent she is. She doesn't seem to understand the meaning of 'no'."

Marcus groaned. "I can't see her now. Ask her to leave a message, and I'll handle whatever it is later."

After Lisa walked out, I said, "My divorce lawyer needs to meet with me again on Monday morning. That means I'll miss another staff meeting. I hope you don't mind."

He frowned and kneeled to face me. "Have you been crying, Carrie?"

Before I could answer, we heard another knock.

He barked, "Damn it" and stood to open the door.

Lisa stepped inside and closed the door behind her. "Neeley said she needed to talk to you now. She said she'll wait as long as it takes." Lisa's mouth tightened in a thin line. "And she's having her calls transferred here while she's waiting." She sighed a breath. "Neeley is expecting me to screen her calls and take messages, and I don't appreciate it."

Marcus stormed out. Lisa and I grimaced, as if anticipating the carnage to follow. She grabbed my arm and pulled me out to witness the onslaught.

Neeley had on a bright yellow, low-cut knit dress showing off her abundant cleavage. "Hi Marcus," she cooed.

"Neeley," he said sternly. "Lisa is not your secretary. You're not to receive calls here, understand?"

Neeley pouted, her green eyes widening in alarm.

"And when Lisa tells you I'm in a meeting and cannot be disturbed, she means it. Please don't disrespect her."

Neeley clutched her chest. "Marcus, dear, I only required a few seconds of your time. Debra Simpson is doing the centerpieces and decorations for the banquet. I'd like you to talk to her about them. I think she's planning to donate her services, but you'll need to call her right away."

"Is that all, Neeley?"

She nodded.

"And you couldn't write that in a message?"

She batted her long lashes. "I wanted to make sure you received the message, Marcus." She glanced at Lisa. "Sometimes they get lost."

He cleared his throat. "I can't remember a time when Lisa has failed to give me a message."

Marcus turned toward me and tilted his head in the direction of his office, a signal for me to follow.

Neeley glared at me. If looks could kill, I'd be a goner, I thought as I dutifully followed Marcus back to his office. "You're swamped, Marcus. We can talk later."

He rubbed his eyes. "Tell me what's bothering you, Carrie."

I squeezed my eyes shut, trying to keep the tears back, but they oozed out anyway.

He wrapped his arms around me. "Is there anything I can do?"

"You've already done everything possible. Please don't worry. It's nothing, just me being emotional. Oh, and before I forget, I put a roll of film with photos of Tatum, Jeremy, Calvin and Leroy on my desk for you to develop. On that same roll, are pictures of Karl Silkman, D.A. Wallace Sheppard, and Assistant D.A. Vernon Abbott. I also snapped Damon Cardoza, the homeless guy who walks to the libraries. And there's a photo of Klan attorney Robert Landingham in this. I can identify everyone once you've developed the photos."

"Okay, thanks, Carrie. I'll get that film developed today."

"Beneath that roll of film is the file Karl Silkman left in the clerk's office."

He touched my arm, sending tingles. "Lisa said you had a call from an Atlanta Policeman about your plans to tag along with undercover officers Saturday night."

I chewed on the inside of my cheek and wished Lisa had kept her mouth shut. "That's right. I've been meaning to tell you. I'm planning to do a story on drugs and prostitution. A few weeks ago, I ran into Kevin Jones. He's a drug enforcement officer. I told him I'd like to tag along with the undercover cops the next time they did a sting or drug bust in our area. He said they were scheduled to go out Saturday night."

Marcus puckered his bottom lip. "Why haven't you mentioned this before?"

I shrugged, not knowing how to explain. "There was so much going on the day Kevin called. I had the bond and Grand Jury hearing to discuss with you, and I considered those things more important."

"You knew I wouldn't want you to go. Isn't that why you didn't mention it?"

Rather than lie, I pressed my lips together.

"I don't want you to go, Carrie. It's dangerous. Those undercover guys carry assault weapons. There's no predicting what will happen. Bullets fly and you could get caught in the crossfire. You say you don't like guns. You won't like their guns."

I exhaled a protesting breath. "Marcus, I've already committed to going. And remember when you told me last night? You said I had power. Are you saying now I have no power to make this decision? And haven't you always told me I need to be on the scene whenever possible? Get interviews firsthand?"

His weary eyes glared into mine. My heart hurt for him. He was worried because of his past and because Susan had died on the job.

"Carrie, I can't forbid you from going. You're your own person. But I'm asking you not to go. I know how dangerous these things are. I don't want you to get hurt. Undercover guys love danger. They need the adrenalin rush. If you go with them, you could get seriously injured, or worse. Do you understand?" He sucked in a raspy breath. "I've got an idea. Lisa and Thomas are attending the Chamber banquet. Thomas bought a table. Why don't we sit with them? I'd love for you to go. I'm sure the undercover cops will understand. You can hang with them another time and when you do, I'd like to be there. Make sure you're safe."

Under normal circumstances, I might have attended the banquet, but I knew my presence would irritate Neeley Nelson, especially if she'd been stalking Marcus. She may have suspected I'd spent the night in the office apartment with Marcus. Had she followed him in the yellow cab, and then followed us to the restaurant? Had she told Kyle I was having an affair? I cringed at the thought.

I refused to make Marcus' life more difficult. I needed to separate myself from him for his protection and mine. "If you'd asked me to attend the banquet earlier, I would have, Marcus, but now that I've already signed the release form, I can't break my word."

He bit his bottom lip. "You mean you signed the form that says if anything happens to you, you won't hold the police department or the city responsible? You mean that form?" His eyes darkened.

"Marcus, I'm going to be fine. I'm not Susan. Nothing is going to happen to me." As soon as I said Susan's name, I regretted it.

He turned his back to me and slammed his palms against the wall. "Damn."

Before I could apologize, he stormed out of his office and ran upstairs.

Chapter Thirty-Eight

I sat at the dining room table and stared at the lovely red roses from Marcus. The buds had opened beautifully.

It felt cold in the house, but the roses seemed to like it. I shivered, pushed my body out of the chair and walked over to the blue marble hearth.

Kyle and I rarely spent much time in this room. He preferred eating in the living room with the television on.

I threw three logs in the fireplace, lit them, and remembered happier times. My parents and I used to eat supper in this room. We'd talk about our day; share the good and bad. If they were here now, they'd probably advise me to apologize to Marcus for mentioning Susan's name.

I didn't mean to hurt him. I wanted to protect him.

I withdrew my Tandy from my tote, turned it on and stared at the blank screen. I needed to write my column, but my foggy mind couldn't focus.

A tiny voice in my head said, "Write about your divorce." I obeyed the voice and allowed my fingers to race across the keyboard, uncensored.

When I finished the column, I typed in the transmit code and checked to make sure I'd entered it correctly. Next, I attached the black contraption to the kitchen phone and dialed the mainframe number.

It seemed to go through, but to make sure, I called the office to alert Marcus.

"Southern Journal, Lisa speaking."

"You're working late, Lisa."

She sighed. "I'm waiting for Thomas. He's helping Marcus in the dark room. Do you want me to give him a message?"

"Yes, tell him I submitted my column, and I'll send the rest of my articles later."

"Do you want him to call you?"

I wanted to say, yes, have him call me, but I didn't want to arouse Lisa's suspicions. "He can call if he wants to or if he has a problem with the column and can't locate it."

"Carrie Sue," Lisa whispered, "Marcus started acting weird after you left."

I closed my eyes. Oh, no. "Weird how?"

"He seemed distraught." She paused. "Maybe I shouldn't say anything, Carrie Sue, but I smelled alcohol on him. I've never known him to drink during working hours. That's why I asked Thomas to come over and help him in the dark room."

I unraveled the phone cord, feeling overwhelmed with guilt, and plopped on the floor. "Maybe he's going through a rough time, and we need to be more understanding, Lisa."

"I'm worried about him, Carrie Sue."

"It's a good thing you asked Thomas to come by and help."

"Thomas loves to help Marcus. You know how much he admires him. I think Marcus reminds Thomas of his son."

Lisa was referring to Jacob, killed in Vietnam. A tragedy. Thomas didn't want Jacob to join the army, but he joined anyway. Thomas and Jacob's mother had divorced. After the split, his son blamed Thomas for the breakup. Unfortunately, Thomas and Jacob failed to settle their dispute before Jacob was killed, according to Lisa.

"As you know, Carrie Sue, Thomas and Marcus have a special bond. I'm hoping they can give each other comfort, but of course I'm not talking about Southern Comfort." She laughed. "If you know what I mean."

"I do."

"Thomas used to bend his elbow too much until I gave him an ultimatum. It was me or the booze, I told him. He started drinking to excess after Jacob died, but somehow our marriage survived. That trip to D.C. helped, I think."

"Was that the time you saw the Vietnam Wall?"

"Yes, and let me tell you, honey, Thomas cried like a baby when he saw that wall. He put a sheet of paper over Jacob's name and shaded it in with a pencil. He had it framed.

It's hanging in the shrine to Jacob we have in our house. Thomas goes in there often, but I just wish he'd talk more about his feelings. He's like Marcus in that way, very reticent. They both keep too much inside if you ask me. I refuse to bottle up my feelings. My Aunt Minnie used to keep everything bottled up and died of pancreatic cancer. Did I tell you I bought a book on Transcendental Meditation? Thomas read it, and I think it helped him. I hope so anyway."

As I listened to Lisa, I felt the need to bend my own elbow with a good stiff drink. I took the Wild Turkey out of Dad's liquor cabinet, poured two fingers, chased it down with a beer and curled up in a fetal position on my bed. I didn't have the energy or the desire to undress and brush my teeth.

I'd drifted off to sleep when the jingling phone jerked me awake. I grabbed the receiver and answered with a grunt.

"Carrie?"

My heart lurched at the sound of Marcus's voice. "Yes."

He exhaled loudly into the phone. "I...don't...like   what's   happened between...us." He was slurring his words.

"I want to apologize for what I said this afternoon, Marcus. I was out of line."

"You don't like to be...controlled. And I'm a control freak. I...need to work on that."

My heart ached for him. I wanted to tell him about my meeting with Debbie and the nasty note, but I knew I couldn't. He'd react badly and might even go after Kyle with one of his guns. "I love you, Marcus. I know I've told you before, but I sincerely mean it, and no matter what happens, I want you to know how I feel. I'll always love you."

I listened to his breathing and waited for him to respond. "I read your column, Carrie."

"I hope you didn't have to search for it in the graveyard of lost stories." Sometimes when I didn't type in the correct code at the top the article, it got lost in what Marcus referred to as "the graveyard."

He cleared his throat. "No, it came in fine...good...sometimes the graveyard won't let go."

"Was my column okay?" I didn't expect a coherent answer.

"Visual and moving, very touching about your parents...how you grieved, and how you were...or thought...you were wrong to make a commitment to Kyle, but you wanted to feel part of a family again...so you married him. I edited out the part about Kyle and the other woman. I thought that might cause a problem with your divorce. Am I making sense?"

"Yes, I was in a trance when I wrote that column." I listened to his labored breathing. "Are you, okay, Marcus?" I bit my tongue to keep from saying I'd drive over to see him.

He sighed a moan. "I'm okay so long as you're okay." He hung up without saying goodbye.

Afterwards, I stared at the ceiling and prayed Marcus wouldn't harm himself or be harmed.

Chapter Thirty-Nine

December 16

I sat on an unforgiving pew inside the stately courtroom of Fulton County Superior Judge Mallard Fortenberry. Only two of the four indicted teenagers faced trial for the murder of Preston Campbell.

One of the youths, Calvin Newson, fourteen, allegedly hung himself inside his cell at the juvenile detention center. The medical examiner said Calvin used a strip torn from a bed sheet he'd tied to a ventilation shaft in the ceiling. After they discovered Calvin's body, they found a hand-written note in his cell. The note accused Jeremy Andrews of shooting and killing Preston Campbell.

Leroy Cortez, sixteen, pleaded guilty to armed robbery and was sentenced to fifteen years in prison. That left Tatum Brookins and Jeremy Andrews.

In a pretrial hearing, Karl Silkman asked Judge Fortenberry to dismiss the charges against Tatum. The judge refused.

Then Karl requested a separate trial for Tatum. The judge denied his request.

During the jury selection process, tempers flared, but eventually nine women, three men and two alternate male jurors were deemed unbiased enough to decide the fate of Tatum and Jeremy.

The defense attorneys wanted to wait until after the holidays to begin the proceedings. They needed more time to prepare, both attorneys said.

"This has been a perpetual rollercoaster," Karl said.

I knew the feeling. My stomach had been reeling since Saturday night. A drug dealer shot one of the uncover cops in the arm. The cop was standing only a few feet from me when he took the hit.

Marcus heard about the shooting on the police scanner and freaked out. I called him to let him know I was okay, but he rudely chastised me for putting my life in danger, and I hung up on him.

Since then, Marcus had gotten into transcendental meditation. The last time I walked into his office he was sitting in the lotus position on the floor with his eyes closed.

He seemed calmer. He even congratulated me on my coverage of the drug bust. The wire service picked up what I'd written. One of the stories covered the bust and the cop getting shot. Another article featured an eighteen-year-old prostitute and drug addict named Summer, who ran away from home at sixteen to escape her father.

She claimed he'd sexually abused her and taught her how to shoot up heroin. A pimp befriended Summer the moment she stepped off the bus, she said. Pimps hang out at bus stations to pick up runaways, an undercover cop told me.

In the raid, Police arrested the pimp, but not Summer. She agreed to check into a drug rehabilitation center. I prayed she'd get the help she needed.

Summer's story reminded me to count my blessings. My parents loved me unconditionally. They were my champions. They had assured me I could accomplish my dreams if I worked hard enough and didn't give up. Marcus had given me the same encouragement, though we'd become distant lately.

I finally told him Debbie wanted me to behave like a virtuous nun to avoid accusations from Kyle and his lawyer.

"Why'd you hide this?" Marcus asked.

His words hit me the wrong way, and I lost my temper. I told him he'd been hiding his personal life for seven years. "If you'd shown any romantic interest in me, I wouldn't have married Kyle," I blurted out.

I probably needed TM, too. I could have used meditation before, during and after my meeting with Kyle on Monday. I vomited twice in Debbie's bathroom.

Kyle was a cheat. That I knew, but I didn't know to what extent until I saw the photos the private investigator produced.

There were several of Kyle with more than one woman; some of them featured Kyle and Maryann making out at the Shady Rest motel. Others showed him kissing a skimpily clad brunette, a young blonde, and a woman who looked old enough to be his mother, but he wouldn't kiss his mother on the mouth like that.

After Kyle saw the pictures, he wanted to speak with me in private. Debbie warned him every word he said would be recorded, but he made his horrible confession anyway. He was a sex addict. He'd been in therapy for years, he said.

"Obviously the therapy hasn't worked," I said.

His addiction began at fifteen when one of his teachers seduced him, he said. Kyle wept during his confession. If this had been anyone else but Kyle, I probably would have felt sympathetic.

He wanted me to attend marriage counseling, but I refused. "You've misled me from day one, Kyle. You knew you couldn't be faithful. Yet you asked me to marry you."

I showed him the threatening note I'd found at my front door. He swore up and down he had nothing to do with it.

In our negotiations, Kyle agreed to sign the divorce papers, but first I had to pay him seven thousand dollars. He said he needed the money for his on-going psychotherapy.

I didn't want our divorce to drag on, so I gave in and agreed to give him the money.

Otherwise, as Debbie reminded me, he would have refused to divorce me until he decided to marry again. "But if he agrees to a divorce now, you wait only thirty-one days. Then the court will set a date. After you meet with the judge, your divorce will be final. You're the plaintiff, so Kyle isn't required to be there."

I regretted writing that column about my impending divorce. After the column was published, total strangers came up to me and shared their divorce stories. Lisa had become a mothering nightmare.

Lord, give me patience had become my mantra as I sat in the uncomfortable pew waiting for the trial to begin.

"All rise," the bailiff shouted.

Judge Fortenberry strode in with a stern expression. Tall and stout, with thick white hair, Fortenberry reminded me of the pictures I'd seen of noblemen in wigs.

"Bring in the jury, Mr. Sheriff," Fortenberry intoned.

After the jury sat, Fortenberry instructed them on the rules. Then he asked assistant district attorney Vernon Abbott to give his opening statement.

Abbott stood and walked toward the jury box, located on the left side of the courtroom. "Good morning. My name is Vernon Abbott. I will be prosecuting this case before you today, but first I'd like to give you a little background about myself."

He pushed his horn-rimmed glasses against the bridge of his nose and smiled warmly. "I was educated in public schools, public colleges, and law school in Atlanta. I have been with the district attorney's office for four years now, and this case is not at all like other cases I've seen. This case is remarkable."

He turned away from the jury for a moment to stare in my direction. "Many of you are already familiar with some of the facts in this case but as you know, we don't try our cases in the news media. Therefore, I want you to erase from your mind everything you've heard about this case. Listen to the evidence as presented and listen to the law as given to you by the judge."

Abbott paused to take off his glasses and rub his eyes. "The evidence will show that the victim Preston Campbell worked part-time at the Methodist Church in College Station. He washed dishes and performed other odd jobs at the church. He elected to walk home rather than take a ride and as Preston walked down in the area behind a grocery store, he was spotted by not one, not two, not three, but four black guys. We will present a chart to you during this trial which will spell out the exact location, but the important thing to remember is, these black guys spotted Preston Campbell and there was a discussion about robbing him. The discussion was heard by all four. However, only two of them are on trial here today. One of the four who is not on trial, is Leroy Cortez. Leroy will testify as to what happened, and we believe the evidence will show that the owner of the gun is Jeremy Andrews."

Abbott pointed to Jeremy. He wore navy blue dress pants and a white shirt. His eyes were wide and expressionless, as he stared down at the defense table. His black hair was short and well-groomed. His skin looked the color of a cardboard box and was at least two shades lighter than Tatum's.

"One of the other four, Calvin Newson, who hung himself in his jail cell, asked for the gun, but he can't be here to testify. We know from Leroy Cortez that the gun was given to Calvin Newson. And we believe the evidence will show that Leroy and Tatum were lookouts for Jeremy and Calvin. In other words, they wanted to make sure Jeremy and Calvin could rob and pistol-whip Preston without getting caught. After Preston was pistol whipped, Jeremy shot him in the back. All four boys left Preston to die. All four boys ran away from the scene, not one, not two, not three, but all four."

He paused and leaned into the jury box. "At this time, I will say no more. I want you to hear the evidence during this trial." He looked at each juror individually. "Thank you for your attention and your time."

Abbott walked back to the prosecution table and waved to Mr. Campbell, Preston's father, a distinguished grey-haired man seated in the pew behind me. Campbell's sad, listless eyes reflected unbearable grief.

Judge Fortenberry glanced at Lovett Boucher, a lanky brown man in a tailored black suit. He sat beside Jeremy Andrews at the defense table. I'd met Boucher during the bail hearing and jury selection. "Mr. Boucher, would you like to make an opening statement?"

Boucher stood. "Yes, your honor." He walked to the jury box. "Good morning, ladies and gentlemen," he spoke with a slight accent, but I couldn't identify its origin. "You are going to hear conflicting stories, but we believe the evidence will show that Calvin Newson, who is not here today, got control of the gun and went up the street to rob and shoot poor Preston. Thank you, ladies, and gentlemen."

After Boucher's brief presentation, Judge Fortenberry glanced over at Karl Silkman, decked out in a three-piece steel-grey suit. "Mr. Silkman, would you like to make an opening statement?"

Silkman stood. "Yes, your honor, I would."

He casually walked to the jury box and stroked his beard like a professor giving a lecture. "Ladies and Gentlemen, I represent only Tatum Brookins." He pointed to Tatum, who looked like a frightened child in a white shirt and black dress pants. His face was the same mahogany shade as the defense table.

"Tatum Brookins has lived in College Station almost all his young life. He lives with his mother and two brothers. His father died about eight or nine years ago. He is a good student, and as you know, the law dictates Tatum's innocence. The prosecution must prove his guilt beyond a reasonable doubt, but the evidence shows he isn't guilty of any crime. In fact, the evidence shows he is innocent. No question Preston Campbell's death was the result of a heinous crime, without justification. It was a crime of extreme violence, a crime that took the life of a young man who had not yet begun to know what the world was all about. Yet without provocation, his life was snuffed out. It is a tragedy for Preston and a tragedy for his parents and for the younger brother and sister he leaves behind, but my purpose today and during this trial is to defend Tatum Brookins and to prove his innocence. Therefore, I'd like to briefly outline for you what I believe the evidence will show. There was a gun, true. The state alleges the gun belonged to Jeremy Andrews. Leroy Cortez apparently had control of that gun. He gave it to Calvin Newson, who ran after Preston Campbell to rob him. My client Tatum Brookins warned the others not to hurt Preston. Tatum said don't go there. Don't get involved. Then he kept walking toward his home. Tatum was far along when he heard a gunshot, and we will prove to you that Tatum said 'hi' to a man delivering laundry. This man's testimony will place Tatum far from the scene of the crime."

I cringed in fear for my friend. What if the Klan targeted Freemont?

Silkman continued. "How do I know this? I know this because when all four boys were arrested, they gave statements, and I expect those statements will be presented to you as evidence. But please, listen carefully: Due to certain rules of evidence, a name may be blotted out of the statements, but not all of them will be blotted out. And the one consistency in these statements concerns my client, Tatum Brookins. Tatum told the others 'No'. He was the conscience of the group, the only one who fought against committing this horrible crime. And furthermore, the evidence will show that Tatum never touched the gun."

Judge Fortenberry pounded his gavel. "Stop arguing the case now, Mr. Silkman. Are you finished?"

"Yes, your honor." He smiled thoughtfully at the jurors. "But I would like to thank the men and women of the jury for their patience and consideration."

Fortenberry nodded his large head at the assistant district attorney. "You may call your first witness, Mr. Abbott."

Abbott announced, "Officer Stanley, Lewis Stanley."

I'd met Stanley before, and I knew he'd helped Nev take the statement of at least one of the witnesses. In his mid-thirties, he had sandy brown hair. He stood about five-ten and was soft around the middle. Stanley approached the witness stand. His smiling face looked like a kindly Samaritan's, even though he wore a police uniform.

After his swearing in, he sat in the witness chair. Abbott asked him to state his name and spell it before he placed a large chart on an easel. The chart denoted streets and landmarks and was positioned between the witness stand and the jury. It was visible to the judge as well and to the public and press gallery where I sat.

Abbott picked up a pointer and asked the members of the jury if they could see the chart. They all nodded.

Abbott questioned Stanley to establish he worked for the City of College Station as a police officer and was working there on the night in question. Abbott handed Stanley the pointer and asked him to explain what happened the night he found Preston's body.

Stanley used the pointed to demonstrate during his testimony. "I received a call over the radio, between eight-thirty, eight-forty-five to go to the area of Hemphill and Virginia Avenue. I couldn't locate anyone at first, so I went down Virginia Avenue, turned around beneath the underpass, came back, went south on Hemphill, turned around and went back north on Hemphill where I found the body of Preston Campbell." He pointed to the spot. "Preston Campbell was hard to find, because of his dark clothing. When I first got the call, the radio operator said a motorist had called in to report someone was lying drunk. When I arrived there, I found Preston Campbell's body. I didn't find any vital signs, but I immediately called for rescue, and asked for a detective to come to the scene."

Abbott asked, "Who did you turn this investigation over to, Officer Stanley?

"Detective Nev Powers, and he called the Fulton County Coroner's Office."

Abbott: "Did you and Detective Powers order the area where the body was found to be sealed off?"

Stanley: "Yes sir."

Abbott showed Stanley a photograph and referred to it as state's exhibit number six. "What is this, Officer Stanley?"

Stanley glanced at the photo. "It's Preston Campbell's body."

Abbott: "Is there anything else pictured here, something smaller?"

Stanley: "There's a pen we found and also a butterfly knife."

Abbott showed Stanley another photograph, which he called state's exhibit number nine. "What is this, Officer Stanley?"

Stanley stared at the photo. "It's the body of Preston Campbell with a bullet-hole in his back."

Abbott: "Do these pictures depict the way the scene looked and the way the body appeared?"

Stanley:"Yes, sir."

After tendering the exhibits for the jury to examine, Judge Fortenberry called Silkman to begin his cross-examination of Stanley.

Silkman asked Stanley to examine what he called "the defendant's exhibit number three," which showed a street sign, a hill and a house a good distance away. Silkman was trying to establish where Tatum was when Preston was killed. Stanley agreed to the location and said the photograph appeared to be accurate.

No one objected and the exhibit was admitted into evidence.

After a brief pause, Silkman continued his questioning. "Officer Stanley, didn't you take the statement of a man named Tim Dillon?"

Stanley: "Yes, sir. Detective Nev Powers and I did."

Silkman: "Was that statement recorded and transcribed?"

Stanley: "Yes, sir, it was."

Silkman: "And were statements taken from Tatum Brookins as well as the other boys who were arrested?"

Stanley: "Yes, sir."

Silkman: "Do you have in your possession a copy of those tape recordings and the transcripts of those recordings?"

Stanley frowned. "No sir. Detective Powers has the tape recordings, and it is my understanding they were transcribed in the

Sheriff's office and presented to the District Attorney."

Silkman nodded. "I have no further questions."

Boucher, on behalf of his client Jeremy Andrews, said, "No questions from me."

Judge Fortenberry excused Stanley from the witness stand and instructed Abbott to call his next witness.

Abbott: "Detective Powers."

Nev sauntered to the witness stand in a three-piece, grey suit, looking more like a dandy lawyer than a police detective. He stated his name for the record and gave his place of employment. He'd been with the College Station Sheriff's Department for five years, he said, and assigned to investigate the alleged homicide of Preston.

Abbott: "Detective Powers, please outline for the court what you did when you came upon the scene."

Nev addressed the jury as he spoke. "We sealed off the area with tape. At that time the paramedics had arrived and were trying to administer first aid, but they found no life signs on the subject. I started a crime scene search. I measured off the area, etcetera. The victim had no identification on him at the time." Nev described Preston's clothing. "The victim wore blue jeans, t-shirt, a light jacket and tennis shoes. A man pulled up in a station wagon, and he asked me what was going on. The man said he was looking for his son. I asked him to get out of the car.

From his identification I saw he was Mr. Campbell." Nev nodded in the direction of Campbell. "We walked down to the scene, and he identified his son."

Abbott: "Did you conduct interviews that evening with regard to this case?"

Nev: "I talked to neighbors and Mr. Campbell, and I talked to Mrs. Campbell, his wife, who is also Preston's mother. I talked to the assistant minister of the church where the boy worked, washing dishes, etcetera. The boy had missed his ride and there was some confusion as to how he would get home. He could have called his parents, but he decided to walk home and then this happened."

Abbott: "How did you go about locating the perpetrators?"

Nev: "We received a telephone call the next day from a bus driver who said he'd seen a white male walking down Virginia Avenue and he saw some black males, crouching down like they were picking up something. It looked as if they were going to throw stones at the bus. Then the driver said he saw them approach the white boy."

Silkman stood and shouted, "Your honor, this is obviously hearsay. Request that the jury not consider this."

Judge Fortenberry: "Ladies and Gentlemen, this evidence should be admitted for the limited purpose of explaining the conduct of the officer testifying on the stand and not for any other purpose."

After a pause, Nev continued. "And we also got a call from tipsters, a female and a male had called. They wanted to know if there was a reward in the case. The woman said she knew something about it, and the man called the police radio dispatch and said he knew a little bit about the case. I instructed the radio operator the next time anybody phoned in to have that person call nine-one-one. The nine-one-one system shows the caller's address on the computer screen. I knew we'd be able to go to the caller's location and apprehend that person. After the tipster called nine-one-one, we were able to send two patrol cars to pick him up. He was using a pay telephone, and we found out his name was Tim Dillon.

Abbott: "Did you bring Mr. Dillon into the station?"

Nev: "Yes and he started telling me about riding the bus with Calvin Newson. He told me little facts he couldn't have known otherwise. For example, he said Calvin told him the victim had only ballpoint pens on him. We hadn't publicized that, and I knew Dillon must know something about the crime. We taped Dillon's statement and Dora Lee Thompson, the Sheriff's secretary, transcribed it."

Abbott: "After you received the information from Tim Dillon, what did you do?"

Nev: "From what Dillon told us, we decided we had enough information for a search warrant. We drew up an affidavit for the warrant on Jeremy Andrews' home."

Abbott: "Had Dillon told you what kind of weapon to look for?"

Nev: "Yes."

Abbott handed Nev a document. "Is this the statement you took from Mr. Dillon?"

Nev glanced at it. "Yes, it is."

Silkman stood up, holding his hand out. "Might we see it?"

Judge Fortenberry said, "Yes."

Abbott said he had no objection, and there was a pause while Silkman and Boucher read through Dillon's statement. Both defense attorneys said they had no objection to the statement, and Abbott asked Nev to read a portion to the jury.

I listened carefully to what sounded like a duplicate of the information I'd received from Dora Lee. Dillon said Calvin said he shot Preston with Jeremy's twenty-two. The Southern Journal had already published all the statements in the newspaper, verbatim.

After Dillon's account was admitted into evidence, Abbott asked Nev. "When you went over to Jeremy Andrew's home with the search warrant, what did you find?"

Nev: "First let me say, we also had arrest warrants. We divided our troupe into two parties. Different detectives went to different locations. I went to Jeremy Andrews' home. We found the family in the house, watching television downstairs. Stanley went with me. As I was inside the house, Stanley searched outside. He found the weapon in the console of a white Camaro. In the search warrant, we hadn't included the vehicle, so I had to get the approval of Mrs. Andrews. She said the Camaro was her car. I asked permission to search the car, and she signed a consent form giving me permission. At that time, we took a photograph of it and put plastic bags over our hands, then got the gun and put it in a plastic bag for fingerprints and forensics. The gun was sent to the crime lab the next day. It was a twenty-two-caliber pistol."

Nev handed the paperwork, including search warrants, signed consent form, and photographs to Abbott. Abbott asked Nev to read the consent form that Mrs. Andrews signed. After he read it, Abbot submitted the documents and photographs for the jury to examine.

Abbott: "What did the state crime lab say about the weapon you found?"

Nev: "Ballistics matched the bullet that came out of Preston's Campbell's body as being fired from the twenty-two gun we found in Mrs. Andrew's car."

Judge Fortenberry interrupted the proceedings to call a fifteen-minute recess. Then he dismissed the jury.

At 11:12 a.m., according to the gigantic courtroom clock on the wall, the jury convened, and Abbott recalled Nev to the stand. "Detective Powers, did you cause any other statements to be taken?"

Nev: "Yes, sir. As I mentioned before, we split up into teams. Different ones went to Leroy Cortez's house, Calvin Newson's house and Jeremy Andrews' house. Everybody came back to the station, bringing the suspects in with at least one parent for each suspect. We advised them of their rights, and took statements from Cortez, Newson, and Andrews."

Abbott: "And what about Tatum Brookins?"

Nev: "We talked to Brookins later. It might have been the next morning."

Abbott: "Tatum Brookins wasn't arrested with the three?"

Nev: "No, we arrested him later."

Abbott: "Do you have all the statements with you?"

Nev: "No, I believe they are in another file, sir."

Abbott said he had no further questions for Nev but wanted to reserve the right to recall him later if necessary. Judge Fortenberry said he could do so. Then he gave Boucher the opportunity to examine Nev.

Boucher asked to borrow Dillon's transcribed statement and instructed Nev to read the paragraph where Calvin said he shot Preston.

After he read the paragraph, Boucher asked, "Dillon said Calvin claimed he shot Preston, is that correct?"

Nev: "That's what he said in his statement."

Boucher: "Did you take Jeremy Andrews' statement without his lawyer being present?"

Nev: "His father was present, as I recall, and he waived his rights to an attorney."

Boucher: "Didn't Jeremy's attorney ask to see him before he gave a statement?"

Nev: "No, I don't recall that he did. At some point I did talk to him, but that's all I recall."

Boucher: "As to Mr. Dillon's statement; he asked for a reward in exchange for the information, isn't that correct?"

Nev: "Yes."

Boucher: "No further questions."

After Boucher sat, Silkman stood and walked up to Nev. "Mr. Powers, did you say an unidentified bus driver said he saw some black males running from the scene on the night in question. He didn't specify the number of males he saw. He didn't say four. Isn't that right?"

Nev: "Yes."

Silkman: "And just so the jury understands. The statement which you have been talking about through your testimony, that is a statement that Calvin Newson made to Dillon, who then repeated it to you. And you were not actually present when Calvin talked to Dillon."

Nev: "Correct."

Silkman: "You conducted a search of Jeremy Andrews' car and found a gun. Is that right?"

Nev: "Yes."

Silkman: "To be clear, that was not Tatum's car. It was Jeremy's car and the Andrews' car, right?"

Nev: "Right."

Silkman announced he had no further questions for Nev, but he wanted to reserve his right to cross-examine him later. The judge said he may do so.

Abbott then called Raymond Peters to the stand. Slim, of medium height, bookish with dirty blonde hair, Peters wore a brown suit and hornrims like Abbott's.

After he was sworn in, he identified himself as the audio-visual technician with the police department. He proceeded to play the tape of Jeremy Andrews' statement, which Dora Lee had transcribed.

I examined my copy as I listened to the tape.

After the recording ended, Jeremy's attorney asked to see the consent form that Jeremy and his father had signed. Then he asked Peters, "Are you aware Jeremy's attorney had asked to be present before this interview was taped?"

Peters: "I think we learned at the end of the interview that his attorney wasn't present, and at that point, I cut the interview off."

Boucher: "I didn't hear that exchange on the tape, and I would like to ask you how long you interrogated Jeremy?"

Peters: "My notes say twenty, twenty-five minutes."

Boucher: "Okay, we've listened to the tape. and it isn't twenty-five minutes long from beginning to end, is it?"

Peters: "No sir."

Boucher: "In fact, I checked the time. It's about ten minutes. No further questions."

Silkman approached Peters. "You are very familiar with these tapes are you not?"

Peters: "Yes."

Silkman: "Regarding your interview with Dillon, he said he only knew three of the boys. Isn't that right?"

Peters: "Correct."

Silkman: "And when he was asked to give the three names, he mentioned Calvin Newson, Jeremy Andrews. and Leroy Cortez. He didn't mention Tatum Brookins, did he?"

Peters: "No sir. But he did say there were four, but he only knew three."

Silkman: "He never mentioned Tatum by name, did he?"

Peters: "Correct."

Silkman asked specific questions about Dillon and Jeremy's statements to reveal Tatum's non-involvement. As I listened, I hoped the members of the jury would have an opportunity to digest all the statements during the deliberation process.

Judge Fortenberry interrupted Silkman to call for a lunch break. Silkman asked the judge for one last question to clarify the date of the interrogations. The judge agreed and then called a recess.

During the lunch break, I took out the peanut butter and honey sandwich I'd packed and ate it while reading over my typed notes. I would have preferred a hot meal, but I knew the court cafeteria was filled with family members of both the accused and the victim, press, and curious spectators. Plus, the jury would be eating there.

At 1:15 p. m. the trial resumed. Abbott recalled Peters to the stand and introduced Tatum's statement and signed consent form into evidence.

Abbott addressed the judge. "Your honor, I have redacted certain names out of this statement so that it could be read into the record. I could go forth with the redacted statement, or I could go forth with the entire statement." He meant he had copies with blacked out names and copies revealing them.

Judge Fortenberry: "What is your pleasure, Council?"

Silkman: "We have no objection to letting it all hang out, your honor. We have nothing to hide."

The judge instructed the prosecution to proceed, and Abbott asked Peters to read Tatum's transcribed statement.

Abbott: "Before you read Tatum's statement, Mr. Peters. I want to point out to the jury that Tatum said the word 'we'."

As Peters read, Abbott interrupted from time to time. It was clear he wanted to establish Tatum as a part of the group.

After Peters read Tatum's statement, I expected Silkman to cross-examine, but instead he said he'd wait until all the statements were read. "I think Tatum's statement speaks for itself," Silkman said.

When Abbott asked Peters to read Leroy's statement, Peters slumped on the stand, looking fatigued, as if he didn't have enough energy to read, but he continued anyway. I referred to the copy Dora Lee had given me. The statements seemed the same.

After Peters finished reading Leroy's statement. Abbott placed Calvin's signed consent form and statement to the police into evidence. Strange, I thought. Calvin allegedly hung himself in his jail cell. He was dead and had no representation.

Abbott instructed Peters to read the signed waiver of rights. Peters complied, and then Judge Fortenberry called for a fifteen-minute recess.

When the jury returned to the courtroom at 3:22 p.m., Peters was recalled to the witness stand to read Calvin's statement to the jury.

On cross, Boucher tried to use the statements to finger Calvin as the trigger man, and not his client Jeremy.

To move things along, Silkman suggested, "It might be easier if several copies of the transcripts were given out with each line numbered." Silkman produced the numbered transcripts for examination. Peters and the two attorneys compared the statements against the originals and agreed to move forward with Silkman's suggestion.

At this point, my eyelids grew heavy as I listened to each attorney pick apart every sentence of these submitted statements. Unlike me, the members of the jury appeared alert and interested.

Finally, Peters stepped down from the witness stand, and Abbott called Charlie McKerry, a tall, thin man with reddish hair and a ruddy completion. Abbott asked a series of questions, and we discovered why McKerry was called to testify. He drove a bus, and on the night in question, his route had taken him through the area where Preston was killed.

Abbott: "Mr. McKerry, tell the jury what you observed the night of December second while driving up Virginia Avenue."

McKerry: "As I turned on Virginia I saw this white boy coming down the bank and then I went on down the street and observed these three black youths, they were coming up Virginia. They turned and went back down Virginia and turned right up Hemphill.

As they got about fifteen- or twenty-feet up Hemphill, one bent over. Looked like he'd picked up a rock and when he stood up, it seemed like he was gonna throw it through the bus window. Then they went on up Hemphill, and I went on up Virginia."

Abbott: "Okay did it look suspicious to you like something was going to happen? What was the relationship between them and the white boy?"

Silkman stood. "Your honor, Mr. Abbott is calling for a conclusion. He should ask Mr. McKerry what he saw, and then the members of the jury can draw their own conclusion."

Judge Fortenberry: "Rephrase, Mr. Abbott."

Abbott: "What did you see as to the relationship between these youths and the white boy?" Abbott handed the pointer to McKerry. "Please indicate the areas you are referring to."

McKerry pointed at the chart. "Looked like to me the black youths that went up Hemphill was gonna pull a prank or hide, jump out and scare the white boy, something like that. I came off Howell Slade Circle and the white boy was coming down the hill. They've got a retainer wall over there to hold the earth back, to keep the rainwater from washing away. He was stepping over it. So, he came up the street, and as I went up Virginia, the three black youths turned up Hemphill to the right. After they turned up

Hemphill, I saw one boy bend over. I thought he'd picked up a rock, but I didn't know for sure. And later I saw on the news where a youth had been murdered in College Station and I said to myself, those boys killed that little boy. That's when I contacted the Police Department."

Abbott: "No further questions."

On cross, Boucher established McKerry couldn't give an accurate description of the black youths and what they were wearing.

Boucher: "No further questions."

Silkman: "Mr. McKerry, You said you saw three black youths, not four. Is that correct?"

McKerry: "That's correct, but there could have been four."

Silkman handed McKerry a bus schedule and asked him if the times on his bus schedule were correct.

McKerry looked it over. "Yes."

Silkman: "Isn't it true you still hadn't left the station in East Point, the next town over, until at least seven-forty-five, and didn't you tell police you were unsure of the time? You thought it might have been seven-thirty or so when you saw the youths?"

McKerry: "That's right."

Silkman: "Mr. McKerry, isn't it possible that the three black males you saw are not the black males accused in this case?"

McKerry: "It's possible, because I can't identify them."

Chapter Forty

December 17

When the court convened Thursday morning at nine-thirty, assistant prosecutor Abbott called Kendrick Franklin to testify. Franklin walked confidently to the witness stand in a pallbearer's black suit and large frameless glasses that made his eyes look like an owl's.

Abbott asked Franklin to briefly tell the jurors about himself and his qualifications.

Franklin turned toward the jury box. "I examine firearms for the Georgia Bureau of Investigation. I've been doing this for nineteen years. I have examined more than forty thousand firearms. I've attended many schools and seminars in the country concerning firearms. I have testified in superior courts in the south approximately sixteen hundred times, and I hold a Bachelor of Science degree in Chemistry and Mathematics."

Abbott: "Tell us about the weapon from the medical examiner's office that you examined in regard to the Preston Campbell case."

Franklin: "I received an RG fourteen, twenty-two caliber revolver. I gave that revolver to you, Mr. Abbott as you requested, to introduce to the jury." He pointed to the exhibit table at the gun inside the plastic bag. "The weapon is safe to examine."

Boucher, Jeremy's attorney, stood. "Your honor, I object to the introduction of that weapon, based on the inappropriate way it was obtained."

Abbott: "Your honor, this is the weapon from the automobile, located at Jeremy Andrews residence. Your honor has heard considerable evidence about it as to the search."

Judge Fortenberry: "Objection overruled, Mr. Boucher."

Abbott pointed to the gun. "Mr. Franklin, please fully describe this weapon, State's Exhibit twenty-three, for us."

Franklin: "It's a twenty-two caliber six-shot revolver. The first time I saw this weapon was when Detective Powers brought it to the crime laboratory. It fires shorts and long rifle twenty-two caliber Empire ammunition."

Abbott: "And did you receive from the Fulton County Medical Examiner's office, a projectile?"

Franklin pointed to the bullet inside a plastic bag. "Yes, I identify State's Exhibit twenty-four."

Abbott: "How did you go about comparing that projectile that was removed from the body of Preston Campbell, with the projectiles you test-fired from that pistol?"

Franklin described in exhaustive detail how he examined the recovered bullet under a microscope and test-fired two cartridges from the revolver that was exhibit twenty-three. He compared the test-fired cartridges and found them identical to the bullet recovered from Preston's body, he said.

Abbott: "So, therefore, it is your expert opinion that the bullet recovered from the body of Preston Campbell was also fired from that pistol?"

Franklin: "Yes."

The gun and bullet were entered into evidence without objection from Boucher or Silkman. Boucher and Silkman had no questions for Franklin.

After Franklin stepped down from the witness stand, Abbott called Gerome Gottlieb, one of the assistant medical examiners, to testify. He looked twenty-something and was almost as tall as Marcus, with black hair and blue eyes, a muscular neck and arms.

Gottlieb gave his credentials. He'd earned a Doctor of Medicine degree and served a residency in pathology. He had been working with the Fulton County Medical Examiner's Office for five months, he said.

Abbott: "Dr. Gottlieb, as part of your duties as medical examiner, did you conduct an autopsy of the body of Preston Campbell?"

Gottlieb: "Yes, sir, I did."

Abbott: "Please describe the autopsied body to the ladies and gentlemen of the jury."

Gottlieb nodded and faced the jury. "The body was that of a teenage white male who measured five feet eight inches in height and weighed a hundred and forty-five pounds. He was clothed in a long blue raincoat and a white, short-sleeved T-shirt. He had on blue jeans and white socks. He wore black and white high-top shoes and a pair of white jockey shorts. The injuries that I noticed to the body were a laceration over the left eye, about a half inch in length, a linear, straight bruise on the bridge of his nose and a gunshot wound to the back."

Abbott asked Gottlieb to step down from the witness stand to show slides he had taken of Preston's body and Abbott instructed the court to extinguish the lights before handing the pointer to Gottlieb.

The first slide, in black and white, showed Preston's body with his raincoat pulled up over his head, lying on his left side in a fetal position. There appeared to be a puddle on the ground under him. "This is a pint or quart of Preston's blood," he said.

As Gottlieb presented the slides, bile rose in my throat. I kept swallowing the sourness to keep from throwing up and closed my eyes as Gottlieb explained how the blood leaked from the wound in Preston's back and got on his hands. I couldn't make myself look at the photos of the bullet wound in Preston's back, nor the ones taken in the morgue.

"When we suspect homicide, we take photographs as the body arrives in the morgue so that we have a record of what the body looks like when it enters our office," Gottlieb said. "The police have placed paper bags over Preston's hands, as you can see here. That's to preserve trace evidence. If he struggled with somebody and got hair or skin under his fingernails, this preserves that evidence."

Gottlieb clicked through the slides. He said one of the photos revealed gashes in Preston's face and nose and over his left eyebrow. "Injuries such as these are consistent with someone striking his face with a pistol," he explained. "And this next photo was taken after we cleaned up the gunshot. It's a high-powered view of the wound. This wound is not completely round. It's more of an oval shape and becomes important, because as we follow the track of this bullet, we can see it passed through Preston from back to front, right to left and in an upwards direction. It passed through his right lung and passed through his heart and caused considerable internal hemorrhage as well as external hemorrhage. He subsequently bled to death from this gunshot wound."

Abbott asked Gottlieb numerous detailed questions to show the brutality of this crime. When I glanced at the jury, I noticed most of them cringed as they viewed these photos.

I exhaled a relieved sigh when Abbott wrapped up his questioning of Gottlieb. Boucher, Jeremy's attorney, declined to cross examine, but Silkman surprised me by asking Gottlieb, "Did you preform the autopsy on Calvin Newson?"

Gottlieb: "Yes, we were on another crime scene and were notified of a hanging at the juvenile detention center."

Silkman: "Did you determine the cause of death?"

Gottlieb: "Yes, we determined it was suicide, death by hanging."

Silkman: "How did you determine it was a suicide?"

Abbott stood: "Your honor, the matter that Mr. Silkman is going into, I'd planned to approach later. There is an exhibit which I would like to introduce. It's a letter that was found in the cell of Calvin Newson."

Judge Fortenberry: "Go ahead, Mr. Abbott, introduce it."

Abbott handed Gottlieb what appeared to be a crumpled sheet of paper. "This is state's exhibit twenty-five. Mr. Gottlieb would you describe what this is, please."

Gottlieb: "Yes, this is the handwritten document I procured from the cell of Calvin Newson at the time we were called to the scene of his hanging."

Abbott asked Gottlieb to read the note but not refer to any defendant by name without a waiver, which meant Gottlieb must read it as "blank" when the other defendants are named.

Silkman stood and said he would like to waive redaction for Tatum and said Leroy Cortez's name should be shown as well, because Leroy pleaded guilty.

Boucher, Jeremy's attorney objected to the names being read.

Judge Fortenberry dismissed the jury from the courtroom until this issue could be resolved. Once they left, Boucher said, "I believe this letter from Calvin Newson would be prejudicial to Mr. Andrews if allowed in."

Silkman: "Your honor, it is very exculpatory with regard to Tatum. Calvin says in here, and these are Calvin's words, not mine, 'Tatum said I best not fuck with that boy'. That's corroborative of everything that Tatum has been saying and goes directly to the heart of the issue of intent. If it's not allowed to come in now, we'd like to introduce it. I can appreciate the problem Mr. Boucher has, your Honor. Maybe this is another reason for severance. We now have a conflict in constitutional rights, but we feel that the Sixth Amendment allows us to introduce it. This letter comes from one of the co-defendants. There's a lot of come-clean about this letter, and I think it sheds tremendous light on what happened."

Boucher: "Your Honor, I object, because there is no evidence as to when this letter was written, or as to the authenticity of it. Calvin Newson is dead and cannot verify that he wrote this."

Both defense attorneys argued back and forth. Eventually Abbott said, "I'm withdrawing this as a state exhibit, and allowing the defense to introduce it as an exhibit if they so choose."

Silkman showed the judge his copy of Calvin's alleged suicide note that had Tatum's name in it. The judge nodded his approval, and after a pause, the jury was called back into the courtroom.

Silkman approached Gottlieb. "I want to show you what has been marked as defendant's exhibit number eight. Without referring to the contents of this, have you seen it before?"

Gottlieb glanced at the document. "Yes, I found this in Calvin Newson's cell at the Juvenile Detention Center the day we were called to his death scene. We found the note under his mattress."

Silkman nodded, as if in agreement, and said he had no further questions.

Boucher stood and asked Gottlieb, "Doctor, did you actually lift up the mattress, or did you have an assistant do that?"

Gottlieb: "I lifted it myself."

Boucher: "Doctor, you expect me to believe that you go around looking under mattresses?"

Gottlieb: "I expect you to believe I examined the scene very carefully. I examined all the areas where I think things such as suicide notes might be hidden. I look inside Bibles, toilets, everywhere. I don't have any assistants to do that type of thing for me."

Boucher: "All right, let's get back to the death of Preston Campbell. Were you able to determine the time of his death?"

Gottlieb: "No. Preston Campbell was put in the refrigeration area of the Fulton County Morgue, which would naturally alter my determination of his time of death."

As soon as Gottlieb stepped down from the witness stand, Abbott called sixteen-year-old Leroy Cortez. He had on a white shirt and black dress pants and appeared a little taller and stouter than Jeremy.

He had already been sentenced to fifteen years for burglary in this case, although his attorney told me she expected he'd receive a lighter sentence and could earn his GED in prison.

After his swearing in, Abbott asked him if he, Jeremy, Calvin, and Tatum were together the night of December second.

Leroy: "Yes."

Abbott: "Tell us what happened at the grocery store before Preston was killed."

Leroy fidgeted before he spoke. "We went into the store and came out." Leroy shifted his body back and forth as if he couldn't find a comfortable position. "I came

311

out of the store first. I left Calvin, Tatum, and Jeremy in the store. I was sitting out on the wall by the store and when they came out, we started walking down the sidewalk."

Abbott: "And you're saying Tatum Brookins was with the others in the Dixie Grocer and they all came out together?"

Leroy: "Yes."

Abbott: "Did you steal a teddy bear when you were in the Dixie Grocer?"

Leroy: "Yes, and Jeremy and Calvin stole cigarettes. Then we started walking down the side of the store. Calvin told Jeremy he wanted to snatch a pocketbook. I didn't say nothing. We started walking down the street. That's when I seen the victim come across up under the bridge. Jeremy said, 'There go a white boy.' Calvin said, 'Let's jump him.' Tatum said, 'Don't fuck with him.' We kept walking by the sidewalk. Calvin said, 'Give me the gun.' I wouldn't give it to him. He asked again. He said, 'Jeremy, tell him to give me the gun.' Jeremy said, 'Give it to him. I gave it to Calvin. I had the gun in my waistband."

Abbott: "And you had the gun with you up at the Dixie Grocer?"

Leroy: "Yes."

Abbott: "When did you get the gun?"

Leroy: "At my house. Jeremy gave it to me, and when Jeremy told me to give Calvin the gun, I gave Calvin the gun. Him and Jeremy ran down the street. Then me and Tatum were standing on the corner. I told

Tatum I was going up the street. Tatum said 'don't go up the street' but I went anyway. I went back up toward where Jeremy and Calvin had gone. That's when I seen Calvin turn around and run to me. We turned around, ran to the corner. That was when we hear the gunshot. Tatum was already gone by then."

Abbott: "Did you see Calvin or Jeremy pistol-whip the white boy, Preston?"

Leroy: "No sir."

Abbott: "Who was with Preston Campbell when you heard the gunshot?"

Leroy: "Jeremy."

Abbott: "Okay, what you are saying is Calvin and Tatum and you were together when the gunshot was fired?'

Leroy: "Yes."

Silkman stood and shouted. "Mr. Abbott is leading the witness, and he's misconstruing and incorrectly restating what the witness said."

Judge Fortenberry: "Do not lead your witness, Mr. Abbott."

Silkman: "Tatum was already two houses down when the gunshot was heard, according to the testimony."

Abbott: "Did you get back together with Jeremy, Calvin and Tatum?"

Leroy: "We met over in front of the trash can in front of Tatum's house and talked about what happened. There was no money. Calvin said he got ready to shoot the boy, but Jeremy jumped on him, Calvin gave the gun to Jeremy and ran from the scene. Calvin said he saw Jeremy hit him and that's why he ran away."

Boucher stood. "Objection, your honor, on hearsay grounds, as to anything Calvin would have said."

Judge Fortenberry: "Sustained."

Abbott: "Your honor, Calvin is a party to the crime. He is no longer here, of course, but if he were sitting here on trial, this evidence would come in and be an exception to the hearsay rule."

Judge Fortenberry: "Calvin is dead and if he were here that would be true, Mr. Abbott. But he is not here."

Abbott: "Your honor, anything that was said by Calvin should be able to come in under the res gestae exception." He was referring to a rule of law that exempted Calvin from the hearsay rule. "What Calvin told Leroy was spontaneous, and not premeditated, and therefore admissible."

Boucher: "However, we still do not have the declarant of those statements here. Even if the declarant were here, those statements would not be admissible."

Judge Fortenberry frowned at Boucher. "Objection is overruled, Mr. Boucher. You may continue, Mr. Abbott."

Abbott smiled and faced Leroy. "What did Calvin say to you about what happened?"

Leroy: "Calvin told the white boy to pull out his money and the boy started throwing pens from his pocket. Calvin said he got ready to shoot the boy. That's when Jeremy jumped on the boy and started hitting him. Then Calvin ran away from them. I had my arm around Calvin when the gunshot went off."

Abbott: "According to the statement you made to Detective Powers, you talked to Jeremy after the shooting and asked him where he shot the white boy. What did Jeremy say?"

Leroy: "Jeremy said he shot him in the back."

Abbott: "Do you see the person in the courtroom who told you he shot the white boy in the back?"

Leroy: "Yes, sir. He's sitting over there." He pointed to Jeremy, who had his head bowed.

Abbott: "Your honor, I'd like the record to show he's pointing at Jeremy Andrews."

Judge Fortenberry: "Let it be noted in the record."

Abbott said he had no further questions of Leroy.

Boucher stood. "Leroy, you pled guilty in this case, because you knew what penalty you would face if you did not. Is that correct?"

Leroy: "No sir, not for sure. I thought it would be life or something. Now I know it's fifteen years or so, for armed robbery."

As Boucher continued to question Leroy, trying to show inconsistencies, Leroy admitted he may have lied on some of the things he told the police, but he remained consistent on what he said about Jeremy shooting Preston Campbell.

Boucher: "Didn't Mr. Abbott and his team coach you on what to say?"

Leroy: "What do you mean coach?"

Boucher: "Didn't they tell you what to say under oath?"

Leroy: "They told me if I lied, I'd get in worse trouble."

Boucher: "No further question."

Silkman stood to cross-examine Leroy. "Tatum said don't go up there two or three times, didn't he? He told you not to go up there, not to go around there. Tatum said those words more than once, didn't he?"

Leroy: "Yes, sir, but I went anyway."

Silkman: "Leroy, did you try to hand something to Tatum to hold?"

Leroy: "Yes, it was my hat, but Tatum said, 'I ain't holding nothing, man'."

Silkman: "Okay, and you've already said when the gunshot went off Tatum was two or three houses away, right?"

Leroy: "Yes, sir."

Silkman: "And in fact Tatum was the only one in the group who said 'no', right? And Tatum had nothing to do with the shooting or the robbery, isn't that what you've said?"

Leroy: "Yes."

Silkman: "Tatum didn't participate in this crime at all, did he? He didn't even serve as a lookout, did he?"

Leroy: "No, sir, he didn't."

Silkman nodded. "No more questions."

As Silkman sat, Abbott stood. "I'd like to ask a few more questions of this witness, your honor." The judge told him to proceed.

Abbott: "Did Tatum see you give the gun to Calvin?"

Leroy: "Yes, sir."

Abbott: "And after the shots were fired, you heard the white boy holler, and if Tatum said he heard the same holler, do you think he was lying?"

Leroy: "No he could have heard the boy from where he was."

Abbott: "Did Tatum Brookins go up the hill and render first aid to the boy who got shot?"

Leroy: "No, sir. He went home."

After Abbott dismissed Leroy and stepped down from the witness stand, Abbott said, "I have one more witness, your Honor." Judge Fortenberry told Abbott to proceed.

Abbott: "I call Hampton Campbell."

Campbell walked to the witness stand and was sworn in. He looked like a grandfather, not the father of Preston. I wondered if his son's death had aged him.

Abbott: "What was your relationship to Preston Campbell, the victim?"

Campbell: "He was my son."

Abbott: "Explain where your son was on the night he was killed."

Campbell: "Preston had gone to church with his mother and the rest of the family. He washed dishes after the Wednesday night supper at the church. When I went to pick them up, my wife was still at choir practice. I drove home and when I went back to pick them up, my other son came out and told me that Preston had already left. He had decided to walk home rather than wait."

Abbott handed Campbell the pointer and asked him to explain to the jury the route his son would have taken to walk home.

Campbell indicated two possible routes his son could have taken to walk those three blocks.

Abbott picked up an eight-by-ten photograph and showed it to Campbell. "This has been marked state's exhibit number eight. What is this?"

Campbell grimaced at the photo and rubbed his eyes. "Preston's legs."

Abbott: "Is that how you saw your son when you came upon him that night?"

Campbell bowed his head and nodded. "I knew immediately it was my son Preston. He had been working out trying to build up his legs to play on the soccer team. I'd bought the high-top shoes for him recently."

After Campbell stepped down from the witness stand, Abbott announced, "The State rests."

Judge Fortenberry dismissed the jury for lunch and instructed them to report back to the courtroom in one hour.

For lunch I'd packed another peanut butter and honey sandwich. I sat on a chair outside the courtroom to eat it and review the trial notes I'd typed.

I looked up when Silkman walked over to say he'd planned to ask the judge for an acquittal.

When the Court was convened, Silkman and I walked in.

Silkman approached the judge's bench. They conferred in private for a few moments. I couldn't decipher what was said, for the talking behind me.

Fortenberry pounded his gavel before he announced, "All right, Mr. Silkman, you may state your motion."

Silkman: "I move for a directed verdict of acquittal, your Honor. There is a plethora of evidence to support the acquittal. Tatum Brookins never intended to rob, murder, or otherwise accost or commit any offense at all against Preston Campbell. There is no circumstantial evidence against Tatum. He did nothing to abet, encourage, procure, or aid in the commission of this crime. Therefore, I'm asking the court for a verdict of acquittal."

Judge Fortenberry: "Motion is overruled."

"Damn," I whispered, not intending for Fortenberry to hear me, but he gave me a stern glance before he asked Boucher to proceed. He called Jeremy to the stand. A bad move, I thought, but I'm not a legal expert. Far from it.

Boucher: "Jeremy, please give your version under oath as to what happened the night Preston Campbell was killed."

Jeremy: "Me, Tatum and Leroy and Calvin met up at Tatum's house and Leroy wanted to go to the store. Leroy toted the gun. We went to the Dixie Grocer. Me and Tatum went to the bakery, but it was closed. We all headed home. But Calvin spotted a white guy. Calvin say he wanted to get him. Tatum say no, don't mess with him. Calvin kept asking Leroy for the gun. He kept saying, 'Give me the gun. Give me the gun.' Leroy pulled the gun out and Calvin snatched it out of his hand. He started running after the guy. I ran, trying to stop Calvin, but I tripped and when I got up there, I heard the white guy say, 'I ain't got nothing but ink pens.' I say to Calvin, 'Come on, leave him alone.' But Calvin throwed him in the bushes and shot him and we ran. We met back up with Tatum where he lives. He asks what happened. Calvin say he shot the guy with a twenty-two, and it don't kill."

Boucher: "Did you put that gun in your automobile?"

Jeremy: "My sister's boyfriend asked for the gun the next day when he came after school. He wanted me to go shopping with him to pay an installment on a ring for my sister. On the way back, we stopped to get something to eat. When we got to my house, he wanted me to tote the gun, but I told him, 'No.' So he put the gun in the car."

Boucher: "When Calvin said, 'Let's get that boy,' what did you think he meant?"

Jeremy: "To rob him."

Boucher: "Did anyone agree with Calvin to rob the boy?"

Jeremy: "No, Calvin just took that gun and ran."

Boucher picked up the pointer and handed it to Jeremy. "Point to the spot where Calvin got the gun."

After Jeremy identified the location, Boucher asked Jeremy, "Identify the spot where Calvin fired the gun."

Jeremy stared at the board for a moment before he pointed.

Boucher: "Okay, Jeremy, now tell me why you told your sister's boyfriend to put the gun in your car?"

Jeremy: "Because my father was in the house, and I didn't want him to know I carry a gun."

Boucher: "Did you know that gun had been used in a crime?"

Jeremy: "Yeah, but I kept it anyway."

Boucher: "Do you regret making the decisions you made the night Preston Campbell was killed?"

Jeremy bowed his head. "Yeah."

Boucher turned to the judge. "I've concluded my questioning of Jeremy, your Honor."

Abbott stood and walked briskly toward the witness stand. "You said you didn't steal cigarettes that night because you knew you were being watched, is that right?"

Jeremy: "Yes, sir."

Abbott: "Did Tatum know y'all were planning to steal cigarettes?"

Jeremy: "Yeah."

Abbott: "Did Tatum know Leroy stole a teddy bear?"

Jeremy: "Yeah."

Abbott: "Did Tatum know y'all had a gun?"

Jeremy: "Yeah."

Abbott: "Do you make a habit of providing a gun to people who you know are going to rob somebody?"

Jeremy: "I didn't know he was gonna rob. I didn't tell him he could have the gun."

Abbott: "But you just told your attorney you knew Calvin had planned to rob, and it was your gun. Didn't you admit that?"

Jeremy: "Yes, sir."

Abbott: "And you were in control of the gun and that's the gun that killed Preston Campbell, isn't that correct?"

Jeremy: "Yes, sir."

Abbott threw questions at Jeremy like a parent scolding a child. Time and again, the teen contradicted his own testimony. I thought the jury had gotten the point, but Abbott continued to grill him.

Eventually Abbott concluded his questioning of Jeremy, and Silkman took his turn: "Jeremy, you agree with everyone else who has testified that Tatum told you, and the others, not to hurt Preston or harass him. Isn't that a fact?"

Jeremy: "Yeah."

Silkman: "And isn't it a fact Tatum told the truth in his statement to police when he said he told you and the others to leave Preston alone?"

Jeremy: "Yeah."

Silkman: "And in other words, when Tatum said 'I ain't fixing to get involved' or whatever it was Tatum said, isn't it a fact that Tatum was telling the truth?"

Jeremy: "Yeah."

Silkman: "And when Tatum said that he never went up there and was never in Preston Campbell's presence, Tatum was telling the truth?"

Jeremy: "Yeah."

Silkman: "Tatum never touched the gun, did he?"

Jeremy: "No."

I thought Silkman's questions and Jeremy's answers proved Tatum's innocence, but at the same time, I wondered if Tatum could find justice, when he shouldn't have been arrested in the first place.

As Silkman concluded his questioning of Jeremy, I glanced at Boucher, expecting him to call another witness on behalf of his client. Instead, he rested his case.

Still standing, Silkman announced, "Your honor, I'd like to call Freemont Jackson to the stand."

Freemont strode into the courtroom wearing a three-piece grey suit. He looked handsome and impressive and seemed relaxed. Unlike me. My hands shook, my heart pounded, and my stomach knotted. He flashed me a confident smile as he was sworn in.

Silkman asked Freemont what he did for a living:

Freemont: "I own and operate Jackson Laundry Service, a business my mama started. It's been a successful business for twenty years. "His resonating voice sounded assertive and sincere.

Silkman: "The night Preston Campbell was killed did you happen to see the defendant Tatum Brookins?"

Freemont: "Yes, that Wednesday night I delivered laundry to Ms. Sikes. I saw Tatum walking alone. I said 'hello' to him, and he greeted me."

Silkman gave the pointer to Freemont: "Please identify where you were when you saw Tatum that night."

Freemont studied the chart and tapped the location of Ms. Sikes' house.

Silkman: "Would you identify for the jury the person you saw that night?"

Freemont stretched out his long arm and directed his index finger toward Tatum. "He's sitting right there."

Tatum smiled at Freemont.

Silkman: "Did it seem strange to you that Tatum would be walking alone?"

Freemont: "Yes. Most young people hang out together at night."

Silkman: "No further question, your Honor."

Abbott stood. "I have a few questions, your Honor. Mr. Jackson, can you tell us the exact time of night you saw Tatum?"

Freemont: "It was after eight, about eight thirty."

Abbott: "But you don't know the exact time, do you? You didn't look at your watch, isn't that right?"

Freemont: "I keep a tight schedule and deliver to Ms. Sikes at about that time."

Abbott: "Do you deliver Ms. Sikes' laundry every Wednesday night?"

Freemont: "Not every Wednesday, but most Wednesdays."

Abbott: "Isn't it possible you saw Tatum Brookins another Wednesday and thought it was the night Preston Campbell was shot and killed?"

Freemont: "No, I'm certain it was that particular Wednesday night."

Abbott: "It was a dark night. How can you be certain it was Tatum Brookins you saw?"

Freemont: "I've been accused of having eagle eyes." The jury laughed. "And there's a streetlight at the corner. That's where I saw Tatum. Also, Ms. Sikes keeps the porch light on. There was plenty of light."

Abbott: "Did you hear a gunshot that night, Mr. Jackson?"

Freemont: "If I heard a loud noise, I probably discounted it as a backfiring car."

Abbott: "But you don't recall hearing a loud noise that night, do you?"

Freemont: "No."

Abbott: "No further questions of this witness, your Honor."

Boucher said he had no questions for Freemont. So Free stepped down. I waved at him as he walked past.

Silkman: "Defendant Brookins rests, your Honor."

The courtroom clock showed 2:35 p.m. Early, but Judge Fortenberry dismissed the jury until 9:30 a.m. the next day.

After the Jurors exited the courtroom, Silkman stood: "Your Honor, I'd like to renew my motion for a directed verdict."

Judge Fortenberry: "Same ruling as before, Mr. Silkman."

Next, the judge called for a conference at the bench. They spoke loud enough for me to hear the order in which the attorneys would give their summations.

Fortenberry allotted each attorney an hour. "Take all the time you want, gentlemen, but remember the mind can absorb only as much as the seat can endure."

Chapter Forty-One

December 18

As I listened to the judge greet the jurors Friday morning, I hoped they'd reach a decision before today's deadline. I didn't want my article to be old news, though I knew our readers would receive more details from our newspaper than they'd get from a daily. Marcus often referred to dailies as McNews, but he admitted they provided a service to readers who preferred brevity. Our newspaper had the reputation of providing comprehensive coverage.

I glanced over my notes as Judge Fortenberry announced, "Mr. Boucher, you will present first. Mr. Abbott will follow him, and Mr. Silkman will speak after Abbott. Then Mr. Boucher will be allowed a second summation."

Boucher approached the jury box. He had on a tailored navy-blue suit. His large brown hands gripped the side of the wooden railing, separating him from the men and women deciding the fate of Jeremy and Tatum.

"Good morning, Ladies and Gentlemen, I would like to first explain the accent you're hearing. I was born in Ghana, but my formal education was in the United States. I believe the United States of America is a great country with a great judicial system. There aren't many places in the world where two black boys who have been accused of murdering and killing a white boy can get a fair trial. But here in America, our Constitution gives the jury the power and the authority to decide the innocence and the guilt of those accused of a crime."

He smiled and paused. He seemed to be studying the jurors' faces. "That's a tremendous responsibility and a high civic duty, but it's yours, Ladies and Gentlemen. You must decipher all the evidence presented and decide the guilt or innocence of the accused. Mr. Abbott and the State have the responsibility of proving guilt, because our law dictates that Jeremy Andrews is innocent until proven guilty beyond a reasonable doubt."

He paused to nod at Jeremy. "Ladies and Gentlemen, I ask you; are you convinced, beyond reasonable doubt, that the State has proven Jeremy committed the act of murder? Did the State convince you? Do you believe beyond a reasonable doubt that he committed an act of aggravated assault, or an act of armed robbery? Or do you have doubts? If you have reservations, you have doubt. And according to our rules of law, you must be able to say with certainty that Jeremy committed the acts alleged by the State. If you cannot do that with a moral certainty, then you must acquit Jeremy, and you must acquit Tatum."

Silkman stood and interrupted Boucher: "Your Honor, I object to the reference to Tatum. Mr. Boucher can argue for Jeremy, but not Tatum."

Judge Fortenberry: "Objection sustained."

Boucher continued. "Ladies and Gentlemen, it is clear the State has the burden of proof. The State must prove every element of the crimes charged. Think of this like a puzzle. Did the State provide all the pieces you will need to convict Jeremy? If there is one piece of the puzzle that doesn't fit, you must discard that piece. As to Leroy Cortez's testimony, he was charged with the same crimes as Jeremy, but he copped out, for fifteen years. Leroy said on the stand he feared he'd face a greater penalty if he had not agreed to a plea bargain. What did he do? He testified for the State. The State and Mr. Abbott want you to accept Leroy's testimony as fact, but you heard him on the stand. You saw his demeanor. What did he say? He lied to police. He admits to lying, but most importantly, did the State show you through Leroy Cortez that Jeremy agreed with Calvin Newson to do anything? Did he agree to rob? No. Did he agree to kill? No. There was no discussion of this, Ladies and Gentlemen.

You can't put Leroy's testimony into the puzzle. It doesn't fit."

Boucher cleared his throat and took a sip of water. "There is no doubt in my mind that you should acquit Jeremy of every charge the State alleges he committed. And I ask you today to consider all the evidence very carefully. No question about it. A precious life was taken when Preston Campbell was killed. There is no justification for that tragedy, but please, don't throw another life away unless you are positive of guilt." He bowed his head. "Thank you for your time."

Abbott stood and pushed his glasses up. He seemed to be looking at each juror individually. "Ladies and Gentlemen of the jury, I told you there wasn't one or two or three, but four involved in this case. There was Tatum Brookins. There was Leroy Cortez. There was Calvin Newson and Jeremy Andrews. The strongest case we have is against Jeremy Andrews. Therefore, I'm going to begin outlining the case against him. The whole tragic scenario that night was like a fire raging out of control. The intent to rob and the access to the gun started the fire. Preston Campbell walked innocently into that fire. Preston was robbed and pistol-whipped, shot in the back and left to die."

Abbott rehashed each bit of evidence, point by point before he mentioned the suicide note left by Calvin. "Calvin had nothing to lose when he wrote in his note that Jeremy pistol-whipped Preston and shot him in the back."

Boucher stood, frowning angrily. "That's an improper argument, your Honor."

Judge Fortenberry: "The court will charge the jury on that matter later."

Abbott continued with his lengthy summation, and eventually defined the difference between malice murder and felony murder. "With malice murder, you must form your intent prior to committing murder. With felony murder, one must only be engaged in criminal conduct or criminal enterprise that is a felony, and for someone to be killed in that process is to be guilty of felony murder."

Abbott attempted to link Jeremy with malice murder. Abbott talked about the gun, which he said is evidence that Jeremy intended to commit a violent act. Eventually, Abbott read selected paragraphs from the statements of Calvin, Jeremy, Tatum, and Leroy, trying to tie all the boys together in this murder.

Silkman stood and interrupted Abbott. "You are misstating the evidence, Mr. Abbott."

Judge Fortenberry: "Mr. Silkman, the evidence is available for the members of the jury to decide for themselves."

Next, Abbott zeroed in on Tatum. "I can almost hear the voice of Preston crying out. Tatum heard it that night. He admits to hearing it. Would anyone but a co-

conspirator leave someone crying from a bullet wound and leave him to die? How could he do that if he wasn't a party to the crime? What type of person would do that? What type of person would leave poor Preston in a pool of blood? No ambulance was called. No First Aid was rendered. And then what did Tatum do? He gets back together with the other boys and talks about the crime."

Abbott reached his long arm upward and pointed at the ceiling. "Ladies and Gentlemen, that night there was a fire burning out of control. That fire is still burning. You need to stop it. You need to throw water on it. Are you going to answer the call? Are you going to throw a bucket of water on the fire of crime in this county? Or are you going to waste that water and pour it away? The eyes of the County are on you. The eyes of the State are on you. The eyes of the Nation are on you. They are looking at this courtroom right now. What are you going to do? Are you going to send a message that it's okay for children to run around with loaded guns? Are you going to send a message that it's okay to carry guns, to put guns in the car, to conceal guns? Are you going to send a message that it's okay to associate with the kind of people who carry guns? Are you going to send a message that it's okay not to call an ambulance? That it's okay to stand and watch? I'm asking you, Ladies and Gentlemen, don't send those messages. Send a true verdict. Jeremy Andrews, malice murder, armed robbery. And for Tatum Brookins send a verdict of armed robbery and felony murder. Give a true verdict, Ladies and Gentlemen. Thank you."

After Abbott's lengthy summation, Judge Fortenberry called for a fifteen-minute recess. As soon as the jury left, he grimaced and hammered his gavel. "There's too much commotion in the courtroom, too many comings and goings. When we bring the jury back in, no one is permitted to get up and leave. Mr. Sheriff, don't let anyone come in after that time."

At ten-fifty-five, when the jurors returned, Silkman stood, straightened his tie, and walked over to address them. "Ladies and Gentlemen, I will try to be as brief as possible, but I need to clarify several misrepresentations you've heard today. First, let me start by saying Tatum Brookins is completely and totally separate from the case of Jeremy Andrews. We may sit on the same side due to the architecture of the courtroom, but we do not sit on the same side of this case. You must apply the evidence you have heard in this case individually and separately."

He stroked his beard, as if it helped him think. "I'm asking you to look at the evidence. Examine it closely, and I'm sure you will reject the State's cut-and-paste theory of criminal culpability. When you look at the total picture and read all the boys' statements presented into evidence, you will find Tatum was consistent. The statements of the other boys prove Tatum was consistent. So please take the time to compare those statements. In those statements, Tatum said 'No, don't go there.' He said, 'Keep walking.' He was the conscience of the group. Tatum is young, and you can imagine how shocked he must have been. But he said 'No, don't go there. Don't do this.' He begged Leroy not to go. Leroy said so himself. Leroy testified as to Tatum's non-involvement on the witness stand. Leroy's statements to the police also corroborate Tatum's innocence. Leroy said he asked Tatum to hold his hat. Tatum said No. Tatum advised the others not to bother Preston. But Tatum didn't know Preston would be shot. Tatum was far away when the gun was fired. You heard Freemont Jackson's testimony. What did he say? He saw Tatum walking alone. Tatum wasn't with the others. However, Mr. Abbott, in his prolonged, yet articulate, summation, wants you to believe Tatum willingly met up with the others. That's simply not true, Ladies and Gentlemen.

Jeremy, Calvin, and Leroy came to Tatum's apartment complex afterwards and stood outside near the trash dump. Tatum had no idea they would be there. But why did police arrest him? Why is he on trial? I'm still scratching my head about that. I don't understand why the State and Mr. Abbott want to link Tatum to this crime. I'm wondering why police didn't talk to Mr. Jackson and interview him. Tatum mentioned Mr. Jackson in his statement to police. Why didn't they take the time to talk to Freemont Jackson? Why didn't they take the time to verify Tatum's statement? And where is the evidence that Tatum intended to rob Preston Campbell? The evidence doesn't exist, Ladies and Gentlemen. Three, four- or five-times Tatum said 'No, don't go there, man.' Does that sound like someone who's about to commit armed robbery? There's not a shred of evidence that Tatum committed a crime. He never touched the gun. He never urged anybody to commit the crime. He never went up the hill. He didn't make a foursome from the threesome. The only action he took was to stay away and urge others to stay away. Think about this: The evidence shows Tatum was standing two-hundred and sixty-five feet away when he heard the gunshot. Mr. Abbott would like you to think he was a lookout, but that's not plausible, and you know it. Jeremy and Leroy both admitted Tatum wasn't a lookout."

Silkman walked over to the defendant's table, took a sip of water, and walked back to the jury box. "Mr. Abbott and the State would like you to believe Tatum was an accomplice in a crime. The judge is going to instruct you that to be a party to a crime you must aid it somehow, abet it, encourage it, procure for it, and recruit it. In other words, you've got to do something to help it along, to be a party to a crime. And to convict Tatum, you have to be convinced beyond a reasonable doubt. Are you convinced, Ladies and Gentlemen? I don't think so. I'm confident that once you have examined the evidence, you'll find Tatum not guilty. I have no doubt a vile crime has been committed, and certainly everyone can see the pain and the suffering of Mr. and Mrs. Campbell.

If you have children, you know the worst thing that can happen to a parent is the death of a child. You'd prefer something happen to yourself rather than to your child, and I'm sure the whole community can feel their pain. This tragedy has affected the whole Atlanta Metropolitan area, the whole State, and beyond. And Mr. Abbott is right when he says the eyes of the Nation are on this case. No doubt the police felt they had an obligation to round up everyone who might be guilty, and sort them out later. Three names popped up and when they interrogated those three boys, Jeremy, Calvin and Leroy, those boys brought in Tatum. That's how his name came up. The police went out immediately, went to his house, and got him. That's within the boundary of the law, for sure.

But after they rounded everyone up, they never sorted everything out. And within a short period of time, they closed the file and brought this case to trial. This case has moved faster than the speed of light, Ladies and Gentlemen. This is a major murder case, a horrible case, a complex case, and it's taken only a few days to close it, indict and go to trial."

Silkman began to talk about the conflicts in the evidence, and the discrepancies in the testimony of the witnesses. "You must examine these statements carefully. If you do, you will see everyone is trying to run with Tatum. Why? Because they knew Tatum had nothing to do with this horrific crime. So now it's up to you, Ladies and Gentlemen. You are the last opportunity to sort this out. If you don't sort it out, it will never be sorted out. Look around you today. This courtroom is full. Courtrooms are rarely full, and this is one of the biggest courtrooms in the courthouse. Everyone is watching you. Camera eyes are on you." He pointed to the cameras. "There are reporters here from every media, from all over the country watching you. Yes, everyone is watching you, and that puts you in a difficult position. But it all comes down to the evidence. You must decide this case on the evidence."

Silkman cleared his throat. "When I was in law school many years ago, I read about a trial that took place in the late eighteen hundreds in Oklahoma. An Indian had been charged with a very serious crime against a rancher. Most of the people in that community at that time wanted to dispense with the trial and go on with injustice. Now this was a time when only men were jurors. I apologize in advance to the women on the jury, but one of the jurors remarked that no man stands so tall as when he stands shoulder to shoulder with someone so small.

The jurors acquitted the Indian. They found him not guilty. Today I'm thinking about that case. Tatum is small. He's a disadvantaged kid. He hasn't had the opportunity to answer the barrage of negative publicity or comments. He doesn't have the skills to articulate. He doesn't have the influence. He is small. And I'm asking you today, Ladies and Gentlemen. Look at the evidence and stand shoulder to shoulder with Tatum. I'm asking you to bring back a verdict of not guilty, because it's the right thing to do." Silkman paused and stared at the jury for a moment. "Thank you for your time and consideration."

When Silkman finished his summation, my cheeks were wet from crying. I wiped my face and glanced at the members of the jury. I tried to read their thoughts. Two ladies in the jury box dabbed their eyes.

I couldn't imagine anyone convicting Tatum, but juries are rarely predictable. The same could be said of judges, and I expected Judge Fortenberry to call a lunch break. Instead, he allowed Boucher to speak.

The attorney for Jeremy stood and attempted to dispute the central points of Abbott's summation. Boucher asked the jury to examine closely the statement from Tim

Dillon. "And ask yourselves why Mr. Abbott didn't bring Dillon in to testify. Police took Dillon's statement. In that statement, Dillon said Calvin told him he shot Preston. Yes, Ladies and Gentlemen. Calvin admitted he shot Preston. 'I shot that boy,' Calvin told Dillon. And the police relied on Dillon's testimony to get a warrant to arrest Calvin and the others. And with that in mind, let's talk about Calvin Newson for a moment. Calvin had no respect for life. He took his own life. And he confessed to Dillon that he shot Preston in the back. In Calvin's own words, he said 'a twenty-two don't kill nobody.' But it did kill someone. It killed Preston Campbell. Yes, Calvin shot Preston in the back and then took his own life. This alone represents a reasonable doubt that Jeremy Andrews did not shoot and kill Preston Campbell. Ask yourselves, did Jeremy act like a guilty person? He didn't throw away the gun, did he? He didn't hide it, did he? If he were guilty, if he had committed this crime, he would have disposed of the gun, but he did not dispose of the gun. Look at the evidence, Ladies and Gentlemen, do the pieces fit together? No, they do not. And if the pieces don't fit, you need to return a verdict of not guilty for Jeremy Andrews. Thank you."

As Boucher sat beside Jeremy at the defense table, the judge dismissed the jury for lunch and told them to return at 1: p.m.

I ran to the bathroom where I ate another peanut butter and honey sandwich. I would have preferred something else, but I needed to isolate myself, review my notes and write. Thoughts of Marcus kept invading my stream of consciousness, but I pushed them away and lost myself in the writing process.

When I realized how much time had elapsed, I rushed to the courtroom to hear the judge instruct the jury on the fine points of law. I wondered why Fortenberry hadn't dismissed the alternate jurors before he began his recitation on the law, but thirty minutes later, when he concluded, he thanked the alternates who then left the courtroom.

Silkman objected to some of the Judge's charges. Boucher echoed similar objections, but the judge said his charges stood.

The courtroom clock showed 2:05 when the jury left to deliberate. They were a varied group of nine women and three men. Their faces looked noncommittal. Eight had dark complexions, from brown to dark brown. Four were Caucasian. They ranged in age from thirty to seventy.

Jeremy and Tatum fidgeted in their seats. I could almost feel their pain. I felt antsy myself, and uncomfortable in the stiff pew. I could only imagine how distraught they must have been while waiting for the jury to decide their fates.

Their attorneys sat pensively while Abbott talked to Mr. Campbell, as if reassuring him justice would prevail in his son's death, but I doubted any amount of justice would help him cope with the loss of his child.

* * *

At 3:30 p.m. someone shouted, "Verdict," and within moments, the jurors entered the court room.

Judge Fortenberry: "Madam Forewoman, have you reached a verdict in this case?"

An attractive, brown-skinned woman stood. "Yes, we have, your Honor."

Tatum and Jeremy stood alongside their attorneys and turned to face the jury.

The bailiff took the paper verdict from the Forewoman and handed it to the court clerk, a fiftyish, grey-haired, fair-skinned woman. Her large, rimless glasses dominated her small, heart-shaped face.

She glanced at the verdict. "In the case of the state versus Tatum Brookins and Jeremy Andrews charged with armed robbery, malice murder and felony murder, the verdict reads as follows: 'We, the Jury, find Jeremy Andrews guilty of armed robbery, guilty of felony murder and guilty of malice murder with recommendations for a lesser sentence on this count.'"

A woman a few pews back screamed. It was Jeremy's mom.

As I watched her grieve for her son, Judge Fortenberry hammered his gavel. "Order, order in the court, or take it outside."

When Mrs. Andrews sobs quieted, the court clerk continued. "Further, we, the jury, find Tatum Brookins not guilty on all counts."

I let out a loud sigh, joining the collective sighing and roar of applause. Someone yelled, "Thank God."

I grabbed my camera to snap a photo of Tatum hugging Silkman. Everyone seemed to be talking at once.

Judge Fortenberry pounded his gavel. "No demonstrations. Take it outside, Mr. Sheriff. Control the noise."

After partial silence had been restored, the judge told Silkman and Boucher to review the verdict. He asked Boucher if he had any witnesses to present before the sentencing phase.

Boucher: "No, your honor."

Judge Fortenberry: "Very well. Mr. Andrews, come forward."

Jeremy hands trembled as he stepped in front of the judge's box.

Fortenberry stared at him for a moment before he spoke. "Mr. Andrews, I will let you serve the rest of your natural life in the penitentiary. I'm merging the felony murder case into the malice murder case, since there was only one murder committed. The armed robbery, count number one, this will be twenty years. On count number two, the malice murder count, the only penalty that can be imposed is a life sentence. I will let the twenty-year sentence on count number one run concurrent with the life sentence imposed."

Jeremy's face showed no expression, though his hands trembled.

Fortenberry informed Jeremy he had the right to file an appeal in the clerk's office, but it had to be done within thirty days, and if he needed a lawyer, the court would appoint one for him at no cost.

I turned and glanced at Preston Campbell's father. He looked sad and lost. I leaned over and asked him how he felt about the verdict.

"I commend Mr. Abbott and the state for their efforts. The legal system did not fail Preston. If there's blame in this case, it rests with the parents of the youths involved. Because of the parents, I have lost my son, and they have lost their sons," Campbell said.

Abbott walked up and placed his arm around Mr. Campbell in a comforting gesture. I asked Abbott what he thought of the verdict.

"I'm pleased," he said. "The jury sent a message, don't mess with guns and don't mess with people with guns."

I asked him what he thought of Tatum's not-guilty verdict.

"Obviously it means that the jury felt when Tatum said 'No' he meant it."

Lastly, I approached Silkman. "I know you're happy with the verdict."

He flashed a wide smile. "Yes, it was obvious from the beginning and from the statements police took that Tatum was not involved with Preston's murder. The Grand Jury acted too hastily in indicting Tatum. There wasn't a whole lot of investigation. But for me, this trial was worth the effort if it prevents another Tatum Brookins case. Police tried to say he was part of a gang, but there was no such gang. No one mentioned anything about a gang during the trial." Silkman shook his head, as if disgusted. "Yet, they tried to feed that crap to the media."

"Why do you think we were told these four teenagers were members of a black gang?"

Silkman frowned. "Hatred and racism."

Chapter Forty-Two

From a courthouse payphone, I called the Southern Journal. Lisa answered. She said Marcus was in the back, pasting up.

"No need to disturb him. Just let him know the jury found Tatum not guilty, and Jeremy guilty. I'll bring in the story with all the details shortly."

I hung up from Lisa, ran to my car, broke all speed limits, racing back to the office. It was a miracle I didn't get a ticket.

When I pulled up in front of the newspaper office, I sat for a moment to admire the Christmas lights. This was the first time in years I'd taken the time to enjoy them.

Adrenalin ran through me as I battled the cold wind and trekked up the stairs. I couldn't wait to see Marcus and let him read my story.

When I pulled open the heavy front door, I expected to see Lisa at her desk, but she wasn't there. On deadline day, she often helped with proofreading and paste-up.

Marcus had his door closed. I stared at the door and took a deep breath before I knocked.

My heart flipped as he swung open the door. I hugged him as tightly as Tatum had hugged Silkman after the not-guilty verdict.

"Did Lisa tell you? Tatum's not guilty. Jeremy got life plus twenty for armed robbery. His lawyer says he's planning to appeal. I've already finished the article. I have loads of photos to give you."

Marcus took my head in his hands. "I saw the verdict before I heard it from Lisa. It came in over the wire service."

I slapped my forehead. "I should have called you right away, but I needed to take more photos and interview everybody."

"I understand. The wire had the bare bones. You'll have the complete story. We'll run your article and photos on the front page above the fold and give you as much space as you need inside."

I talked about the trial and rehashed some of the highlights. His face lit up as he listened and shared my excitement.

"I'm proud of you, Carrie. I want to hear all about the trial and read your report, but first give me the film. Thomas is in the dark room now."

I withdrew the roll from my tote and handed it to him.

He smiled. "I'll be right back."

After Marcus left, I sat in a swivel chair, withdrew my Tandy, and pulled up my article. I read through it and made some final edits.

When he returned, I handed him my computer. He plopped in the chair next to me and began to read what I'd written.

I twisted my hands as I waited for him to comment. He usually found something to correct.

He asked questions to clarify a few points as he edited. "Great work, Carrie."

"Thank you. I had a great mentor."

He smiled and attached my computer to the mainframe for printing. "Is that so? I've heard he's a grouch and a hard-nosed perfectionist."

I laughed. "I rather like his hard nose."

He stood, turned the lock on his door and pulled me up to wrap his arms around me. "What's going on with us, Carrie?"

"For one thing I've been misdirecting my anger at you."

He kissed my forehead. "Don't apologize. I've misdirected my anger for years. You're entitled to your feelings and your anger." He paused. "Why don't we start over? I'll try not to shut you out, and vice versa. You've kept things from me because you were afraid I'd overreact. You're probably right. From now on, if you feel I'm trying to regulate and direct your life, and you don't like it, tell me. If something bothers you, let me know. If I do something that hurts you, tell me. I can change. In return, please don't hide important things from me, okay? I'd like for us to communicate better and work out a compromise that suits us both."

"Okay, that sounds doable, Marcus. I'm feeling better now that Kyle has signed the divorce papers. At first, I was afraid he and his money-grubbing lawyer might come after you. I didn't want them to charge you with something ridiculous like alienation of affection."

Marcus frowned. "As far as I know that statute isn't even applicable in Georgia. Last time I checked, women are no longer considered chattel. You're now deemed capable of making your own decisions, which are probably much more thoughtful than those of any man I know."

I jumped at the knock on his door.

"Not now," Marcus shouted. "I'll be out in a minute."

I cringed, wondering if the person on the other side of the door had been eavesdropping.

Chapter Forty-Three

December 19

On a chilly, cloudless day, an estimated two hundred Klansmen in hooded white robes marched through the middle of College Station. My stomach soured from the sight, but I pushed aside the creepiness. The fewer than predicted Klansmen meant the Klan had become a dying organization, I hoped.

I'd already taken one roll of film of the parade. Marcus had positioned himself near City Hall where the march was scheduled to stop. I couldn't locate him in the crowd, but we'd planned to reconnect later at my house. I'd invited him and Freemont for supper. I'd also invited Karl Silkman and Tatum Brookins, but they'd declined.

"Tatum is struggling to catch up with all the school he's missed, and I have another engagement," Silkman said. "It's my wife's birthday."

Before I'd left that morning, I found a message in the roses from Freemont. His note said he would arrive at my house around 5:30 p.m. if not before. "I'm joining the counter- demonstration today. If you see me, wave," he wrote.

I wrote back saying, "Don't join the protest. The All-People's Congress has urged black residents to stay away from the march."

Even if Freemont had read my message, I figured he'd ignore it, but I hoped he'd control his temper and not get into a confrontation with the KKK.

I basically gave Marcus the same instructions about controlling his anger. When I saw him earlier, he looked angry enough to start a war. He hated the Klan, even though he knew the law upheld their right to march, and since it was a newsworthy event, we had to cover it.

I searched for Freemont in the group of people yelling, "Hey, hey, ho, ho, Racist Klan has got to go," but with all the angry protestors, curious onlookers, local police, National Guard officers, and Ku Klux Klan members packed together, I couldn't find him.

One Klansman in a pointed hat and mask with eye-slits carried a sign that said: Support White People.

Another sign said No National Birthday for MLK - referring to the holiday commemorating Dr. Martin Luther King's birthday.

A tall dark man, dressed in black, bowed his head, as if in prayer. I asked him what he thought of the march.

"I came out to see what was taking place," he said. "It's a plague. It hurts me to see my brothers like this. In the sight of God, we are all one. There is no color in the sight of God. My prayer today is Father forgive them for they know not what they're doing."

I asked him if I could take his picture. He agreed, and after I snapped him, I walked up to one of the Klansmen.

"Why don't you remove your mask?" I asked. I didn't expect him to grant my request, but I'd become feisty and disgruntled from what I'd seen today.

"No," he shouted. "Don't take my damn picture." I stared into his eyes through the holes in his mask. I thought he looked and sounded familiar. "In an all-white community, like Cumming, we wouldn't need burglar bars."

Where had I heard that voice before?

I tried to identify it as I recalled the history of Cumming. In the early 1900s, black youths were arrested and hanged for allegedly raping two white women. A vigilante group, known as the Night Riders, terrorized all the black citizens, firing into their homes and killing their livestock. Fearing for their lives, these black citizens fled, leaving behind their property.

My face burned as I tried to control my anger. "Why are you afraid to show your face and have your picture taken?"

He spit on the ground. "You better get out of here, little lady, before you get hurt."

"Are you threatening me?"

"You heard him," another Klansman shouted. He lifted a beer bottle in the air. "Get out of here if you know what's good for you."

I laughed at his shrouded face. "I'm not afraid of you, but you're afraid of me. If you weren't afraid, you wouldn't hide behind a costume."

The beer-toting Klan member yelled "bitch."

When the bottle hit my head, I saw flashes of light. Darkness swallowed me.

When I opened my eyes, I saw Marcus' face.

"Carrie, say something." He lifted me up.

"What do you want me to say?"

"Can you stand?"

"Yes," I answered, though my legs felt like jelly.

"I need to get you to a doctor, but first, I'm going to kill the son of a bitch who hit you." He flagged down a National Guardsmen. "Keep her safe and out of the way," he ordered.

I watched in horror as Marcus lunged at my attacker. "You fucking low-life scum." He pounced on top of the Klansman.

A curious crowd formed a circle around the fight, blocking my view. "Stop," I yelled and tried to push my way through the crowd.

The Guard entrusted with my safekeeping pulled me back as if he needed to protect me from the carnage. "If someone hurt my woman, I'd do the same."

I grimaced. "I'm my own woman."

As I said these words, Marcus walked toward me. His hands looked bloody, but at least he was alive, and didn't appear seriously injured. A few in the crowd cheered him.

He pointed to the beaten man on the ground. "I want him arrested and charged with assault. Lock him up. He doesn't deserve to freely walk the earth." My attacker had lost his hooded mask, but I couldn't see his face for all the blood. He appeared to be unconscious and incapable of walking anywhere.

Chapter Forty-Four

After three hours in the hospital emergency room, I'd learned I had one heck of a hard skull. My forehead and the top of my head were the best places to hit me, the doctor said. I suffered no internal bleeding but had a mild concussion from the impact.

Marcus tried to change my mind about cooking supper. He offered to take us out to a restaurant instead, but I'd already bought all the ingredients for the Lobster Newburg and steamed the lobster tails. Also, I'd prepared a green salad before I'd left for the Klan march. All I needed to do was add tomatoes to the salad and cook the Newburg and rice, I told him.

"Okay, but I'll do the cooking," he insisted.

He stood in my kitchen, studying the recipe like it was a complicated math problem. He refused my help. I tried to talk to him, but he scowled, still angry about what happened at the march. I wanted to remind him he'd promised to share his feelings, but this didn't feel like the right time.

"Would you like a shot of Dad's Wild Turkey, Marcus?"

He shook his head. "Haven't you heard I'm fucking meditating now?"

I remembered the day I walked into his office and saw him sitting in a lotus position on the floor. The memory struck me as funny. I pressed a hand to my mouth but couldn't smother my giggling.

He glared at me as if I'd lost my mind and then started laughing, too.

Once we'd regained our composure, Marcus opened one of the bottles of chardonnay he'd bought and poured us both a glass. I sipped the wine and contemplated the close relationship between tragedy and humor.

He drank his wine and methodically combined the lobster, butter, brandy, cream, egg yolks, nutmeg, and cayenne pepper in a heavy saucepan. After the ingredients were heated through, he offered me a taste.

"Yum, Marcus. This is better than I remembered."

He smiled. "I merely followed the recipe."

I heard the grandfather clock chime six times. "I wonder what's keeping Freemont. He said he'd be here at five-thirty, or before. He's usually early. He makes a point of it."

Marcus glanced at his watch. "It's only six." He gave me a reassuring hug. "But if it makes you feel better, why don't you give him a call?"

Marcus placed the warm French bread, rice, Lobster Newburg, and salad on the table, as I dialed Freemont's number. It rang and rang.

When the machine came on, I left a message after the beep. "Supper's ready. Where are you?"

I rushed outside to see if he'd left another note in the roses. No note, but I smelled something burning, like a fire close by. Instinctively I knew Freemont was in trouble.

I ran back inside. "I have a horrible feeling, Marcus. I smell fire in the air. We need to drive over to Freemont's place right away."

Marcus didn't hesitate. He guided me out the door, and we jumped in his jeep.

From a half-mile away, I noticed the fiery cross. "Oh, God, please God, no."

I froze in fear as I recalled the photo taken in the early 1900s of a group of men who hanged Leo Frank, a Jewish American man, from a tree. Frank, an Atlanta factory superintendent, had been convicted of murdering Mary Phagan, one of his employees. The caption read, The Knights of the Ku Klux Klan as vigilantes for Mary Phagan. In the photo there was a burning cross in the background.

Marcus pulled up beside Freemont's white van. He opened his glove compartment and withdrew a Glock. "Carrie, keep your head down and stay in the car. I'll search the house and grounds."

"No, Marcus, I'm going with you."

"I'll be back in a minute." He handed me the keys to his jeep. "Drive back to your house and call nine-one-one. We need to report this."

I jumped out. "No, I'm coming with you."

"Damn it." He walked around to my side and pushed me behind him.

Chapter Forty-Five

We found Freemont on his back. He was lying on his front porch. In his right hand, he clutched a handgun. His t-shirt and his left hand were covered in blood.

"I shot one of the bastards," he growled.

Marcus ran inside to call paramedics while I knelt beside Freemont and tried to comfort him. "You'll be okay, Free. Stay calm."

I trembled in fear for my friend and remembered the pictures of Preston Campbell in a pool of his blood. He'd bled out, according to the trial testimony. Oh, please, God. Grant a miracle.

Freemont gritted his teeth. "Get the video."

I placed my hand on his head. "Video? What do you mean?" I thought he was talking out of his head.

"The security system."

Then I remembered. "The one Jeff installed? Are you thinking it may have captured a video of who did this to you?"

"Yeah."

"Okay, I'll get it."

Marcus walked out carrying a blanket. He covered Freemont. "Hang on. Help is on the way." He touched Freemont's neck. "Good pulse in the carotid artery. Do you know who shot you?"

"Klan."

"Where were you hit?"

Freemont tapped his upper left chest with his bloody hand.

Marcus turned to me. "I have gauze and bandages in the jeep. I'll get them. I'm going to apply a little pressure on the wound to slow down the bleeding."

Marcus returned with a black bag of his first aid stuff and a Nikon. He passed me the camera. "Take photos of the burning cross."

I bit my lip. For crying out loud, how could Marcus expect me to take pictures when my best friend was bleeding to death?

I turned away to snap the burning cross and told myself to woman up. Stop crying. Stay calm for Freemont's sake.

"Marcus, there's a video tape in Freemont's security system. He asked me to get it. He must be thinking we'll find evidence on it."

Marcus pressed gauze to Freemont's chest. "Okay, get the tape and I'll have Jeff look at it."

We waited for what seemed like an eternity before paramedics arrived. Marcus and I backed away as they worked on him. Freemont looked unconscious by the time they'd loaded him into the emergency van.

I wanted to ride in the van with Free, but Marcus said it would be better for him if we didn't interfere and allowed the paramedics to do their thing.

When we arrived at the hospital, Freemont was already in surgery. We couldn't see him, a nurse said.

Marcus guided me to a cushioned bench near a payphone in the waiting area. I rested my head on his shoulder. He wrapped his arms around me.

His eyes looked wet, and his body trembled, though his voice sounded firm. "I need to make a few phone calls, Carrie."

I listened as he talked to Jeff Daniels. Marcus gave him a summary of what had happened and asked him to come by the hospital and pick up the video tape I'd retrieved.

As I listened to Marcus, I wondered if Freemont had a premonition he was in danger. Had he received threats? Why had he faced this alone? Why didn't he say he feared for his life when he bragged about his security system?

These questions bothered me as Marcus made one call after another. As soon as he hung up from Jeff, Marcus talked to his friend with the Georgia Bureau of Investigation and asked his help in apprehending Freemont's assailants.

A police officer in uniform walked up to us. He introduced himself as Vance Straub, with the Atlanta Police Department.

I told him about the burning cross, how we found Freemont, and what he said about shooting one of the Klan members in self-defense. In response, Straub said he planned to question Freemont. "If and when he can talk," he said.

After Straub left, I nervously paced the waiting room. "Why haven't we heard anything from the doctors?

Marcus took my hand and forced me to sit. "We'll know something soon, Carrie. He's tough. He'll make it."

I glanced at the circular clock on the waiting room wall. It read,10:15 p.m. "It's been hours. We should have heard something by now."

Before Marcus could respond, Jeff walked in. Marcus handed him the tape. "We need information on this right away."

Jeff nodded, took the tape, and without a word, he left.

"Why don't we get something to eat?" Marcus asked.

I remembered the Lobster Newburg. I should have asked Jeff to go to my house, eat what he wanted, and store the remainder in the fridge, but under these traumatic circumstances, I wasn't thinking straight. "I'm afraid to leave. What if the doctors come out and we miss them?"

Marcus walked to the vending machine in the hallway and returned with two bags of peanuts and a carton of orange juice. I refused the peanuts but took a few sips of the juice.

"Freemont knows every twig of the woods behind his house, Marcus. Why didn't he escape? I didn't even know he owned a gun. If he hadn't had a gun, maybe he wouldn't have gotten shot."

Marcus exhaled loudly. "If he hadn't had a gun, we may have found him hanging from a tree."

I groaned. "Not if he ran away. Freemont is fast. He runs like a gazelle. He could have called nine-one-one the moment he saw them and escaped into the woods."

Marcus tilted my chin up and studied my eyes. "I think we're going to have to agree to disagree on this."

"But surely you agree that bigoted and insane people and children shouldn't have access to guns, Marcus. Look what happened to Preston Campbell. These kids nowadays think guns are toys. Last week a MARTA policeman arrested a fourteen-year-old with a fully loaded sawed-off shotgun under his coat. You saw the crime report. You know. When I have children, I don't want guns anywhere around the house. Period."

Marcus's eyebrows hiked up. "How many children are you planning to have?"

I thought about his question before I answered. "Two or three maybe. I'm an only child and I wish I'd had siblings. But, of course, Freemont is like a brother." I started sobbing again.

Marcus wiped my eyes and nose with his handkerchief.

After I'd calmed down, I asked him, "What about you? Did you ever think of having children?"

"I love kids. I enjoy my nephews, Josh, and Jonah. They're seven and nine. I try to talk to them as often as possible. I wish they lived closer."

"But do you ever think about having children of your own?"

"Sure. But I'd like to get married first."

Chapter Forty-Six

Dr. Green beeped us through a metal door. We walked past the nurses' station.

My heart thudded when I saw Freemont. He looked like a bronze statue in repose, too large for the narrow hospital bed. A nurse studied the beeping cardiac monitor and adjusted the bag of liquid that fed into his arm.

I touched his cheek. "Hi Free."

His eyes popped open.

"Doctor Green said you're a lucky man. The bullet missed your vital organs. They're planning to keep you a day or two. Then you can go home. How are you feeling?"

He grimaced. "Woozy."

Marcus stepped beside me. "Hi Freemont, we have your video tape. Jeff is looking at it. He's very methodical, as you probably know. Also, I've called in the GBI. We're going to pursue this until we get the bastards who shot you and desecrated your front yard."

Freemont stared at Marcus and nodded. I'm not sure he understood. His eyes appeared glassy and unfocused.

Marcus continued. "Last night you said you couldn't see their faces, but can you tell us anything that might help? Can you remember how many you saw? Can you describe what they were driving?"

"There were four or five. They drove up in a green pickup."

Freemont's eyes closed.

I knew he needed to sleep. "We'll be back to see you tomorrow, Free. I love you."

We left intensive care and walked through the waiting room where we ran into Jeff Daniels. He had already examined the tape and traced the owner of the pickup.

Chapter Forty-Seven

December 20

I jerked awake when I heard the tinkling piano. I recognized the tune, *Close to You.*

I stretched and rubbed my throbbing head. Sunshine streaked into the room through the diaphanous blue curtains. The time on the radio clock registered 10:35. I'd slept late in Marcus's house, in his bedroom, lying on a giant sleigh bed. The walls were a deep shade of blue. A large, mahogany desk took up one corner of the room. A phone sat on top of the Atlanta yellow page directory. Beside it were a stack of newspapers and a framed family photo.

I studied the photo. A bearded Marcus was standing between an older man who resembled him. Probably his dad, I thought, and the lovely dark-haired woman must be his mom. A younger woman sat on a bench, in front of them, between two boys. Had to be his sister and her children.

In the yellow pages, I located the hospital's number. I picked up the desk phone and called.

An operator answered.

"Can you tell me the status of Freemont Jackson? I'm Carrie Sue Justice. Freemont is my neighbor and close friend. He was brought in last night. My stomach knotted as I waited for her to find out.

"Satisfactory and stable."

I thanked her and said a silent prayer of gratitude, though my anger bubbled inside. I wanted to destroy the Klan.

I took deep breaths to relax as I listened to the tinkling piano. I was nude and didn't remember getting undressed. My bra, underpants, sweater, and jeans were folded on the arm of a yellow wingback chair near the bed. My boots stood beside the chair.

I recalled falling asleep in Marcus' jeep. I should have asked him to take me home to pick up my tote. During our rush to Freemont's house and the frantic drive to the hospital, it was the last thing on my mind.

A door from the bedroom led to the master bath, a gleaming space, with white and grey tile, a Jacuzzi tub and separate enclosed shower. In the medicine cabinet I found aspirin. I swallowed two with a gulp of water, washed my face and brushed my teeth with Marcus' toothbrush. I had a purple bruise on my forehead from the blow I took yesterday. My hair stuck out in all directions. I picked up a black comb from the sink counter and raked the tangles out.

As Marcus played *On Top of the World*, I crept back to the bedroom and opened the walk-in closet. I grabbed one of his white shirts and slipped it on. The shirt tail reached my knees.

I followed the music and found Marcus, sitting shirtless, behind an ebony grand piano. His back was turned, and he didn't see me walk in. My heart warmed as I watched him. His graceful hands glided across the black and white keys. His bare feet worked the pedals. He played with exuberance, devotion and integrity. I knew without a doubt I loved and trusted him. I'd never known him to lie or cheat. He told the truth as he saw it. I'd sometimes despised his grumpiness, toughness, and perfectionism, but I'd never stopped admiring him as a mentor and supervisor. Now I loved him as my soul mate.

The décor in this room was a mixture of vintage and contemporary furniture, an interesting blend of colors, blue, red, white, grey, brown and black. The room suited him. I felt at home, cozy and warm. A fire crackled in the stone hearth.

As if he sensed my presence, he stopped playing and turned. "Hi, Carrie."

"Hi, yourself, you play beautifully. Don't stop."

He stood and walked toward me.

He pulled me into an embrace. "My shirt looks much better on you than me."

I squeezed him, trying to block out the horrible events of yesterday.

He touched the sore spot on my head. "How're you feeling?"

"I'm okay. More importantly, Freemont is listed as stable and satisfactory. I just called the hospital."

He smiled. "Yes. I called, too. Good news."

He massaged my neck and shoulders. "How about a cup of coffee and some breakfast?"

"Sounds great."

"After we eat, I'll try to loosen up your tight muscles." Marcus led me to the kitchen and pulled out a rustic straight-back chair for me to sit. There were eight of these chairs around what looked like a farmhouse table. The kitchen was huge, with stainless steel appliances. "I love your house, or what I've seen of it. Can I help you cook?"

He shook his head and moved around the kitchen with ease as he prepared breakfast and talked about the remodeling he'd been doing. He seemed relaxed, yet exuberant about his home.

"As you know, I've been renovating this house forever. All the rooms had flowered wallpaper. I thought I could paint over it. That didn't work. I eventually stripped off the paper and repainted. This kitchen used to be small. I had walls torn down to enlarge it. I liked the original parquet flooring. I've kept most of it."

"I think what you've done is beautiful, Marcus."

"I've tried to make it livable. Having you here makes this place feel like home."

My heart fluttered. "Aw, that's so..."

He interrupted. "Sweet?"

"Very sweet."

He leaned over, kissed my forehead, and served me a plate of what he called a farm-hand breakfast: eggs, bacon, grits, and wheat bread.

I thanked him and tasted what he'd given me. "Delicious, you're a good cook, Marcus."

"I'm glad you like it. I learned out of necessity and discovered I enjoy cooking. Maybe I should retire from the newspaper business and become a chef." He laughed.

"You can cook for me anytime." I winked.

"That's good to know."

We ate, and eventually got around to discussing what Jeff and his GBI friend had uncovered. They'd traced the license plate of the green truck to Mathew Powers. The driver backed into Freemont's driveway, and the license place was visible in the video.

"I've met Mr. Powers, but don't know him very well. I've known Nev his son since high school, but we weren't close. We attended different schools. I had one date with him, but it wasn't pleasant."

"Why wasn't it pleasant, Carrie?"

"In the movie theatre I saw a friend of mine and talked to him briefly. Nev didn't like it. They got into an argument. Nev punched him. He said my friend reminded him of the drunk driver who caused his mom's accident. Nev's brother lost his life in the accident, and his mother was paralyzed."

"Was the friend you talked to in the movie black?"

"How'd you know?"

"I guessed." He frowned and didn't say anything for a moment. "Godwin, my GBI friend, has already interviewed Mr. Powers at his home."

"What did Mr. Powers say?"

"He claimed he drove into town during the Klan rally and parked his truck. When he returned, the truck was gone. He said he reported it missing to his son, and Nev was able to locate it. It was found parked near City Hall. Blood splatters in the front seat, Godwin said. They're sending a sample to the crime lab."

"Do you think Mr. Powers told the truth?"

"He acted nervous, Godwin said, and when Godwin asked Powers why he was jittery, Powers said he was upset about his wife. She has severe health problems, he said, and is an invalid from that auto accident you mentioned."

I nodded. "The accident happened when Nev was a child. It was his twin brother who was killed."

"Mr. Powers had a bloody bandage on his arm. He claimed he was shot, accidentally, on a recent hunting trip."

"What do you think, Marcus?"

He shook his head. "His story sounds fishy. Unfortunately, the interview with Powers was brief. Nev came in and provided an alibi for his father. He was rude. Told Godwin to get out, but don't worry. We'll get whoever's responsible for shooting Freemont."

"I've heard Nev make racial slurs, but do you think he and his father are Klan members?"

"Wouldn't surprise me." Marcus touched the bruise on my head. "Why don't you go lie down while I clean up, Carrie?"

I pushed my chair back and stood. "I'm fine. Let me help you."

He shook his head. "No, I want you to rest. Go to bed. I'll wake you up in a bit."

I headed toward the bedroom and rehung Marcus' shirt. The aspirin, strong coffee and food had knocked out my headache, but hadn't increased my energy level. I couldn't keep my eyes open.

I eased my body onto Marcus' bed and pulled the covers up. My muscles and joints were stiff, but I understood why. I'd been hit over the head and stressed out over Freemont. I'd probably empathetically absorbed his discomfort.

I soon drifted off to sleep, but jerked awake when I heard Marcus's voice. "Carrie, why don't you flip over on your stomach, and I'll give you a rub down."

"How long have I been sleeping?"

"Not long." He squirted baby oil in his hands.

I inhaled the sweet aroma and turned on my stomach.

He started massaging my tight neck.

"Ouch," I said when he touched a tender spot.

"Sorry, I'll be more careful. Imagine your body melting into the bed," Marcus whispered. His hands began to knead my shoulders, and eventually worked their way down my back. I could feel my body relaxing and soon I drifted off to sleep again but awoke as he stroked my butt.

Eventually, we made love.

"Aw, Carrie," he cried out as we both found our pleasure.

I smiled. "Thank you."

His dark eyes seemed to study my face. "I should be thanking you, Carrie." The muscles in his jaw clenched. "And I need to tell you something."

"Is it a bad thing or a good thing?" I'd had enough bad news for a lifetime.

He stroked my hair. "I guess you'll have to be the judge." He paused, as if measuring his words. "I'm not sure I can be the man you deserve. I don't know if I'll ever stop having nightmares about the war." He sighed.

I studied his eyes. They looked haunted.

"I never thought I could love again, Carrie, or deserved to love again. Remember what you said in your column about your brown thumb?"

"Yes, but what does that have to do with us?"

"You thought you were jinxed and that's why you couldn't grow anything. But you planted the roses, and they lived."

"Freemont said I'd jinxed myself."

Marcus nodded. "What you said about those roses delivered a symbolic message to me."

"What do you mean, Marcus?"

"Because of what happened in the past, I was afraid I would jinx you and something terrible might happen."

I hugged him. "I knew you were obsessed about my safety because you felt responsible for your wife's death. That's why I hid things from you. I didn't want you to worry excessively about me."

"Yes, Carrie, but I want you to trust me enough to share with me despite my need to protect you. I love the woman you are, and I want you to feel free to express yourself. When we first started working together, I was grieving and miserable. To say I was grouchy is an understatement."

"You were grouchy with a capital G."

He laughed. "True, but your love has changed me. He paused and stroked my face. "I never expected to feel this kind of passion for anyone. Maybe it's my age now, or my past, or the lessons life has taught me. But I think it's also the kind of woman you are. You have so much to give. You've given me more than I can ever repay. You've given yourself, Carrie, and that's a priceless gift. I still don't believe I deserve you, but I want us to be together, even though I'm not sure I'm what you need. I'm trying to be a better man. Not burden you with my fears, but I don't know if I can ever let go of the past."

"I want you to share your fears, Marcus. Everyone feels afraid sometimes. I have separation anxiety. I think it's a result of losing Mom and Dad." I waited for him to respond.

He smiled. His eyes gleamed with love. "Despite everything, I want you to know you're the only woman I need. The only woman I want. Once you're officially divorced, I'd like for us to make a permanent commitment. Think about it and when you're ready, I'll deliver a proper proposal." His lips brushed mine. "And I'll try to show you how much I love you."

If it's possible for a heart to burst from love, mine would have exploded. "I feel the same. I never thought I could love anyone as much as I love you, Marcus. You're my soulmate."

Readers we need you.

Please leave a review, even a one liner counts, and has a big influence on our future sales.

Like Carrie Sue Justice, Sandy Semerad has worked as a newspaper reporter, broadcaster, editor in Atlanta and earned her B.A. in Journalism from Georgia State University. Prior to her career as a journalist, Sandy modeled in New York City and Atlanta. She was raised in Geneva, Alabama but now lives in Santa Rosa Beach, FL with husband Larry and their spoiled Shih Poo Elvis. Sandy has two daughters, Rene and Andrea and a granddaughter Cody. *Justice's Journal* (previously *A Message in the Roses*) is her third book. It's loosely based on a murder trial she covered in Atlanta. The location and names of those involved have been changed, and Sandy used poetic license to alter events. *Justice's Journal* is a prequel to *Carrie Sue Diary,* an award-winning best seller. Visit her website at www.sandysemerad.com.

BWL Publishing

bwlpublishing.ca